DANCING ANGELS

ALSO BY ALICE DUNCAN

DANCING ANGELS

A MERCY ALLCUTT MYSTERY
BOOK 10

ALICE DUNCAN

ePublishing Works!

November 2025
ISBN: 978-1-664457-775-2

ePublishing Works!
644 Shrewsbury Commons Ave, Ste 249
Shrewsbury, PA 17361, USA
www.epublishingworks.com
Phone: 866-846-5123

For the special folks at Daisy Daze, who keep pulling me out of hot water, no matter how difficult the task. Don't know what I'd do without them.

You're only given a certain spark of madness. You mustn't lose it.

ROBIN WILLIAMS

ONE

Alfred A. Knopf published Dashiell Hammett's books. Very well. I'd better not even attempt getting my manuscript past Mr. Knopf's editors.

Bobbs-Merrill published the *Charlie Chan* books by Earl Derr Biggers. Charlie Chan came a little closer to my heroine than Sam Spade did to my hero, but still… Skip Bobbs-Merrill too.

Unfortunately, most of the good mystery and detective fiction released in the previous few years (1920-1926) had been published in Great Britain. Agatha Christie, John Buchan, Dorothy L. Sayers, Anthony Berkeley, Freeman Wills Croft… Well, you get the picture. They were all British. I'm not.

I spent, therefore, what seemed like a hundred hours in the Los Angeles Public Library on Fifth and Hope opening mystery and detective novels and flipping to the verso page, attempting to find a publisher that might agree to look at my humble effort. The task proved daunting, and not simply because the USA didn't publish much mystery and detective fiction; there were also precious few female American authors in the stacks. Mary

Roberts Rinehart stands out as a brilliant exception, but I doubted I was anywhere near her league.

Nevertheless, I finally chose a publisher, packaged my opus in brown paper, tied it securely with string and tape and, with my heart pounding like a bass drum in a speakeasy band, took it to the local post office. I'd addressed the parcel to Halliday, Smith, and Ransom, Publishers. Because I didn't know the names of any of their editors, I inscribed my parcel to the Editor of Detective Fiction. Then I prayed there was such a person.

I nearly screeched, *"Give it back!"* after the postal clerk stamped my parcel and tucked it into his outgoing mail bin. When I walked out of the post office, my nerves jumped like water on a hot skillet, my skin got all goose-bumpy, and my heart raced so fast I feared I might faint. I barely made it all the way to my little Moon Roadster.

Once there, I managed to open the door and more or less collapse into the front seat, pressed a hand to my thundering heart and called myself (silently) seventeen types of ninny. I'd probably have called myself even more synonyms except I had to get back to work. My brave deed had been accomplished during my lunch break.

After a few tense seconds during which I took in deep breaths and let them out slowly, I pushed the starter button. Determining the worst of my nerve-storm to be over, I summoned the courage to maneuver my machine into traffic. I swear, Los Angeles was getting more crowded every day.

When I finally finished writing my book, I didn't tell anyone. Never, ever, would I admit that I'd sent it to a New York publishing house. It was my secret. I anticipated rejection from the publishing house, but I didn't crave pity or condolences from my friends. More, I didn't want anyone to tell me I was stupid for having tried.

Traffic was heavy, and the poor police officers standing in the middle of intersections manning semaphores seemed even braver to me than *I'd* been. While I might anticipate rejection after sending my book to a publisher, at least I hadn't risked life and limb in order to do it. The mechanized semaphores at some intersections weren't much better. Every thirty seconds or so, a bell would ring and either the "Go" signal would go up, or the "Stop" signal would go up. People in L.A. always seemed to be in a hurry, and some of them didn't wait until the intersection was devoid of other autos before motoring on.

It was probably lucky that traffic *was* so heavy that day; otherwise, I'd have been an edgy wreck worrying about my poor book chugging its way across the vast United States from L.A. to New York City. Bah.

Stop it, Mercy, I lectured myself. *Think about something else.*

Easier said than done.

Finally, I found a parking spot about a block north of the Figueroa Building. Fortunately for me, I always wore sensible shoes to work, so I scurried like a frightened rabbit down the hill to my place of work, passing other places of business as I did so. I smiled as I passed the Murray Dance Academy. It would be fun to…

Then I had a brilliant idea. Or maybe it wasn't. But it couldn't hurt to try. The best way to keep my mind from dwelling on my poor orphaned book would be to keep busy. And the Murray Dance Academy might just come in handy, by Jupiter! Every now and then my heart would thud heavily, but I determined not to expose my nervous state to anyone.

Mr. Buck, the custodian at the Figueroa Building, smiled at me and opened one of the double glass doors for me as I approached the building. "Thanks, Mr. Buck," I said, smiling at him in return.

"You're more than welcome, Miss Mercy," said the kind-hearted Mr. Buck. "Hope you had a pleasant lunch."

Lunch? Oh. Guess I'd forgotten all about lunch, hadn't I? Rather than say so, I lied. "Yes, thank you. I got a tamale and a glass of lemonade from the vendor on the corner."

"I hear those tamales are quite tasty," said Mr. Buck. I'm sure he hadn't wanted me to see his nose wrinkling at the notion of eating Mexican fare for lunch.

"They are *very* tasty," I affirmed, wishing I'd actually stopped at Pedro's tamale cart. Oh well. Too late now. I'd just have to starve until dinner. Nertz.

My pal Lulu LaBelle sat behind the reception desk in the lobby of the Figueroa Building, buffing her long, long fingernails. I'd met Lulu one hot July day about a year and a half prior. Every single time I'd seen her at her desk, she'd been doing something with her fingernails. She used to paint them a bright, bright red. In recent months, however, she'd toned down her appearance. Rather than eye-poppingly loud colors, she now wore tasteful and subdued clothing suitable (according to me, anyhow) to an office setting.

"Hey, Lulu," I called breezily as I strolled to the reception desk.

"Hey, Mercy."

"Did you and Rob go out to lunch together?" I asked slyly. Lulu and an attorney named Robert Gabriel, who was a friend of my boss Ernie Templeton, had been seeing each other for a few months.

Because Lulu no longer wore inches of pancake makeup to work, I saw her cheeks turn pink. "Yes. He took me to the Brown Derby." Lulu lifted her shoulders, clasped her hands to her bosom, and smiled broadly. "He is *so* good to me, Mercy."

"I'm glad, Lulu." It was only the truth. A few months ago, Lulu'd had the bad luck to attract the attention of a phony "talent scout" who'd got himself murdered. No big loss to the world. I'm sure that's a rotten thing to say, but it's the truth.

Anyhow, Lulu had been suspected of his murder. That's when she met Rob, because he acted as her attorney. Not that she'd needed an attorney because she hadn't done anything to the rat except run away from him.

But never mind that.

"Say, Lulu," I said, "do you remember when I asked if you'd like to take tap-dancing lessons with me?"

Tilting her head, Lulu said, "Uh...yes! I remember that. It was when we stayed at your sister and brother-in-law's castle in Beverly Hills. I thought you were joking."

A side note here: My sister Chloe and her husband Harvey lived in Beverly Hills. Harvey Nash owned and ran an extremely lucrative motion-picture studio in Los Angeles. Lulu and I, along with my boss Ernie, had stayed there for a couple of weeks after the Nashes' first child was born. While their home wasn't precisely a castle, it came darned close.

Anyhow, I'd liked the way our shoes clacked on the Nashes' marble staircase, and the sound had made me think about tap dancing. A few horrible things then happened so quickly, I'd forgotten all about those lovely clicking sounds until I walked past the Murray Dance Academy on my way back to work, thus prompting my perhaps-brilliant idea.

"I wasn't joking! I think it would be keen to take tap lessons. There are dance studios all over Los Angeles. People can learn everything from ballet to the Hawaiian hula dance. Heck, there's a dance studio right up the street from here. I think we'd be great, and then we could show off our talents to Ernie and Rob!"

That's when I lost what was left of my mind and attempted to execute a dance step, not that I knew any. The soles of my sensible shoes didn't appreciate being asked to perform an exercise to which they weren't accustomed on a carpeted lobby floor. I darned near fell over. How embarrassing. Lucky for me, nobody else was in the...

"Careful there, Irene Castle!" Ernie's voice came to me from the doorway.

"Yeah. Be careful, Mercy. What were you doing anyhow?" said Rob Gabriel, who stood next to Ernie and… Oh, crumb.

"Are you all right, Mercy?" asked Phil Bigelow

The three men stood in a clump at the front door of the building. Mr. Buck peered at me through the window glass in evident alarm.

Heck and darnation!

"She's trying to tap dance," said Lulu, grinning.

"Not really," I said as I felt heat creep up my neck and invade my cheeks. "I just thought it might be fun to take tap-dancing lessons. I just…tripped, was all."

Ernie hurried over to me and took my arm. "You all right, Mercy? There's nothing here to trip over."

"Of course I'm all right," I said, irked. "I didn't lift my foot high enough and stumbled. That's all."

"You're blushing up a storm," Ernie said, confirming what I already knew.

I chuffed out an annoyed breath. "Almost falling over for no reason in front of other people is embarrassing," I said.

With a shrug, Ernie said, "If you say so, kiddo."

I absolutely hated it when he called me *kiddo*. I didn't object, deciding I'd already made a fool of myself. No sense digging the pit any deeper.

"I do say so," I said through gritted teeth.

"Well, let's get back to work then, shall we?"

"Fine with me," I muttered.

"Lulu and I are going to the Hollywood Bowl this evening. The New York Philharmonic is playing," said Rob Gabriel.

"How upper-crust of you," said Ernie with a grin.

"Upper-crust boloney," said Rob. "A client gave me four tickets. They have packed dinners there too. It might be fun to dine and listen to some pretty music under the stars."

"I had to go to the New York Philharmonic when I lived in Boston," I said, remembering the experience without fondness.

"But if you join us tonight, you won't have to sit with your parents," said Lulu, laughing.

"Valid point," I said, "but I'm sure Mrs. Buck has already planned dinner for us. She might even have something cooking right now."

"Well, she'll have to feed Caroline and Sue anyhow," Lulu reminded me.

"Yes," I said, "but I don't like to spring things on her. She works really hard to fix good meals for us." I didn't intend to sound priggish, although I did.

I'd been trying with all my heart to transition from my privileged beginnings on Boston's Beacon Hill to the mean (and sometimes not-so-mean) streets of Los Angeles. I wanted to be of the laboring classes, to be a single working woman who had to live on her earnings. So far, I'd had mixed success, although Ernie hadn't fired me yet.

"That's true," said Ernie. "The poor woman works her fingers to the bone to clean that enormous house and cook for you too."

"I pay her well," I snapped, and instantly wished I hadn't. Ernie claimed he'd known from the second I'd first set foot in his office that I "came from money," as he phrased it. It was probably true. He had well-honed detective instincts, darn it.

"I know you do, Mercy. Just joshing you. Am I invited to dinner, or do I have to sit in the cold and listen to classical music at the Hollywood Bowl tonight?"

"You know you're always invited," I reminded him icily.

I honestly didn't intend to be icy. Guess my innards were still a wee bit knotted. Well, I knew they were, but I was trying to hide my anxiety. Mixed results on that front too.

"In that case, let's dine at your place. I can't imagine a packaged dinner, whatever that is, possibly competing with one of Mrs. Buck's feasts." Putting an arm around my shoulder, Ernie steered me toward the elevator. I felt a little stiffish and tried to relax. Ernie Templeton, you see, was not merely my boss. Since shortly before the end of last year, we'd also been seeing each other in our off hours.

"C'mon, Mercy, let's get to work. We'll take the elevator. The other guys'll have to walk up the stairs."

"Hey!" said Phil Bigelow, pretending outrage.

"Not fair," said Rob Gabriel, likewise pretending.

By Jupiter, we were all pretending that day! Except Lulu, who seemed her usual happy-go-lucky self. When I first met her, she'd been hoping to be discovered by a movie producer and become a star on the silver screen. After her experience with the loathsome "talent scout," her ambitions had swerved. My brother-in-law had been impressed with her abilities in the makeup department, and she now had her sights set on being a makeup artist in the flickers. I figured her chances at employment by one of the studios were better as a makeup artist than as an actress, and her career would last considerably longer than those of women who had to rely on their looks for money.

But enough of that. "What are Rob and Phil doing here?" I asked, hoping to divert Ernie's attention from my failed attempt at tap-dancing to business.

"You've read about the death of Frederick Lewiston?" Ernie asked.

Glancing up at Ernie—he was a good deal taller than I, and I don't think I've yet mentioned his absolutely *gorgeous* blue eyes—I said, "The wealthy businessman? Yes, I've read about it. The newspapers all reported that he fell out of a window of the

Ambassador Hotel. That doesn't sound like an easy thing to do, actually. Do you think he jumped?"

"He went out of a window at the Ambassador, but there's some uncertainty as to whether he did it by himself or had help."

My itchy nerves perked up. I said, "Really?" Oh, boy, a murder case! Not, mind you, because I approve of murder, but murder cases were much more interesting than those involving spying on straying spouses, which was most of what Ernie's business consisted of.

"Really. And you're not going to get involved."

"Of course not," I said innocently. "What makes Phil think Mr. Lewiston was murdered?"

"*Might* have been murdered," Ernie corrected me.

"What makes Phil think Mr. Lewiston *might* have been murdered?"

"A few things don't add up," said Ernie, not enlightening me one little bit.

The elevator clanked to a stop on the third floor, and Ernie opened the cage. I carefully stepped into the hallway—the elevator almost never stopped at precisely the same altitude as the hall—and waited for Ernie to exit the thing. I saw Phil and Rob standing outside Ernie's locked office door.

Ernie said no more, darn it, so it was a slightly peeved Mercy Allcutt who walked to the door at his side. Ernie unlocked the door. I became calmer when I stepped into my work environment, mostly because I felt at home there.

The office was also the place where I wrote most of my book, but I'd never tell Ernie so.

TWO

Once I got to my desk, I finally relaxed completely. I tucked my handbag and hat in the bottom right drawer of my desk. That drawer should have been filled with file folders. The P.I. business waxes and wanes, though, and lately business had been waning. A jealous wife here, a stolen handbag there. Most of Ernie's cases were as boring as...well...Boston. However, as mentioned before, Ernie hadn't fired me yet.

He also didn't invite me to his office when he, Phil, and Rob entered it. They were going to discuss the Lewiston case; I just knew it. And they were leaving me out. This was typical. Ernie never wanted me to be involved in his cases, even though I'd been of great help to him a couple of times. He hadn't yet, however, promoted me to the position of P.I.'s assistant. I remained his confidential secretary.

I was a darned good confidential secretary, though. I'd defied both of my parents, several aunts, uncles, and cousins, and taken shorthand and typing at Boston's Y.W.C.A. According to my family, taking the courses was outrageous all on its own. When I moved to Los Angeles and obtained a real, honest-to-goodness *job*, my parents might have suffered apoplectic fits, were they inclined to do such things. They weren't. I do believe my mother was crafted of granite, my father of bronze. They exuded all the charm, love, and warmth of those two substances.

"Mercy," called Ernie from his office. "C'mon in here for a minute, please."

Hoorah!

Or maybe not.

I picked up my secretarial pad and two sharp pencils—I always had sharpened pencils in a cup on my desk—and went into Ernie's office. Phil and Rob rose from their chairs when I entered. Ernie made a stab at rising but didn't make it all the way to his feet before he sat again.

Because Rob had been gentlemanly enough to offer his chair for my sitting pleasure, I smiled at him and sat. He pulled up the chair that generally sat in the corner so it faced Ernie's desk.

With my pencil poised over my pad, ready to take notes or dictation or whatever Ernie wanted of me, I smiled at him. "Yes?" I asked sweetly.

"Phil has a proposal for you," said Ernie, surprising me.

Plopping my pad and pencil in my lap, I turned my head and peered at Phil. Phil was, according to Ernie, the only honest copper in the entire Los Angeles Police Department. It might have been true. Ernie had been an L.A.P.D. officer for a couple of years after he moved to Los Angeles from Chicago, but the corruption rife in Los Angeles had so disgusted him that he'd quit the force and opened his own business as a private investigator.

"Oh?" I said, curious. "What kind of proposal?"

"Just wanted to know if you'd be willing to take minutes at a meeting Ernie and I have set up."

"Sure," I said. "What kind of meeting? I thought you had coppers on the force who take shorthand."

"They do," said Ernie, taking over from Phil. "But Phil wants to keep this particular meeting on the sly."

"On the sly? That sounds as if you don't trust your own people, Phil," I said.

"He doesn't," said Ernie, again taking over Phil's role.

"Not true, Ernie," said Phil, at last speaking for himself. "I just want to be extra careful about this. It involves important people."

"Oh," I said. "You mean if it involved plain old folks, you wouldn't care?"

"There you go again," said Ernie, grinning. "You really ought to curb your Socialist tendencies, Mercy."

"I'm not a Socialist," I snapped. "I just think we should all be treated the same, no matter who we are."

"So do I." Phil spoke rather loudly, I suspect to keep Ernie and me from sniping at each other anymore. "In this particular case, an L.A.P.D. officer might be involved. I hope he's not, but I don't want to take any chances."

"I will be happy to take notes for you," I said primly. "When and where will this meeting take place?"

"Tomorrow afternoon. Two p.m.," said Phil. "At the Ambassador Hotel."

"Oh!" I said, excited. "Does this involve stuff about the Lewiston case?"

Ernie, Phil and Rob all gazed at me with disapproval writ large on their respective features.

Ernie spoke first. "There is no Lewiston case, Mercy."

"Poppycock," I said. "You told me yourself that Lewiston might have been murdered! That would make it a case. Why else would you hold a meeting at the Ambassador?"

"Any number of reasons," said Ernie. "Possible fraud. Money missing from the Cocoanut Grove's till. Fellow running out on his bill. Guy operating a numbers racket from his hotel room. Gangsters from Chicago trying to corner the market on illegal booze. The list is endless."

I frowned at him. He was correct, darn it. But I'd bet, if I did anything so foolish as to bet on things, that the meeting Phil aimed to hold concerned Mr. Lewiston and his demise. Because I didn't want to incur anyone's wrath, I didn't say so.

"Very well," I said instead, bowing to forces greater than I, even if they *were* lying to me.

"Thanks, Mercy," said Phil.

Turning to my boss, I asked, "You're going to be at this meeting too, right?"

"Yup. And so is Rob. He's been hired by one of the people involved."

"Involved in what?" I queried. "I'd like to know what I'm getting myself into, if you don't mind."

"Nothing violent," said Ernie. "I know that's not what you wanted to hear, but Phil's recently received reports of grifters cheating people out of their money."

"What's a grifter, and what does a grifter do to cheat people of their money?" I'd never heard of a grifter before. My L.A. street-speech education was expanding, by golly!

"A grifter is a plausible fraudster who charms people into investing in non-existent oil wells, railroads, and parcels of land in other states. Stuff like that."

"Oh," I said. "Like those folks who bought land in Florida, thinking they were buying plots on which they could build houses, and the land turned out to be swamps infested with alligators?"

"Right," said Ernie.

"The fellow who hired me," said Rob, "gave another fellow several thousand dollars to invest in a gold mine in Colorado. So far, there have been no gold sightings, and my client is becoming suspicious."

"Why'd he give the other guy money? He must have been persuaded that the gold mine exists, was full of gold, and that it could earn a good profit."

"Exactly," said Rob.

"That's it?" I asked. "Your client gave money to a fellow he now doesn't trust?"

"More or less, yes," said Rob.

"Your client sounds pretty gullible," I opined. "Didn't the man selling the shares show him evidence of the gold mine's existence and expected profitability?"

"Yes, he did," said Rob.

"Well, then, what's your client's beef? Not every investment makes a fortune. Surely he knew that going in."

"Yes, he knew that. But the man selling shares keeps asking for more money," said Rob.

"In that case, your client is a sucker if he keeps paying. I know some of my father's business associates invest in railroads, mines, banks, and so forth before those enterprises begin making money, but most of them know what they're getting into. They also have spare cash to invest in such ventures. They don't just hand over thousands of bucks to dubious gold mine owners."

"Her father's a banker in Boston," Ernie told Rob and Phil, I presume to explain my knowledge (small though it was) of investment schemes.

"He owns the Boston Bank of Commerce," I corrected my boss. "I don't admire my father, my father's business, his friends, or his ethics, but when folks put money into his bank, he invests it in already-successful ventures. I don't know what he does with his own money, but he doesn't take chances with money belonging to his depositors."

"You sure about that?" asked Ernie. "The employees in your father's bank never lend money to people who want to buy stock shares on margin?"

I squinted at him, surprised, never having considered that my father or anyone employed by him might do anything the least bit dangerous or dubious. "I honestly don't know," I admitted. "He's always railing against speculation and peculation. I can't imagine him changing the habits of a lifetime and allowing his staff to gamble with their depositors' money."

"Your father sounds like an honorable man," said Rob.

I shifted my squint from Ernie to him. "No, he's not. He's a rich man who wants to remain rich. He guards his vaults like a dragon guards his golden hoard."

"Poetic mental image," muttered Ernie.

"It's the truth," I said. "Anyhow, what's to say your client isn't just an idiot? Gold isn't as easily come by as it was in the eighteen-hundreds, you know. Maybe he speculated on something not worth speculating on. According to my father, speculating with your money unless you have that much money to lose is a fool's game."

"He said that, did he?" Ernie was grinning at me again.

"Of course he didn't use those words," I said. "But that's what he meant."

"Sometimes there's a fine line between honest gold mine purveyors and dishonest ones," said Rob.

"I guess," I said. "Anyhow, I'll take minutes at your meeting, Phil, but I don't know what you expect to achieve by it."

"We're hoping to determine if Rob's client bought shares in a legitimate goldmining operation."

"How can you do that without taking a trip to Colorado and looking for yourself?" I wanted to know.

Ernie answered my question. "Good idea, but Rob's client doesn't want to take such a long trip. If Rob and I look over the gold mine owner's paperwork, we might be able to tell if he's legitimate or not."

"That sounds really boring," I said. "You're not going to spend much time on this case, are you, Ernie?"

"Not every single case I take results from murder and mayhem you know, Mercy."

"Of course I know that. Sometimes you have to find lost Pekingese dogs. Or tail cheating husbands."

"Don't forget lunatics who stray from their cages," said Ernie.

"Mr. Brentwood is *not* a lunatic!" I said, my temper flaring in spite of my efforts to remain calm. "He's got problems communicating, but he's a brilliant artist. Just because he…well, gets lost sometimes, it doesn't mean he's crazy."

"If you say so." Ernie knew full well that the odd Mr. Brentwood wasn't crazy; he was just being difficult. Ernie. Not Mr. Brentwood.

"Piffle," I said. "But *is* this your next case, Ernie? A man selling shares in a gold mine?"

"Not so much him as his purported mine," said Ernie.

"Same thing," I grumbled.

"I work for whoever pays me," Ernie reminded me.

"You're right," I said, defeated. "It sounds awfully uninteresting though. I won't have to do anything except take notes for the meeting tomorrow, will I? I honestly don't care about fictitious—or even real—gold mines in Colorado."

"You only have to take minutes for one meeting," Ernie promised.

"Very well." My voice sounded glum. I felt glum. I'd been hoping Ernie had been hired by someone to look into the circumstances surrounding the death of Mr. Lewiston. "But I don't find financial stuff awfully exciting."

"Lucky for you that you don't have to," said Ernie.

I know it was childish, but I stuck my tongue out at him.

He, Phil, and Rob all laughed, so I guess they didn't mind.

THREE

Caroline Terry, Sue Krekeler and I gathered at Lulu's reception desk that afternoon shortly after five p.m. Caroline, Sue and Lulu all lived and boarded at my large home on Bunker Hill in Los Angeles. I'd bought the place from Chloe and Harvey when they moved to their mansion in Beverly Hills. Some folks (primarily Ernie) considered my Bunker Hill home a mansion. It was big, true, but it was also close to work. Better, it was near the charming one-block-long funicular railroad called Angels Flight, which took folks from Olive Street to Hill Street every few minutes all day, every day. Hmm. Truth to tell, I'm not sure it operated on Sundays.

Most days, we girls walked the couple of blocks from my home to Angels Flight, gave the conductor our respective nickels, and rode either *Olivet* or *Sinai* (Angels Flight's two railroad cars) to Hill Street. From there, we walked to our respective workplaces. Because I'd driven everyone in my Roadster to work that day, I aimed to drive us all home in it as well.

"Do you two want to take tap-dancing lessons with Lulu and

me?" I asked Sue and Caroline as we waited for Lulu to get off the telephone.

"Tap dancing?" said Sue. "I didn't know you could take tap-dancing lessons."

"Sure," I told her. "The Murray Dance Academy is only a few doors up the street from this building. They teach all kinds of dancing. I think you can even learn to waltz or tango there. You must have passed the studio when you walked here from your job."

"Did I? I guess I wasn't paying much attention. Why do you want to take tap-dancing lessons?"

With a shrug I said, "Just thought it might be fun. I like going to Vaudeville shows and watching the tap dancing. When I lived in Boston, Chloe and I made a trip to New York City and saw *Shuffle Along*. It was great, and all those people tap dancing in a chorus line was downright inspiring."

"I haven't seen many Vaudeville shows," said Sue, wistfully.

"We weren't supposed to see *Shuffle Along*, but we did anyway," I told her.

"I thought that was a show full of Negro people," said Caroline.

She would.

"It was," I said. "It was also great. And heck, everyone tap-dances nowadays."

"Do they?" Caroline sounded skeptical.

"Fred and Adele Astaire tap-danced in *Lady Be Good*. They're as white as you are, Caroline." I didn't intend to sound as censorious as I felt, but I realized Caroline had sensed the bite of my words when next she spoke.

"I didn't mean there was anything wrong with Negro people dancing," she said. "I just didn't know anyone could do it was all."

Both Sue and I peered at Caroline in puzzlement.

"Well, you know what I mean, don't you?" she asked.

"Not really," I told her. "Dancing is universal. Everyone in every culture in the world dances. At least I think they do."

"I love to dance," said Sue. "And I think it would be fun to learn how to tap dance."

"So do I," said Lulu as soon as she hung the receiver on the switch-hook. "I wish people wouldn't wait until two minutes to five to call the building."

"Don't blame you," I said. "Want to walk up to the Murray Dance Academy and inquire about dance lessons before I drive us home?"

After not eating lunch, I was practically starving to death, but I didn't want to let on. No way in heck would I admit I'd sent my book to a publisher and felt anxious about it.

My stomach didn't cooperate, taking that opportunity to growl. Loudly.

Lulu said, "You sure? You sound hungry, Mercy."

"I am a trifle peckish," I admitted. "That single tamale for lunch didn't last as long as I'd hoped it would."

"A tamale?" Caroline gaped at me. "Where did you get a tamale?"

"From the fellow who has the food cart on the corner." Defying a lifetime's worth of my mother's stern admonitions about proper etiquette, I pointed to the corner. It no longer housed the tamale cart.

"Oh," said Caroline.

"I like Pedro's tamales," said Lulu.

"I don't think I've ever eaten a tamale," said Sue.

"Anyhow, I can't go with you to the dance studio," said Lulu. "I have to get ready to go to the Hollywood Bowl."

"That's right!" I gave Lulu a big smile.

"You're going to the Hollywood Bowl?" Sue sounded envious.

"What's playing there?" asked Caroline.

"The New York Philharmonic." Wrinkling her nose, Lulu said, "I'm not much of a classical music person. I prefer music by Al Jolson and Gene Austin."

"I like them, but I also like classical music. I'm sure you won't be surprised when I tell you my mother never let Chloe or me listen to jazz or anything the least bit modern on the radio. Or watch it at the theaters," I said.

"Not surprised," said Lulu.

Sue nodded.

Caroline just stared at me.

Lulu said, "How'd you get to see *Shuffle Along*?"

"We didn't tell Mother that's where we were going, of course."

"Of course," said Lulu.

"Let's skip the dance studio for today," I said. "We can visit tomorrow on our lunch break, Lulu. We'll sign you up too, Sue, if you want us to. Oh, heck, you can come with us. You work right up the street."

"Thanks," said Sue happily. "This should be fun."

"I'm sure you'll have a good time, but I don't think I'll join you," Caroline said. No surprise there. Caroline was a nice young woman, but she was straightlaced and rigid and didn't approve of people having fun.

Lulu nudged me when she walked out from behind her reception desk. Bending slightly, because she's taller than I am, she whispered, "I'm glad she's not going to take classes with us. She's a wet blanket." Sue and Caroline had already started for the front doors, so they couldn't hear us.

I whispered back, "Yeah. She is."

"I've never been to the Hollywood Bowl before," Lulu said then in her normal voice. She sounded thrilled.

"I'm sure you'll have a great time. It's a beautiful place, but even though it's late spring, it will get cold after the sun sets. You'd better take along a wrap. The two times I went, it got chilly even though it was summertime."

"Can I borrow that black evening coat of yours?" asked Lulu. "I don't have anything that will go with my new evening dress."

"Sure. You're wearing the new red velvet one you got last Saturday at the consignment shop in Chinatown?" It was a lovely dress and suited Lulu to a T.

"You don't think it's too red, do you?" Lulu asked worriedly. "I'm not wearing loud colors ever again in my life."

Understandable decision on her part, given that it had been her astonishingly bright clothing that had caught the eye of the evil man who'd nearly killed her.

"Oh, no! It's a lovely gown, and the red isn't too vivid. It's a beautiful, subdued color."

"You think it's subdued?" Now she sounded wary.

"It's a perfectly lovely dress," I reassured her. "I'd have bought it for myself if it had fitted me properly. It looks gorgeous on you. It will definitely be chilly at the Bowl though. You don't have anything with sleeves?"

"G'night, Miss Mercy and Miss Lulu," a voice piped up from behind us.

Lulu and I glanced over our shoulders to find Junior O'Fannin's freckled face grinning at us. He rushed ahead and opened one of the big glass doors before Caroline and Sue got to it. He bowed deeply as he held the door open.

"Thank you," Sue and Caroline chimed in a surprised duet.

"Thanks, Junior," I said, wondering if he expected a tip for his trouble.

"Sure thing, Miss Mercy," said Junior.

Lulu said, "Kind of you, Junior."

"Any old time, ladies," Junior told us.

Junior was a nice kid. He worked in the Figueroa Building as

31

a runner for various attorneys, carrying briefs and so forth all over Los Angeles on his bicycle and on foot. He also performed odd jobs for others when they asked him to do them. When he wasn't fetching and carrying for folks in offices in the Figueroa Building, he whiled away his time in the basement of the building helping Mr. Buck. He helped Mr. Buck because he was a nice kid and Mr. Buck was a stellar person; the rest of us had to pay Junior for his services. Junior and his sister Glynis lived in a fatherless home, and their hardworking mother needed all the help she could get in the making-a-living department.

I didn't have time to dwell on the O'Fannin family's poverty, however, because as soon as we stepped onto the sidewalk, Lulu said, "An evening dress with *sleeves*?" She sounded downright shocked.

"You sound shocked," I said.

"I am shocked. I've never seen an evening dress with sleeves before."

"Oh. Well, you know me. I'm not exactly at the forefront of the fashion industry, but hasn't anybody ever designed an evening gown to wear at outdoor parties? Or evenings out at the Holly-wood Bowl?"

"I don't think so," said Lulu. "None of the movie magazines show actresses in evening dresses with sleeves."

"In that case, be sure to take a blanket as well as my coat. And a pillow to sit on. Those seats are hard."

"Gee, you're making me almost sorry Rob's taking me to the Bowl," said Lulu.

"Don't be silly," I said, sorry for having dented her antici-pated enjoyment, however slightly. "You'll have a wonderful time. Just be sure to wrap up if it starts to get nippy."

"I can do that," she said.

"You know, I read in the *Times* that an American opera will be performed at the Hollywood Bowl sometime this summer. I can't remember the date, but I'd like to go. Maybe I can talk Ernie into taking me."

"You can talk Ernie into almost anything," said Lulu with what sounded suspiciously like a snigger.

"Cut it out, Lulu," I huffed. Then deciding she was actually correct, I went on. "The opera is called *Shanewis*, and it's about Indians and people in high society and how they interact. I read a review from when it was on Broadway, and it's a well-regarded piece."

"Sounds like a tragedy to me," Lulu opined.

After thinking over her words for a second and a half, I said, "You're right. I don't have to see shows about races not getting along with each other, do I? We see stuff like that all day, every day, don't we?"

"I never really noticed until I met you," Lulu reminded me.

Her words gave me pause, which was probably a good thing. Anyhow, we'd made it up the street to my Roadster, and I didn't feel like lecturing Lulu—or Sue and Caroline—about the inequities endemic in our American society, so I let the subject drop. I still wanted to see *Shanewis*, though. Maybe. It would probably only make me angry and sad. Still, I decided to look up the Hollywood Bowl's concert schedule in the newspaper that night. Glutton for punishment, wasn't I?

But everything was well again as soon as I parked the Roadster at home, and we were greeted at the front door by my darling apricot-colored toy poodle, Buttercup. Her nubby tail waved like a fluffy flag. I picked her up, and we all petted her and told her she was a good girl. She knew that already, but she appreciated our confirmations.

"Oh, boy, it smells good in here," said Lulu, sniffing. "I'm almost sorry Rob's taking me to the Bowl."

"You can't beat one of Mrs. Buck's dinners," I acknowledged, my stomach growling in corroboration.

I put my darling pup on the floor and said, "C'mon, Lulu, let's get you appropriately clad for your big night out."

"Thanks, Mercy. Do you really think it'll get cold later on?"

"I know it will," I told her.

As luck would have it, both Ernie and Rob showed up at my front door at about six p.m. Both men entered the beautifully tiled entryway, sniffed the air and said, "Smells good in here."

Opinions were unanimous, by gum.

Lulu was ready in her lovely red velvet gown and my warm velour evening coat. She appeared slightly shy when she walked under the arch from the living room and into the entryway. As shyness and Lulu were a couple of words I never thought I'd think of together in the same sentence, I stared.

Rob stared too.

Ernie didn't bother staring. He came in, grinned, and stood at my side along with Buttercup. Leaning over a bit, he whispered in my ear, "I think they're both smitten."

"I think you're right," I whispered back.

"I'm glad you brought along a wrap," said Rob after he'd greeted Lulu with a chaste kiss on her cheek. "But I've got something that might keep you a little warmer. It gets cold at the Bowl after the sun sets."

And darned if he didn't whip out from behind his back a fur stole!

Lulu clapped a hand to her mouth and stared, speechless.

"Turn around," urged Rob, "I'll drape it over you. I couldn't afford mink, but this is pretty soft."

As if the scene were choreographed, Lulu obediently turned, Rob draped the fur stole over her shoulders, and Ernie, Lulu and I all reached out to feel the softness of the stole for ourselves. Rob was correct. The fur was soft as a...whatever animal it had come from.

"Lulu, that's gorgeous!" I said, happy for my friend, if not for the animals that had sacrificed their lives for her beautiful stole.

"It is, isn't it?" she said, a suspicious quaver to her voice. She petted her new stole as if it were Buttercup.

Lulu and Rob then took off to the Hollywood Bowl, and the rest of us gathered in the living room and chatted until Mrs. Buck called us in to dinner.

"I have a feeling this is better than a boxed meal at the Hollywood Bowl," said Ernie as he forked up some roasted chicken and mashed potatoes.

"It's delicious," said Caroline.

For once, everyone in her vicinity agreed with her.

FOUR

On Wednesday morning, Lulu was a little bleary-eyed, but she fairly glowed with happiness as she returned my velour evening coat.

"I'll never say anything bad about classical music again," she told me.

Taking my coat, I asked, "What was on the concert schedule?"

"I don't even remember. But it was wonderful, and Rob is so sweet to me."

"I'm glad of that. You deserve a nice man like Rob."

"Thanks, Mercy." Lulu sat on the sofa and glanced absently around my sitting room.

"Would you mind hanging my coat in the closet?" I asked her.

"Hmm? Oh. Sure." Lulu seemed to be lost in a love-induced trancelike state that morning.

Because the day was predicted to be a fair one, I'd set out a sensible, lightweight, blue-checked suit with a long-waisted jacket that had a tie belt at about hip-level. In those days, women weren't supposed to have curves, and this outfit was one with which I didn't have to wear a bust-flattener. I was glad of that, because those stupid things hurt me, a victim of unfortunate curves.

As I got ready for work, Lulu waltzed to my closet and hung up my black velour coat.

"Wish I could wear my fur to work today," she said pensively as she floated back to me.

I'd just stuck my right foot into a sensible brown shoe and propped the foot on the vanity stool. As I bent to tie its shoelace, I peered over my shoulder at Lulu, who'd again taken a seat on the sofa. "Do you think your fur stole would be appropriate for your job?" Then I wished I hadn't asked the question. Ever since we'd first met, Lulu had been attempting to spruce me up to little avail.

"Of course it's not," said Lulu with a laugh. "Don't worry, Mercy. I'm not going back to my old ways. But, golly, is that thing warm and comfy."

"I'm sure it is."

"That's a nice suit," said Lulu, surprising me.

I'd just finished tying my left shoe. I stood up, turned and stared at Lulu. "You think so?" I glanced down at myself. Then I looked at myself in the mirror. "It's pretty much like my other office clothes, isn't it?"

"But the blue matches your eyes," declared Lulu.

I stepped a little closer to the mirror and squinted into it. "By Jupiter, you're right." I felt almost dapper, which was better than feeling dull and boring. Both Chloe and Lulu had said more than once that most of my clothes were dowdy. "Thanks, Lulu."

"Sure." She heaved a gigantic sigh. "I can't believe how well Rob treats me."

It sounds mean, but I hoped Lulu wouldn't rattle on all day about her wonderful Rob. I was happy for her, but Ernie sure didn't treat me like any fairy princess, as Rob treated Lulu. Ernie and I were more liable to scrap and squabble than be all lovey-dovey. Ah well.

As we sat at the breakfast table, conversation centered primarily around Lulu, although she didn't participate a whole lot.

"Did you enjoy the concert last night?" asked Caroline.

"Yes, I did." Lulu smiled dreamily.

"What was playing?" Caroline.

"Hmmm?" Lulu.

"I wondered what the New York Symphony Orchestra played last night." Caroline.

"Don't remember." Lulu. With a shrug.

"Lulu's not interested in music this morning." Sue.

"Hmmm?" Lulu.

"It's not worth the effort, Caroline." Me.

"I don't understand." Caroline.

Neither Sue nor I was surprised by Caroline's confusion.

We working girls couldn't linger over breakfast, no matter how delicious it was. Not long after we sat down at the table, therefore, Buttercup walked us to the front door. She appeared disappointed when I patted her and told her we'd be back after work. I'm almost sure she didn't really get lonely during the days; after all, Mrs. Buck was there unless she took her shopping basket and Angels Flight to the Grand Central Market, which was directly across the street from Angels Flight's Hill Street terminal. If you could call such a tiny arched structure a terminal.

As usual, we walked from the bottom of Angels Flight to the Broadway Department Store on Fourth and Broadway, where we bade Caroline farewell for the day. Caroline worked at the hosiery counter at the Broadway. When we got to the Figueroa Building, Lulu, Sue and I stopped for a chat before Lulu and I entered the building.

"Sue, do you want to go with us to the Murray Studio at lunchtime?" I asked. "You can walk down here, or we can meet at the studio."

"I'd love it," she said. "I think tap-dancing lessons will be fun."

"I think so too," I agreed. They'd also take energy and keep me from dwelling on the fate of my first novelistic endeavor. I pictured my poor little manuscript on its way to New York City. It might have made its way to Arizona or Nevada by this time.

Stop thinking, Mercy!

"Let's meet on the way to the studio," said Lulu.

"Good idea," I said.

"Great with me," said Sue.

"Then maybe we can get lunch at the diner across the street," I said. "They have tasty sandwiches." I recalled the meeting at which I was supposed to take minutes that day. "I can't take too long, though. I have to attend a meeting Ernie and Detective Bigelow have set up.

"Rob's going to be there too, isn't he?" asked Lulu.

"Yes," I said, surprised, although I'm not sure why. "Did Rob tell you the reason for the meeting?"

"Hmm?" asked Lulu.

Sue and I exchanged a couple of indulgent smiles.

"Well then, we'll meet at the studio," Sue said.

"See you there," I told her. Then I took Lulu by the arm and gently guided her to the entrance of the Figueroa Building. Mr. Buck, who always left my home on Bunker Hill before my tenants and I did, kindly opened the door for us.

I took the stairs to the third floor and walked to the office. After unlocking and opening the door, I hung my hat, a floppy white felt toque to which I'd attached a ribbon the same blue color as my checked suit, on the hat rack beside the door. Then I wound the clock on the wall, straightened the pictures, made sure the cunning rug I'd bought in Chinatown didn't have any wrinkles in it, and walked to my desk.

There, I opened the bottom right drawer and deposited my handbag. Next came the second drawer on the right side of my desk, from which I withdrew the feather duster I'd brought to the office. Then I went to work dusting everything in the outer room—my space—and in Ernie's room. When Ernie first hired me, the state of housekeeping in the Figueroa building was appalling. That's because the former custodian, a strange fellow named Ned, was lousy at his job.

A little over a year earlier, I pushed Ned down the elevator shaft. I didn't do it on a whim. He was attempting to kill me at the time.

Bah. I didn't like to think about it.

Anyhow, by the time Ernie strolled casually into the office, I'd dusted everything, wound the lovely pagoda-shaped clock on my desk, and sharpened all the pencils in the pencil cup. I looked up from where I'd been straightening the message pad on my desk and smiled at him. "Good morning."

"Is it?" He didn't sound convinced.

"Yes, it is. What's the matter with you?"

"Nothing." He grinned at me. "I just like to rile you every now and then." As ever, he had a copy of the *Los Angeles Times* tucked under his arm. Also as usual, he stepped into his office and flung his hat at the hat rack beside his desk. Unlike most days, he said, "Hey! Got it in one!" Meaning he'd managed to get his hat to land on a peg and not the floor.

"That doesn't happen often," I muttered.

"True," he agreed.

I decided to tell him about my plans for the day. Aside from taking minutes. He already knew about that part.

"Lulu, Sue and I are going to sign up to take tap-dancing lessons at the Murray Dance Academy up the street from here."

Glancing up from the headlines, which were dismal—people were still attempting to blow up the pipelines to the California Aqueduct system—he said, "Yeah?"

"Yeah. I mean yes. We all think it will be fun."

"Tap-dancing? You want to learn to tap dance? You guys plan on going into Vaudeville or something?"

Exasperated, I said, "Of course not. We just thought it would be fun to learn. It's also good exercise."

"Huh."

"Want to go with us?" I said for the heck of it.

"Why would I want to take tap-dancing lessons?"

"I have no idea." Gesturing to the newspaper on his desk, I said, "Ranchers are still trying to blow up the aqueduct system, eh?"

"Yup. In a way, I don't blame them."

"No?" I wasn't quite as surprised by his remark as I'd have been when he'd first hired me. "But if they succeed in blowing up the Aqueduct, L.A. won't have any water."

"True. Which is why folks in Inyo and Owens are attempting to do it. They need the water for their ranches and orchards and so forth."

"Bother. Isn't there enough water for all of us?"

"Beats me," said Ernie. "Hurts too."

"Funny," I said, unamused.

"Spoilsport," said Ernie.

"Anyhow, I presume you don't want to take tap-dancing lessons with Lulu and Sue and me, right?"

"Right," he said. "I was tapped out a long time ago."

"Ha-ha," I responded to his terrible joke.

He only shrugged, grinned, and said, "But you ladies have fun."

"We will. Thanks. We're going to visit the studio on our lunch hour."

"Be sure to get back to work in time for the meeting at the Ambassador."

"I'm *always* on time for my job, Mr. Templeton," I said, a trifle irked. "In case you hadn't noticed."

"Calm down, Mercy. I've noticed, believe me." He grinned up at me before his gaze traveled back to the newspaper. "Be sure to pay attention at the meeting. We need all the opinions we can get about the guy selling shares in his so-called gold mine."

"You already sound skeptical. Why doesn't Rob's client just demand his money back if he's unhappy with the seller?"

"The seller has allegedly invested his money in the mining operation. He's supposed to bring proof to the meeting today."

"Well, if he brings proof, that'll mean he's legitimate, won't it?"

"Depends on how good the proof looks."

I sighed. "How boring. I wish you'd get an interesting case."

"Don't knock it. Money's money. If I don't make enough money, I can't pay my secretary. Even if she doesn't need the mazuma."

"Stop talking about my money, Ernest Templeton," I demanded.

He saluted me.

"Bother," I said and went back to my own desk.

FIVE

Ernie and I took the elevator from the third floor to the lobby a little after noon that day. Lulu looked as if she had the telephone glued to her ear when we walked up to the reception desk.

"People have been calling the building all day," said Junior, who stood at the reception desk. "I don't think Miss Lulu has had a free minute since she walked in here this morning."

"I'll connect you with Mr. Orchard's office," said a frazzled-looking Lulu. She glanced up at me and shrugged, as if trying to tell us she'd be with us if the telephone ever stopped ringing. Finally, after glancing at the clock on the wall and discovering it was already ten past noon, Lulu hung up her receiver, reached under her desk, retrieved the OUT TO LUNCH sign she put on her desk at lunch time, and whooshed out a huge breath.

"Busy morning?" I asked.

"I'll say it was busy," she agreed. "Hey Ernie."

"Hey Lulu," said Ernie. "I hear you ladies are taking tap lessons."

"Yeah!" Lulu sounded enthusiastic.

"Well, good luck to you," said Ernie with a big grin. He strode off to the front door and walked to his Packard, which sat right smack in front of the Figueroa Building. That's because Mr. Buck saved the parking space for him every day.

"Let's get out of here before somebody asks me something else," Lulu said, clapping her hat on her head as she skimmed around the end of her desk and joined me. "The morning has been too darn busy."

"The dance studio is close by," I told her. "It's just a few doors away."

The kindly Mr. Buck opened the front door for us when we left the building. We thanked him and began walking.

Not long after we set out, I saw Sue traipsing down the street in her white nurse's uniform. She wasn't precisely a nurse but she worked in a dentist's office, and they required that she wear the uniform. Sue didn't mind, especially since her dentist paid for her uniforms. She also didn't have to figure out what to wear to work every day.

"Hmm," I said after thinking about Sue's arrangement for a second or two. "I wonder if Ernie would like me to wear a uniform." I waved at Sue, who was in the process of maneuvering her way through the heavy pedestrian traffic.

"What?" asked Lulu.

"Nothing," I said after I'd squinted at Lulu and deemed her to be lost in dreamland once more. I thought it was keen that she and Rob were so fond of each other, but I was also kind of jealous. Don't tell anyone, please.

"Hey Sue!"

Sue heard me and waved. She hurried the rest of the way to Lulu and me. "Is this the studio?" she asked.

Thinking the wording on the door, MURRAY DANCE ACADEMY, was self-explanatory, I nevertheless said, "Yes."

"Good! I've been looking forward to this all morning," said Sue.

"Really? I'm so glad." As my motive in suggesting we take tap was far from pure—I didn't want to dwell on the fate of my first authorial effort—I was happy both Sue and Lulu seemed enthusiastic about the idea. Rubbing my hands together, I then opened the door for Sue. As Lulu had managed to lose herself in romance again, I took her arm and led her into the building.

"Good day to you, ladies," said a good-looking fellow with slicked-back hair, smiling at us. "Charles Murray here. What can we do for you today? Looking to take some dance lessons?"

Because I was the one who'd suggested this expedition, I boldly walked up to the counter behind which Mr. Murray stood and said, "Yes. We want to take tap-dancing lessons."

"Tap, eh? We can do that."

"Thanks." Sue joined me at the counter. As I'd hauled Lulu up with me, she was already there, although I'm not sure she knew where precisely where "there" was.

"You're in luck," said Charles. "We offer beginning tap-dancing classes during the day and in the evenings."

"We're all working women," I said with probably undeserved pride. "What time in the evening do your classes start?"

"Beginning tap starts at seven-thirty p.m. and lasts until nine p.m. We also offer two tap lessons on Saturdays. They begin at ten-thirty and last until noon. The evening classes are on Tuesday and Thursday. Most of our tap classes are taught either by Miss Marian Murray or Miss Lucille Murray. The Murray ladies are not merely my sisters, but they're also professional dancers who have starred in Vaudeville productions and learned at Jack Donahue's studio in New York City. Miss Marian Murray also danced with Fred and Adele Astaire. They're both true professionals and wonderful teachers."

Sue and I exchanged a couple of glances. I said, "Sounds

good to me." Turning to the man, I asked, "How much do the lessons cost?"

Then I hoped like heck the lessons weren't expensive. After all, both Sue and Lulu had to live on their earnings. I tried to live on mine, but I often had to dip into the legacy left for me by my great-aunt, Agatha. She was about the only member of my family whom I'd liked. My parents thought Great-Aunt Agatha was scandalous because she'd divorced two husbands! They also believed Aggie should have left her money to my idiot brother, George.

"Fifty cents per lesson per class, ladies. We don't ask that you sign a contract, by the way. We prefer it if our students *want* to come to classes and not feel forced to come."

"Let me consult with my friends for a bit." I dragged Lulu to the end of the counter. Sue followed. In a whisper, I asked, "What do you think? Is fifty cents per lesson too much?"

"I don't think so," said Sue. "If we go both evenings and on Saturdays, we'll only spend a buck and a half each week. I think it's a good deal." In a whisper, she added, "I read in a magazine that Jack Donahue's Studio is *the* place to learn jazz dancing. And Fred and Adele Astaire are stars."

"True," I whispered back. "If he's telling the truth, both Miss Murrays sound as though they've earned their places in the dance-teaching world."

"Especially if they danced with Fred Astaire," agreed Sue.

Suddenly perking up and paying attention, Lulu said, "Fred Astaire? He's funny looking, but he's a *great* dancer! I wouldn't mind dancing with him."

"I doubt he'll attend our classes," I told her. "But according to that guy"—I hooked a thumb over my shoulder toward the man at the counter—"both Miss Murrays have danced with the Astaire team."

"Oh, my," said Lulu. "Dancing with Fred Astaire. Imagine that…"

Shaking my head, I decided not to remind her that Mr. Astaire would almost certainly not come to the Murray Dance Academy and dance with us. I also decided I'd pay for Lulu's tap-dancing lessons. And Sue's too, if she needed help. Aunt Agatha would definitely consider the expense worthwhile. Also, if my parents ever learned about us dancing to jazz music, they'd be incandescent with rage. So it should work out perfectly.

Returning to Mr. Murray at the counter, I said, "Thank you. Do we need to sign anything?"

"Will you be joining us tomorrow evening?"

As the next day was Thursday, I said, "Yes, please. And we'll come on Saturdays and Tuesdays, too." I glanced at my companions. "Is that all right with you, Sue and Lulu?"

"Sure," said Sue and Lulu together. I hoped they danced as well as they spoke. For that matter, I hoped I'd learn tap as easily as I'd learned typing and shorthand.

"In that case, I'll just take down your names. That way, Miss Murray will know to expect you. You may pay for each class before you enter the studio."

"Oh, and what about shoes?" I asked, wishing I'd thought of this significant necessity earlier.

Leaning over the counter, the young man smiled and said, "I'll let you in on a secret. Most of our students don't go out and buy new shows strictly for tap lessons. You can achieve almost the same effect by using bottle caps."

"Bottle caps?"

"Yes. You'll need three bottle caps per shoe. Hammer two caps on the heel of your shoe—it's best to use shoes that don't have high heels—and another one onto the toe. Instant tap shoes."

"My goodness," said Sue.

"That sounds easy," agreed Lulu.

"Ingenious," I said.

"If you decide you want to continue tap-dance and become more professional, there are special shoes made for tap-dancing, but they cost considerably more than bottle caps."

"I can imagine." Turning to Lulu and Sue, I said, "I'll bet Mrs. Buck saves bottle caps."

"She probably does," agreed Sue.

"Great idea. Thanks," I said.

"Absolutely," said the young man.

"May we please have a look at where we'll be taking lessons? I mean, may we see the…uh, the room?"

"The studio? Of course you may," Mr. Murray said, sounding delighted that I'd asked. He gestured to a door a few paces down the hall from us. "Just go in there. Miss Murray is conducting a class, so please try not to disrupt her or her students."

"Thank you very much." I turned Lulu and she, Sue, and I walked to the door he'd pointed out. I heard clicking noises emanating from the room itself. When I pushed the door open, we saw approximately a thousand children dressed in tutus or tights listening to a beautiful, blond-haired woman who stood in front of them.

Good heavens, I had no idea so many children wanted to learn jazz dancing!

"Remember now, children," said Miss Murray. "Shuffle, hop, step. First the right foot and then the left. Ready?"

I hadn't noticed the pack of mothers bunched at the back of the room until one of them called out, "Start with your right foot, Lenny!"

Looking slightly peeved, Miss Murray said, "Lenny is doing a fine job, Mrs. Autley."

Whichever Miss Murray this was—Marian or Lucille—she

went to a phonograph sitting on a table at the front of the room, lifted the arm and put the needle on a disk spinning on the turntable. I whispered to Sue, "That's a spiffy machine, isn't it?" It appeared to be all-electric, so Miss Murray didn't need to crank it to life.

Sue nodded vigorously.

"Wow, that's swell," said Lulu.

Suddenly *Kansas City Stomp* by Jelly Roll Morton filled the air. Loudly. Lulu gave a start of alarm and squeaked.

"Shhh," I told her. She blinked a couple of times and focused on the children attempting to dance.

The kids began tapping when Miss Murray did. The directions she'd given—shuffle, hop, step—didn't sound too difficult, but some of the kids appeared uncoordinated. One of the boys shuffled a trifle sideways and bumped into a girl with Mary Pickford ringlets. She shoved him away, and he bumped into another child, this time a boy. The second boy didn't merely shove the first boy, but took a swing at the first boy's chin with his clenched fist.

A mother bolted from the cluster at the back of the room and grabbed the second boy's raised arm. "Stop that, you rotten little thug!"

Poor Miss Murray gave a well-deserved—in my view—roll of her eyes and lifted the stylus off the spinning disk. "Mrs. Autley!" She spoke loudly. "Please take Lenny home."

"It's not Lenny's fault!" squawked Mrs. Autley. "That horrid boy hit him!"

"I know," said Miss Murray. "Dickie, you already know that Lenny has a little trouble with his footwork. I'm sure he didn't mean to bump into you."

"He did so!" cried the puncher, whose name evidently was Dickie. "He's not just clumsy, he's a bully!"

"Yes, he is!" said the girl into whom Lenny bumped first.

49

It seemed to be the cue that the rest of the mothers were waiting for. As a gang, they surged onto the dance floor and headed to their respective children. They all spoke at once, so I didn't hear specifics, but I got the impression that Lenny regularly did damage to his fellow classmates. Glad Lulu, Sue and I weren't like that.

And those *mothers*! Goodness gracious sakes alive, they all seemed to hate each other as well as each other's children.

"Let's get out of here," I told my friends, not bothering to whisper as a whisper couldn't have been heard above the uproar.

"Great idea," said Sue.

"Yeah," said Lulu. "Cripes, we won't have to take lessons with those kids, will we?"

"I hope not," I told her.

The three of us exited the studio in a hurry to find Mr. Charles Murray in conversation with a man in a summer suit, looking worried. Mr. Murray, not the man in the summer suit. He just looked smug. Both men glanced up as we entered the room.

Speaking before I could catch my breath, Sue said, "We aren't going to have to take classes with those kids, are we? I don't think we want—"

The poor guy (Mr. Murray) interrupted Sue. I'm sure he didn't mean to be rude. "No, no! Those children are attempting to break into the motion pictures. They need some skills before a studio will work with them. Their...um...mothers sometimes want their kids to get into the business more than the children themselves do."

The summer-suited man frowned first at Charles Murray and then at Lulu, Sue, and me. He didn't speak.

"I noticed that," I said. "But we won't have children in our tap classes?"

"No. There are two classes on Saturdays, one for adults and

one for children." He gave us a smile that, I believe, was meant to be reassuring. "Miss Marian Murray generally teaches the adult classes. Today our other tap teacher, Miss Lucille Murray, was… uh…under the weather, so Miss Marian stepped in."

"Nice of her," I said. "Those kids don't look easy to deal with."

"It's probably not the kids," said Lulu, surprising me. "It's their mothers."

The summer-suited man gave a loud guffaw.

"Yes!" the young man said upon a relieved puff of breath. "That's exactly what the problem is. I mean, they're not a problem, but…" He slid a hand over his slicked-back hair. "Well, you won't have children in your classes."

"Thank you." I turned to my companions, "Want to grab a sandwich?"

"Sure," said Sue.

Lulu had become occupied in studying some of the framed photographs hanging on the walls. "Look," she said, pointing. "It's Fred and Adele Astaire."

"We have an autographed photo of Vernon and Irene Castle too," said Mr. Murray proudly.

"That's terrific," I said, "but we need to get back to work. See you tomorrow evening." I grabbed Lulu's arm and she, Sue, and I headed to the door.

As we stepped out onto the sidewalk, a skinny, rat-faced man bumped into me. I nearly went flying. He said, "Oomph. Watch where you're going!" and charged into the dance academy.

"Well," I said, gathering my ruffled senses together. "And I beg *your* pardon too."

"What a boor," said Sue.

"He looks like a weasel," said Lulu.

"He has the manners of a pig," I said.

"Our pigs were nicer than that for the most part," said Lulu, who had grown up on a farm in Oklahoma.

"I'm glad to hear it," I said to my friends as we stood on the sidewalk. It wasn't quite as crowded as it had been upon our arrival, perhaps because everyone was lunching somewhere. "Want to eat at the Figueroa Diner?"

"Sure," said Sue. "But look there!" she said, pointing at another dining establishment. "Is that a Chinese place?"

"Yes," I said. "It's a Chinese place, and they have good food. Want to eat lunch there?"

"Sure!" said Sue.

"You bet!" said Lulu.

So we maneuvered around the people on the sidewalk, turned right at the next street, and went into the Canton Palace. Ernie and I had eaten food from the place before. The son of the owners, Fong, was a pal of Junior's.

Oh my, it smelled good in there.

A white-clad Chinese waitress smiled at us and gestured for us to take seats at a table across the room. The place was pretty full, but a busboy was busily wiping down our table as we approached. Guess earlier diners had already eaten and left.

"I'm glad we're here and not at the diner," said Lulu after we'd seated ourselves.

"Me too," said Sue. "I don't get to eat Chinese food very often."

"Ernie has a friend who has a restaurant in Chinatown, so we go there quite a lot," I said. Then I took a second to be amazed that I used "we" when referring to Ernie and me. We were an acknowledged couple, by Jupiter! I stopped myself before I could join Lulu in dreamland.

"Charley Wu," said Lulu, clearly still in the here and now. Looked as if I'd be in dreamland by myself if I went there. "I love his pork and noodles."

"So do I." I nodded.

A waiter appeared at our table and handed us menus. "Thank you," I said, believing it was only good manners. He bowed slightly and floated away again.

"Oh my," said Sue. "They sure have a lot of options."

"They sure do," I said.

"Look at this," said Lulu, pointing at her menu. "They have pork and noodles here too."

"So I see." I scanned more options. "Oh, but look here. They serve rice fried with chicken and pork and vegetables. They call it chow fan. If I order that and you two want the same thing, we can split it for only ten cents a plate extra. So that would mean you could have a good Chinese lunch for only ten cents each."

"You'd have to pay thirty-five cents though," said Sue.

"That's all right with me," I said. "I'm not terribly hungry after that big breakfast Mrs. Buck served us."

"I'm starving," said Lulu. "I didn't eat much breakfast because I kept thinking about my date with Rob at the Hollywood Bowl."

Sue and I laughed. The waiter showed up again, and I asked for the chow fan for three. Inspired, I added, "Oh, and please bring us an order of pi qui." I *love* Chinese spare ribs.

"For three?" the waiter asked.

"Yes," I said. To Lulu and Sue, I said, "I'll pay twenty cents extra so you can have some too."

"Thanks, Mercy," said Sue, sounding surprised.

"Mercy's always good to us," said Lulu.

"Piffle," I said. Then I felt myself blush.

The waiter bowed and wafted off, and a busboy brought us tea.

"I love the dishes they use in Chinese restaurants," said Sue, picking up her tiny teacup and admiring it.

"So do I," said Lulu.

"As do I," I said and fanned myself with my menu.

While I was still wielding the menu, the waiter reappeared with food. He nimbly removed the menu from my hand and set the food before us. Boy, was that a good lunch!

After lunch, however, I had to take minutes at a sure-to-be boring meeting. What I wanted to do was take a nap. Too bad for Mercy.

SIX

"Wake up, Mercy," said Ernie at about twenty minutes to two that afternoon.

Jerking in my swivel chair, I lied. "I'm not asleep."

"Fibber."

"We had Chinese for lunch. Made me sleepy."

"Well, keep those baby blues open for a while yet. We have to meet Phil, Rob, his client, and the possible grifter at the Ambassador."

"Fine with me," I said, opening the bottom right drawer of my desk and removing my handbag. Then I grabbed a few pencils and my secretarial pad. Whether I wanted to be or not—not, is the correct answer—I was ready.

I retrieved my floppy cloche hat from the hat tree next to the front office door, plopped it on my head, and Ernie and I walked to the elevator. When we arrived on the ground floor, Ernie took my arm. The lobby was full of people, all of whom seemed to be gathered around Lulu's reception desk.

Wondering if a terrible accident had befallen her, I steered Ernie towards the desk. What I heard was Lulu saying, "Dr.

Graves's office is room 241. Mr. Swedlow's office is room 327. Let me call Dr. Gregory's office to see if he's expecting you."

She didn't say all of the above to the same person, but to different people clumped before her desk. I was impressed with her knowledge of who worked where, but Ernie and I didn't stop long enough for me to tell her so. It was just as well. I'd only have interrupted her. Besides, her telephone had started ringing. Poor Lulu.

"Got an appointment?" asked Mr. Buck as he opened the front door for Ernie and me.

"Yup," said Ernie. "At the Ambassador."

"Nice place, the Ambassador," said Mr. Buck.

"It is," said Ernie. He opened the passenger side door of his Packard and I slid in.

When he got behind the wheel, Ernie said, "Wonder how he knows what the Ambassador's like."

"Why wouldn't he?" I asked, surprised.

"He's a Negro. The Ambassador only allows colored people in through the kitchen entrance. I expect they hire cleaning staff and waiters who are Negroes, but both of the Bucks' kids have college degrees, don't they?"

Startled, although I don't know why—I'd learned soon after my move to Los Angeles that classes (or castes) abound in our supposedly classless country—I said, "Yes, they do."

"Then they probably aren't working as maids or janitors at the Ambassador."

"I think their daughter is teaching school in Los Angeles somewhere. I don't know what Calvin's doing."

"Me neither," said Ernie.

"I think it stinks that they won't let anybody but white people through their front doors," I grumbled.

"Sorry I brought up the subject," said Ernie. "I know how you get."

Rather than rant and rave at Ernie, who didn't deserve it, I kept my outrage to myself as he drove. The traffic at almost two p.m. on this Wednesday afternoon wasn't awfully bad, and Ernie and I arrived at the Ambassador in plenty of time to get to the meeting. Phil and Rob were there already and met us in the beautiful lobby of the hotel as soon as we walked through the doors. Rob had another fellow at his side.

Darned if he wasn't the rat-faced man who'd plowed into me outside the Murray Dance Academy! Oaf. I didn't say so.

"Miss Mercy Allcutt and Mr. Ernest Templeton, please meet Mr. John Horshank. Mr. Horshank appreciates you both attending the planned meeting today."

"Yes, I do," said Mr. Horshank in a high and squeaky voice. His voice suited him, I decided on the spot. I also decided he looked more like a ferret than a rat, although I suppose it's not nice to say so. He also wore big, horn-rimmed spectacles, and I think he wore one of those old-fashioned shirts with detachable collars. And he'd been incredibly rude to me.

As the only female there and having been drilled in my child-hood nearly to death about manners and etiquette, I held my hand out for Mr. Horshank to shake, which he did. His grip was weak and clammy, and I wiped my hand on my skirt, trying not to be obvious about it.

"We've bumped into each other before," I said.

"We have?" said Mr. Horshank, displeased for some reason.

"Outside the Murray Dance Academy about an hour and a half ago," I reminded him.

"I wasn't there. Don't know the place."

Why the big fat liar!

Little skinny liar.

"Do you have a rude twin brother?" I asked.

"*Mercy*," hissed Ernie. Piffle.

"No, I do not." I could tell Mr. Horshank was peeved by my questioning.

Because Ernie seemed annoyed with me already and would only become more so if I set Mr. Horsefeathers straight, I said with a syrupy smile, "We're happy to help."

"We are indeed," fibbed Ernie.

Mr. Horshank nodded.

"Has Mr. Madison arrived?" asked Ernie.

"Who's Mr. Madison?" I asked in my turn.

"He's the one with the gold mine," said Phil under his breath.

"Ah," I said.

Not long after that, another man showed up. He was introduced to me as Mr. Clive Madison. A large man with a jovial manner about him, I disliked him instantly. What a pill I was, huh? Ah well, it was but the truth.

The meeting turned out to be just as boring as I'd expected it to be. Several other men joined the party, which was held in a special conference room at the Ambassador. Coffee and tea were provided to the attendees, and the room was set up more or less theater-style.

During the meeting, Mr. Madison handed around lots of paperwork, including survey maps, blueprints, supposed assay reports, diagrams, city charters, endorsements, and so forth. I dutifully took notes and logged in all the exhibits. After about an hour and a half of that, Mr. Madison asked if anyone had questions. I had questions, but I wasn't about to ask them.

Mr. Horshank asked about the money he'd already invested in the so-called gold mine. Mr. Madison showed him ledgers allegedly attesting to how the already-invested money had been put to use. Mr. Horshank seemed satisfied. Then Rob asked a couple of questions. So did Ernie. So did Phil. So did several other men.

Before I lost my mind entirely, the meeting ended on a happy note, with everyone shaking hands and thanking each other. Have no idea for what. If I could peg Mr. Madison as a male-factor the instant I saw him, I don't know why all those men seemed so happy with him. One of the mysteries of life, I reckon. Or maybe men were just stupid.

When Ernie, Phil, Rob, Mr. Horshank and I got back to the lobby, I asked, "Want me to type up these notes, or was that all for show?"

Mr. Horshank blinked at me. This gesture made him look like a blind mouse. Golly, am I being an old meanie, or what? But he'd bumped into me and blamed me!

"Wouldn't hurt," said Phil after contemplating my question for a second or two.

"If you wouldn't mind," said Rob, smiling.

"Why not?" said Ernie.

"Because Mr. Madison is a crook? You want evidence and a written record?" I asked.

"A *crook*!" Mr. Horshank seemed appalled, and the eyes behind his cheaters grew as large as pie plates. Now he looked like a bug-eyed frog.

Very well, I'm going to stop comparing the stupid man to rodents and amphibians. It's not a nice thing to do. Of course, neither is nearly running a woman down on a sidewalk, not apologizing for it, and then denying he'd done it.

"Well, yes," I said, gazing from man to man to man. And to man. Almost forgot Ernie. "He's clearly cheating the people he wants to attract to his bogus gold mine."

He behaved precisely as the villain in my first novel behaved, in fact.

"Now wait a minute, Mercy," said Rob. "All that paperwork looked legitimate to me. Why don't you believe it was?"

"My father," I said succinctly. "And the newspapers."

"Very well, you've talked about your father the banker

59

before," said Ernie, fixing on my first point. "Aside from being a banker in Boston, what does he have to do with a gold mine in Colorado? Besides, I thought you two didn't get along."

"We don't," I said.

"Well, then, why do you cite him as a source?" asked Phil

"As I told you already, my father's a banker. The people in his bank have dealt with shifty customers like Mr. Madison for eons. If his claims were legitimate, he wouldn't have needed so many pieces of paper. He could have just shown you the business's bank statements. I didn't log any bank statements into evidence. Or core samplings. Anyhow, the surface gold deposits have already been found and depleted. You have to dig deep in order to find gold these days."

"How do you know that?" asked a huffy Mr. Horshank.

"Because I read a lot," I told him. "These days, you need a major fortune to find underground gold deposits. I didn't see any geological surveys or information regarding digging equipment. Or any core samples. You'd need advanced equipment, and he didn't show anything at all about mining equipment. He'd already have had to invest in geological surveys and core samples. In that meeting, Madison talked about 'start-up' costs. I thought this mine had already been started."

"It has!" said Mr. Horshank.

"Then why's he still asking for start-up money?" I asked, believing the question to be relevant.

"How could *you* know anything about gold mining?" asked Mr. Horshank, as if I were a mere nothing.

"Feminine intuition," said Phil.

"Feminine intuition, my foot!" I declared. "Your precious Mr. Madison is as crooked—my apologies to Buttercup—as a dog's hind leg!"

"What do buttercups have to do with anything? Your secretary is out of line, Mr. Templeton."

"Mr. Templeton isn't responsible for my behavior," I snarled at the ferret-faced Mr. Horshank.

Drat. Sorry. I forgot I wasn't going to do that any longer.

"All right now," said Ernie loudly. "Mercy will type up the meeting minutes. Who needs a copy?"

"We do," said Rob.

"I'd like a copy," said Phil.

"Fine," I said. "I'll type them up this afternoon or tomorrow morning."

Taking one of my arms, Ernie led me to the entryway. The last thing I heard before the doorman, after first bowing politely, opened the front door for us, was Phil saying, "So how much does Madison need if we want to invest in the mine?"

Deciding I'd probably said too much already, I didn't talk when Ernie started his automobile and aimed it back toward the Figueroa Building.

After several silent minutes, Ernie said, "Is it really true that surface gold deposits have already been found?"

"And depleted," I said. "Yes. The so-called California Gold Rush started before the middle of the last century. In the seventy-five years since then, operations like the Comstock Lode, the Carlin Mine, etc., have found all the easy-to-get gold. You can't, for instance, pan for gold and expect to find huge gold nuggets shining amongst the pebbles and rocks any longer. They were all found and taken away years ago."

"Interesting," said Ernie.

"And Phil was asking how much it would cost him to invest in Mr. Madison's non-existent mine! Please tell him not go do it, Ernie. Phil has a lovely wife and a darling daughter, and he doesn't need to be losing money on a...what did you call him? A grifter?"

"That's the word all right," said Ernie in a musing kind of

61

voice. "So you've really read all that stuff about gold in newspapers?"

"Yes. And books."

"Good for you!"

Surprised, I said, "You really think my information is worthwhile?"

"You bet I do. It makes sense. I have a feeling Phil might see the light too, if I talk to him."

"Of course, Phil would take the word of a *man* over that of a mere *woman*. Feminine intuition, my left hind foot!"

"Just one more inequity in his harsh old life, I reckon," said Ernie. He was smiling, drat him!

"Iniquity is more like it," I snarled.

"Hey, I'm on your side, Mercy," he said. "Horshank's stupidity isn't my fault. Nor is Phil's, although I'm surprised he fell for it."

"I thought you fell for it too."

"I kept an open mind during the meeting. Mr. Madison comes across as a plausible salesman."

"Unless you know anything about what he was trying to sell."

"True."

"Besides, he didn't come across as plausible to me, even when we were first introduced."

"Now *that's* feminine intuition," said Ernie.

"It is not!" I said indignantly. "When my parents entertained at home in Boston, I met many, *many* Mr. Madisons. They all had that jovial way about them, and everyone thought they were great fellows until one of the Mr. Madisons took off with their money. They thought they were investing in everything from railroads to parcels of buildable land in Louisiana. The land, of course, was swampy and full of alligators, and the railroads didn't exist."

"Really?" said Ernie, not as if he didn't believe me, but rather as if he was intrigued by what I said. "That's interesting."

"Well, you know, Ernest Templeton, we women aren't invited to participate in much of anything, so we learn a lot by observing. Even my father has been fooled once or twice, although he's so tight with a buck he's harder to swindle than most unsuspecting boobies."

"That's interesting too."

"So glad you think so."

"Hey, Mercy, I believe you. I honestly didn't realize how much you'd learned by observing your parents and their friends. No wonder that book you're writing is so good."

I stiffened up like Lot's wife after looking back at Sodom. "What do you know about my book?" My voice sounded strained, probably because it was. So was I.

"You caught me reading it a few months back. Don't you remember?"

"Oh," I said. "Yes, I do remember that."

"I thought you captured people's personalities truly well from the little bit I read."

"Really?" Still strained.

"Yes. Really."

"Thank you."

Ernie gave me a slanty-eyed look before he said, "You're welcome."

Neither of us spoke again until we returned to the Figueroa Building.

SEVEN

By the time we got to the office, it was darned near time to quit for the day. I wasn't sorry.

Although the lobby was full of people, Lulu saw us and waved when we entered the building. Ernie and I stopped at her desk for a minute or two. Fortunately, we were the only two lobby-dwellers who approached her. The rest of the mob headed in other directions.

"Was the meeting as dull as you expected it to be?" she asked.

"More boring, actually," I told her. My voice didn't sound as strained as it had a few minutes earlier, probably because I felt safe in the lobby. Not that I felt unsafe with Ernie, but when he mentioned my book...I can't explain it very well.

"Don't believe her," said Ernie. "It was a fascinating meeting and filled to the brim with exciting details."

"That bad, huh?" Lulu wasn't fooled.

"More than that bad." I attempted a laugh and managed a small giggle. I lectured my inner self to calm down. "Might have been interesting to an alienist or a psychiatrist."

"Why?"

"A person could learn a lot from the confidence trickster, Mr. Madison. The room was full of mugs and saps he aims to cheat. Madison had them eating out of his hand."

"Ow," said Ernie.

"It's true though," said I.

"Golly," said Lulu. Then she said, "Hey, Ern, did Mercy tell you about the tap class we signed up for?"

"We didn't have much time to talk about the class," I said.

"She mentioned taking tap lessons but not that you've signed up for them," said Ernie.

"It was a hoot," said Lulu. "I'm glad we won't have little kids in our tap classes. And those *mothers*! They were as bad as Mercy's mother, only in a different way." She glanced at the clock on the lobby wall. "But it's almost five already! You're not going to make Mercy work overtime, are you, Ernie?"

"Heavenly days, no!" said my boss, slapping a hand to the portion of his body that might possibly contain a heart.

"What about typing up the minutes?" I reminded him.

"Eh, do that in the morning. There's no rush."

"If you say so. But if you value Phil's friendship, try to dissuade him from investing with that sharper."

"Wow, is the great L.A.P.D. detective on the wrong scent?" Lulu sneered magnificently. Not sure if I've mentioned this before, but she and Phil had been at odds a couple of times since I came to work for Ernie.

"Not if I can help it," said Ernie.

"Nertz," said Lulu.

"Oh, and Rob's client—the one he fears is being duped by Mr. Madison—is the same rude boor who ran into me outside the dance studio!"

"You're kidding!" said Lulu.

"No, I'm not," I told her.

"What happened?" asked Ernie.

"Let me take all this stuff upstairs to the office, and I'll tell you there," I said, brandishing my pencils and pad. "Glad I didn't have to cart all those fake exhibits around too."

"Fake exhibits?" said Lulu.

As I walked toward the door to the staircase, Ernie said, "She'll tell you all about it later."

Catching up with me before I could start climbing, Ernie pressed the elevator button, and it began its clanking descent to the first floor from wherever it had been. "Come on up with me, Mercy. You don't have to trudge up all those stairs."

"Thanks, Ernie." My heart, which had seized up and frozen solid when Ernie mentioned my book, had thawed out quite a bit. "I should tell you about the dance studio. Those kids were pure heck, and their mothers were *ghastly*."

"True stage mothers, were they?"

"Is that what they're called? Stage mothers? It sounds about right. They clearly want their cherubim to become stars on the silver screen. Some of the kids weren't as happy about the careers their mothers planned for them as the mothers were."

"And did the kids behave like cherubim?"

"I don't know about all of them, but at least one of them was called a bully by several of the other children. The rest of them didn't appear overjoyed to be there either. Tap-dancing didn't look like so much fun when they were doing it."

"I'm sure." Ernie chuckled.

"But Sue and Lulu and I will enjoy ourselves, I'm sure. And the man at the counter told us how to make tap shoes."

"You can *make* tap shoes?"

"Yes. Use bottle caps. Tack two caps on the heel and one tap on the front, and you've got improvised tap shoes."

Opening the cage to the elevator and gesturing for me to leave it before he did, Ernie said, "Yeah, I can see how that might work. If you have bottle caps. You guys drink a lot of beer in Mercy's Manor?"

It was idiotic of me to be shocked, but I was anyway. "*Beer?* Why would we—" Glancing back at my boss, I realized he was teasing me. Again. "Darn you, Ernest Templeton."

"Hey, it's not my fault you guys need bottle caps."

"Other beverages come with caps on them. Not just beer."

"You'd better hope so if you aim to collect a bunch of them."

When Ernie unlocked the outer office door and we walked in, the telephone was ringing. I hurried over to my desk, dumped my pads and pencils on it, and picked up the receiver. "Mr. Templeton's office. Miss Allcutt speaking."

"Hey, Mercy," said Phil Bigelow. "May I speak to Ernie?"

"Sure. Just a minute." I waved at Ernie to go into his office. "It's Phil," I told him.

"Thanks," said Ernie, and went into his office. He didn't bother tossing his hat at the rack, probably because he didn't intend to stay there for long. I heard him say, "What's up, Phil?" as I gathered my fallen objects and put them into their proper places.

The topic of discussion at Mercy's Manor that night was how to create tap shoes. After dinner, Mrs. Buck raided her stash of bottle caps—"I keep them in case we need them for something," she said—we went to our rooms to find a pair each of old shoes we didn't mind hammering taps on to.

We went upstairs in a clump, and Caroline said possibly the only amusing thing I'd ever heard come out of her mouth. "You should call them cap shoes instead of tap shoes."

Lulu, Sue, and I laughed. Sue said, "You sure you don't want to join us, Caroline?"

"No, but thank you. I think I'll read the *Modern Priscilla* magazine I bought today."

"Yeah?" said Lulu. "Would you like to look at the latest copy of *Photoplay*? I just got it yesterday."

"No thank you," said Caroline. "*Modern Priscilla* will suit me fine. There's a sweater pattern in this one that I think is swell."

"How nice," said Lulu. She stared after Caroline as Caroline walked to her room. As soon as the door closed, she said, "She'd rather knit than read about the stars and the flickers? Well, it doesn't surprise me."

"No, nor I," I said. "But let's see if we can find old shoes to put bottle caps on." Bad grammar, Mercy!

Nobody but my mother, far away in Boston, would care.

We rooted around in our closets. By the time we'd gathered our shoes and gone downstairs again, Mr. Buck was waiting for us with a pile of bottle caps, a box of carpet tacks, and a hammer. He did a great job of nailing our taps to the soles of our shoes. And we had fun tapping in the upstairs hall after he was done. I even attempted the "shuffle, hop, step" move Miss Murray had tried to teach her young students, but I didn't have much success.

The following morning at work, I typed up the minutes of the meeting I'd attended the afternoon before. I made two carbon copies, put one in the file and handed the original and a copy to Ernie. The rest of the day went the way days usually do. I fielded a few telephone calls and wrote down appointments on the office calendars. Ernie had already left the office by the time five o'clock rolled around, so I locked the office behind me and took the stairs to the lobby. Caroline and Sue joined us, and from there Lulu, Sue, and I tramped to Angels Flight and then went home.

At about seven-fifteen that evening, Lulu, Sue, and I got into my pretty blue Moon Roadster and drove back toward the

Figueroa Building. Fortunately, the City of Los Angeles had invested in streetlights, so I wasn't as frightened as I usually was about driving at night. Anyhow, it wasn't really dark yet.

"But it will be when we go home," Sue pointed out. "So it's good you parked here, under a lamp."

"Thanks," I said, pleased that Sue didn't mention cowardice as my motive.

When we walked through the front door of the Murray Dance Academy, Miss Marian Murray was deep in conversation with the same Charles Murray who'd been at the counter yesterday. I didn't hear much of what they said, because I'm not a snoop—

Oh, who am I trying to kid? I'm a first-class snoop. Unfortunately, Miss Murray and Mr. Murray stopped speaking after I'd heard only a sentence or two. Those sentences were moderately interesting, however.

"Don't do it, Charles. It's stupid to risk your money unless you know considerably more about the scheme than you know now."

"But he showed me the paperwork," said Charles.

Shaking her head, Marian said, "I still don't want to do it."

"But it's a sure thing, Marian. Profits will double in six months."

"Anyhow, it's *our* money," said Marian. "And I don't want to risk my part of it or Lucille's on what sounds like a fishy scheme."

"There's nothing fishy—" Charles saw us and clammed up.

Marian saw us too, smiled broadly and walked over to greet us, holding out her hand. "Good evening! Charles told me that three lovely ladies would come tonight to take our beginning tap class."

"That's us, all right," I said.

We shook hands and introduced ourselves to Marian. I positively *longed* to ask the siblings what the perhaps-fishy scheme was in which Charles wanted to invest. A gold mine in Colorado perhaps? I managed to curtail my curiosity, but a brilliant plan began formulating itself in my brain. Maybe. Might not have been brilliant. Sometimes it's difficult to tell at first.

Anyhow, back to the dance studio.

After inspecting our bottle-capped tap shoes, Marian told us we were all set. We paid our money and followed her to the dance studio. No cluster of children met our eyes, thank heaven, nor was there a pack of rabid mothers gathered at the back of the hall.

"We'll use this room over here," said Marian, directing us to another door. It led to a smaller, mirrored room. "It might be disconcerting at first, but it's a good idea to watch yourself in the mirror after you learn the basics, because you can perfect your moves better if you can see them.

"That makes sense," said Lulu.

"It does," I said, delighted. "We came yesterday when you were teaching a class of children."

"Please," said Marian in a world-weary voice. "Don't remind me. Most of the kids—with at least one exception—are okay, but their mothers... Well, all I can say is, I'd rather teach you three."

For the record, Lulu, Sue, and I wore old day dresses. Marian wore an outfit that reminded me of the gym bloomers I'd had to wear at school in Boston.

"Where do you get an outfit like yours?" asked Lulu of Marian.

"Most stores carry gym slips or gym bloomers," Marian said. "You're fine as you are for tonight. Unless you want to keep up with tap-dancing, there's no need to buy a special outfit or special shoes. If you *do* decide to continue tap, these shoes are swell." She bent her knee and lifted her leg so we could view her shoes. Low-heeled, patent-leather, black shoes, they reminded me of the "Mary Janes" my mother made me wear for the first sixteen years of my life, only Marian's pair had big metal plates attached to the toe and heel of each shoe.

"My goodness," said Lulu. "May I feel them?"

"Sure," said Marian. "They're just leather shoes with taps riveted to them. The brand of these is Capezio. There are stores in Los Angeles that cater specifically to dancers and other folks in show business who need footwear especially crafted for dance. They sell ballet slippers too, if you want to learn how to dance *en pointe*."

"You mean on our toes?" asked Lulu.

"Exactly."

"No way," said Sue. "I'd fall over for sure."

"Me too," said Lulu.

"Dancing *en pointe* is rough on a person's feet, too," said Marian. "I don't recommend it for ladies your age."

"Hey, I'm only twenty-two!" said Lulu.

With a laugh, Marian said, "I'm not calling you old. I'm just saying that you really need to begin when you're a youngster in order to learn ballet properly. And it's still extremely hard on a person's feet even when you start young."

"How do you spell that brand name? Capezio?" I asked, reaching into my handbag for my note case. It was a cunning item I'd purchased in Chinatown months earlier. It held note paper and a pen in a special holder.

"C-a-p-e-z-i-o," said Marian.

"Sounds Italian," said Lulu.

"I believe the man who started the company came from Italy," said Marian. "Another good brand is Miller and Ben's."

"Miller and Ben's," I repeated, dutifully jotting down the name on my notepad.

"Yes," said Marian. "Capezio or Miller and Ben. They make reliable footwear for dancers. Believe me, when you dance a lot, your feet get a brutal workout. It pays to buy good shoes if you aim to dance onstage or professionally."

"Oh, but we're just…girls," said Sue. "We're not professionals."

With a light, silvery laugh, Marian said, "None of us were professionals in the beginning. It takes time and hard work in order to become a dance pro."

"I'm sure it does. Anything anyone does in a creative field takes time and hard work," I said, thinking of my unpublished writing career. "And luck."

"Especially luck," said Marian as if she knew.

I had a dismal feeling that luck might play a prominent role in becoming a published author, darn it. I decided not to think about it, but to pay attention to the task at hand.

"Very well, ladies," said Marian, lightly clapping her hands. "It looks as if you're the only beginning tappers here this evening, so you'll get special attention from the teacher. Why don't you line up in a row there, leaving space between you so you don't bump each other?"

"Yeah, like Lenny bumped What's His Name in the class yesterday," said Sue.

"Who's Lenny?" asked Lulu.

"You didn't notice Lenny bump into that other kid? Dickie?" I asked.

"Guess I was thinking about Rob," said Lulu, her cheeks taking on a pretty pink color.

"You're better off not seeing him," I told her.

"Not seeing *Rob*?" Lulu was horrified.

"No," I clarified. "You're better off not having seen Lenny."

"Ah," said Lulu.

"That's for sure," said Marian.

"Is he generally a problem in your classes?" I asked, curious.

"I don't teach the children very often," Marian said. "Lucille,

72

my sister, usually takes the class, but she was unable to teach yesterday. I may never forgive her." She laughed again.

"I don't blame you," I said.

We lined up like good little girls and began our very first tap-dancing lesson. We shuffled, hopped, and stepped as directed, and I think we did a creditable job. We had a little more trouble with flap, ball, change, and a step called the chop suey.

"Very good, ladies," said Marian after we'd been shuffling, hopping, stepping, flapping, and ball-and-changing for a few minutes. "Let's see how well you dance to music." She went to the gramophone, lifted the arm and placed the needle on the disk.

All I can say for sure is that we did our best.

"I'm exhausted," said Lulu when we limped back to my little Moon Roadster. "And I'm not coordinated like you two are."

"You did fine, Lulu," said Sue, who seemed to have a better grasp of rhythm than either Lulu or I.

"We just need to practice," I said, hoping I was right.

"If we practice in the upstairs hallway, we're liable to scuff the floor beyond repair," muttered Lulu.

"Hmm. That's true," I said. "Maybe we can tap outside. The weather's warm enough."

"Tapping on the driveway," said Sue, laughing. "Sounds like the name of a song."

"It does, kind of," said Lulu. "I almost fell over when we were trying to do the chop suey."

"I did too," I said. It was the truth. "I thought taking tap lessons would be fun, but maybe I was wrong."

"You weren't wrong!" said an animated Sue. "It was lots of fun! I love it."

"Very well then," I said, feeling slightly more chipper than when we'd first left the Murray Dance Academy. "Can't hurt to keep practicing."

"Practice makes perfect," said Sue.

"I'm gonna have to practice the chop suey a whole lot," said Lulu.

"Same here," I said.

Buttercup was delighted to welcome a bedraggled trio of worn-out tap-dancers back to our home on Bunker Hill.

We all slept well that night.

EIGHT

F riday morning, however, found at least one of last night's dancers (me) stiff as a board and hurting. I doubt my legs and feet had ever been called upon to do so much work. Perhaps I should walk down to Hill and then up to Olive instead of taking Angels Flight every day.

I decided to start that particular exercise routine on Monday. It was all I could do to walk across the floor to the powder room on Friday. Buttercup, as ever, cheered me on.

"Oh lord, Buttercup, how am I going to walk downstairs?"

Buttercup didn't have an answer for me. Fortunately, the more I limped around in my sitting room, the more mobile I became. My muscles still hurt, but I could move more easily. As always, I'd set out the day's office attire before going to bed, so at least I didn't have to think and hurt at the same time.

A knock at my door sent Buttercup wagging to see who was there. I was in the process of tying my sensible shoes, so I called, "Come in!"

The door opened. Lulu said, "I can hardly move this morning!"

Sue stood right behind her. "I'm sore all over!"

"Join the party," I said, and groaned when I put both feet on the floor and stood up straight again.

"I guess I knew dancing was difficult, but I didn't know it would be harder than physical exercise classes at school!" said Sue. She had a happy smile on her face in spite of her achy body.

"We didn't do much exercising at my school," I said. "We mostly just played tennis. I hate tennis."

"I suppose it's good for you though," said Sue, walking into my sitting room.

"I don't like tennis. I liked badminton, because the birdie doesn't go as fast as tennis balls go. Maybe my eyes are bad. I had trouble following the path of the ball in tennis."

"All we ever did was run around the track," said Lulu of her own experience in Oklahoma. "We were in pretty good shape to begin with, because we farmed. You have to be strong to do farm work. I haven't done any for quite a while."

"You roped a bad guy a few months back," I reminded her. "It was thrilling to watch too."

"Oh, yeah," said Lulu. "I did do that, huh?"

"Did you really?" Sue was wide-eyed.

"She did." I grabbed my hat and handbag and walked to the door, down the hallway and to the staircase. There I clung to the banister rail as I went downstairs. "She was a heroine."

"Good for you, Lulu!" Sue seemed entirely too enthusiastic that morning. Unless my aching body made me fail to appreciate her bounce.

I wasn't surprised to find Caroline already in the breakfast room by the time we laggards managed to maneuver down the stairs and get to the room from which the good smells emanated.

"You gals got home late last night," said Mrs. Buck as she brought the coffee pot into the room and poured for us. "Did you enjoy your dance class?"

"Yes!" said Sue. "It's hard work, but it was fun. Wasn't it?"

"Uh-huh," said Lulu uncertainly.

"Yes," I said, deciding I should appreciate Sue and attempt to emulate her happy attitude.

"And did those bottle caps on your shoes work well enough?" asked Mrs. Buck.

"Very well," I said.

"I'm glad to hear it. Mr. Buck asked about whether they worked or not. You be sure to tell him they did when you get to work, Miss Mercy."

"I will," I said.

Breakfast was, as ever, delicious. I felt slightly less weak and sore after I polished mine off. The walk to Angels Flight helped loosen me up even more. Friday at work was relatively boring, but we all survived. Ernie and Rob both came to dinner at Mercy's Manor on Friday night.

It's probably a good thing we didn't have to take another tap class that evening. Instead, Ernie and Rob took all of us to the flickers. Even Caroline enjoyed *The Winning of Barbara Worth*, starring Ronald Coleman, Vilma Bankey, and Gary Cooper. I thought Vilma was beautiful, and Gary Cooper was…well, spectacularly handsome. Ernie looks a little bit like Mr. Cooper.

On Saturday, we three adventuresses felt a little less stiff and sore. At breakfast, we discussed the motion picture. Lulu, Sue, and I also discussed taking the tap class that day.

"Yes!" Sue said with intense enthusiasm.

Caroline gave her a side-eye. "I thought all that dancing made you sore."

"It did," said Sue. "But it's so much fun! I definitely want to continue. Exercise is good for a person."

"Yes, I suppose that's so," said Caroline. "But tap-dancing isn't awfully dignified, is it?"

"Who cares about dignity?" asked Lulu sharply. "Tap is fun. We're all young women. We should have fun."

This from a woman who, a few minutes before we went downstairs for breakfast, had come to my room and told me she wasn't sure about taking any more tap lessons. "I didn't know I was so out of shape," she said despairingly.

I'd felt the same way until Sue and Caroline's conversation at the breakfast table. Now I was firmly on Sue and Lulu's side.

"Exactly," I said. "I had to be dignified when all the other little girls in the world were playing with their dogs and dolls. There's nothing the least bit undignified about being able to dance, no matter what kind of dance. Besides, as Sue said, the exercise is good for us."

Lifting her eyebrows, Caroline said, "Very well. I just thought something a little less strenuous might be better for you."

"Eh, strenuous is good," I said, although I have no idea why. "Builds muscles."

"Ballet dancers must be strong as heck," said Lulu in a musing voice. "And Marian Murray said they have to dance on their toes, which is bad for their feet."

"*En pointe*," I said. "Yes. I don't think I'd want to do that."

"Do you think the Astaire siblings know ballet?" asked Caroline.

"Probably," said Sue. "They both point their toes a lot."

Upon that note, we finished breakfast. I don't know what Caroline expected to do with the rest of her morning but Sue, Lulu and I all went upstairs and retrieved our tap shoes. We then walked to Angels Flight and took the car *Sinai* to Hill Street. From there, we walked to the Murray Dance Academy. We were early for our lesson.

When we entered the lobby, a swarm of children was already in evidence. A lovely woman who looked almost, but not quite, identical to Marian Murray seemed to be herding them and their mothers into the large dance studio.

"Ah, there you are," said Marian, spying us. "Welcome. We'll use the smaller room again today. The children take up all the space in the large studio."

"Is that your sister Lucille?" I asked, gesturing to the retreating gaggle of children and mothers.

"Yes, that's Lucille," said Marian fondly. "We've been dancing together for most of our lives. We were on the Vaudeville stage in New York City when we were no more than toddlers."

"That must have been wonderful," breathed Sue in rapture.

"It was hard work," said Marian in a voice meant to quell undue romanticism. "We had one of those mothers too." She gestured to the kids and mothers entering the large studio.

"I'm sorry," said Lulu. "My first name is Lucille, too, but everyone's always called me Lulu."

"Lulu suits you," said Marian.

"I loved our first lesson," said Sue.

Marian smiled at the three of us. "You weren't too sore the next morning?"

Lulu, Sue, and I exchanged glances. "Actually," I said, "we were."

"But it was worth it," Sue hastened to say.

"Yes, indeed," I affirmed.

"Yeah," said Lulu.

I don't think Marian believed Lulu or me, but she gave us another friendly smile. An additional woman joined us that morning for beginning tap.

So, with Marian leading us, we attempted to execute our tap steps as we stared at ourselves in the huge mirror in front of the studio. Staring at ourselves in the mirror was disconcerting at first, but we shuffled, hopped, stepped, ball-changed, and chop-sueyed our way through the next one and a half hours.

79

The lady who'd joined in the class with us left after about the first half-hour. I have a feeling Lulu would have liked to leave with her, but Lulu wasn't a giver-upper. Neither was I, although I rather wanted to quit too. I was dripping and exhausted at the end of our lesson.

Sue, on the other hand, while glowing with perspiration, was almost euphoric. Lulu and I watched her slanty-eyed as she gushed to Marian.

"I've never had so much fun in my life!" Sue told her.

"I'm so glad," said Marian. "You worked very hard, and you seem to be a natural. You pick up the steps really well."

"Thanks!" said the beaming Sue. She joined Lulu and me as we wiped our brows with our hankies and sat to change our shoes. "This is the best idea you've ever had, Mercy!"

"Really happy for you," I whimpered.

"You're good at this, Sue," said Lulu. "I'm not so great."

"You just need more practice."

"You think so?" Lulu wasn't buying Sue's message. I could tell.

"I wish your excitement were contagious," I told her. "I'm beat to a frazzle."

"Oh, you just need to soak in a hot bath and take a nap. You'll be fine in no time."

"Sounds good," said Lulu. I could tell she was skeptical.

"We can rest up tomorrow," I said, feeling guilty because I aimed to rest on Sunday and not attend church services.

"I'm going to practice," said Sue, unlacing her tap shoes. She replaced them with sensible low-heeled oxfords.

I'd already changed into my walking shoes and wished I'd driven us to the class that morning. But I hadn't, so we'd have to walk to Angels Flight, take one of the cars up to Olive and then walk two blocks home. I didn't want to. Heck, I didn't want to walk out of the dance academy.

My mood, however, didn't matter. I squared my shoulders and said, "Very well. Let's go home."

"Want to stop at a lunch counter for food first?" asked a perky Sue.

"No," Lulu and I chorused.

When we opened the studio door into the lobby, I realized I'd managed to forget about all the children and their mothers who'd danced in the larger room. They were straggling out, appearing about as worn out as I felt. As we trod past the desk, I heard Charles and Marian in whispered conversation.

"I can't believe you did that, Charles! That money isn't just yours, you know. Lucille and I earned most of it!" Marian was clearly angry with her brother.

"But it's a sure thing," Charles whispered back. "It will pay off enormously."

"You're an idiot, Charles Murray. Lucille and I didn't agree to this so-called 'investment scheme' of yours."

"But you'll reap the profits along with me. You'll see. Just wait a little while."

"Guess I'll have to," grumbled Marian. "Nothing I can do about it now. That shyster has probably already left the country."

"Don't be—" Charles saw our disheveled trio and shut his mouth.

Boy, I really wanted to know what kind of investment scheme Charles had bought into with his—and, evidently, Marian and Lucille's—money. Too bad, Mercy Allcutt. In a way, it's unfortunate that we didn't linger and I didn't ask, but I was fatigued beyond bearing just then.

"You three did a great job today," Marian said, smiling with what appeared to be genuine pleasure. "Hope you'll continue tap classes."

"We will," said a happy Sue.

"We will?" whispered Lulu.

"We will," I said firmly. "No quitting."

By golly, as the three of us left the dance academy, I saw Mr. John Horshank scurry up the street. He ignored us and barged into the academy's building. "There's that rude Mr. Horshank again," I muttered. "I'll bet he's the one trying to get Charles to invest, and I'll bet he wants him to invest in the gold mine that isn't there."

"Huh." Lulu limped even more than I did on our way to Angels Flight.

She and I let out a relieved "Ahh," once we were seated in the car *Olivet*. Unfortunately, the ride only took about a minute. Then we had to rise and walk out of the carriage. At least it took us up that steep, steep incline between Hill and Olive. The same hill I'd contemplated walking up and down to and from work. Silly me.

"You know," said Sue as we began our trudge back to Mercy's Manor, "we should be walking up and down that hill instead of taking Angels Flight every day. The walk would help strengthen our muscles."

"Sue Krekeler, you're nuts if you think I'm going to hike up and down that hill every day!" Lulu cried with more energy than I could summon.

With a shrug, Sue said, "Just a thought."

"After our muscles get used to the unaccustomed exercises we get with our tap lessons, maybe we can try walking up and down the hill," I said in an attempt to soothe feelings. Deciding a change of subject wouldn't come amiss, I said, "I wonder what Marian and Charles were arguing about."

"Dunno," said Lulu.

"I didn't know they were arguing," said Sue, surprised. "I didn't hear them."

"Guess I'm snoopier than you are," I told her.

My response drew a laugh from Lulu, so that was a good thing.

"You don't know what they were beefing about?" asked Sue.

"Some kind of investment. Marian didn't want Charles to invest in something, but he did it anyway. Marian was peeved with him for sinking her and Lucille's money into some investment opportunity. I'll bet it's that silly nonexistent gold mine."

Lulu tilted her head. "Wasn't that meeting Rob, Ernie, and you had to go to about investments and a gold mine?"

I nodded. "Yes. Some crook is trying to convince people in L.A. to invest in a gold mine in Colorado that doesn't exist."

Squinting at me, Sue asked, "How do you know it doesn't exist?"

"He's spinning a long list of lies," I said. "Before I moved to California, I read everything I could find about the gold frenzies in California, Nevada, Alaska, and Colorado."

"Why in the world did you do that?" asked Sue as if reading about gold mining was an unnatural act.

"I wanted to learn about the state I aimed to live in," I told her. "Colorado and Nevada were involved in the rush for gold, too. And Alaska."

"You read the strangest stuff," muttered Lulu.

"You're smart, Mercy," said Sue. I guess she thought Lulu's judgment to be slightly harsh.

"I suppose it was rather an odd thing to read about," I said, siding with Sue. "But I learned a lot. There's no gold left unless you dig underground for miles, and the guy who held the meeting was talking about picking up gold from the ground."

"You can't do that?" Lulu said.

"Not any longer," I said.

"Too bad," said Sue.

"I guess."

Even talking about that stupid meeting bored me. I was glad when we got home. After I let Buttercup outside to do her duty as a dog, we found some waxed-paper-wrapped sandwiches the kindhearted Mrs. Buck had left for us in the kitchen and ate them with some lemonade she'd also prepared. Then we all went upstairs. I took Sue's advice and soaked my tired, achy body in a warm bath. Then Buttercup and I napped.

NINE

By Monday morning, I decided I was going to live to take another tap lesson on Tuesday evening. So did Lulu. There was no doubt about Sue. She had become totally enchanted with tap-dancing.

Good for her, was all I could say about that.

Phil called Ernie's office early on Monday. "May I speak to Ernie?" he asked.

"As soon as he gets here, I'll ask him to call you," I told Phil, who ought to know by this time that I was the only person in our firm who arrived at work at the stroke of eight o'clock.

"Thanks, Mercy." Phil sounded glum.

"What's the matter, Phil?"

"It's a situation I need to talk about with Ernie."

He didn't end his sentence with a preposition! How about that?

"Very well." I tried not to feel miffed that Phil wouldn't tell me his news.

"I'm sure Ernie will explain it to you," said Phil.

I wasn't, but I hoped he would.

When Ernie strolled into the office at around eight-thirty, which was a trifle earlier than he generally showed up. I waved a message at him. "Phil called."

"Why'd he call so early?"

"Don't know," I said. "I didn't ask."

"What's he want?"

"He wouldn't tell me."

Ernie's eyebrows lifted over his startlingly blue—in truth, they were almost turquoise—eyes. "That bad, huh?"

I shrugged.

With the *Los Angeles Times* tucked under his arm, Ernie took the message from my fingers, glanced at it, crumpled it up, and went to his office. There he threw his hat at the hat rack, missed, grumbled something under his breath, and continued to his desk where he swished his hat from the floor and hung it on the rack. He sat in his swivel chair, and I heard him pick up his telephone receiver and dial Phil's L.A.P.D. number. He didn't shut his door, so I listened hard.

Still couldn't hear anything until Ernie raised his voice. "What do you mean, he's gone? Where'd he go?"

Phil must have said something because Ernie stopped talking.

"People don't just disappear, Phil. He's got to be somewhere."

More silence from Ernie.

"Did he mention anything about Madison's gold mine?"

Very well, this might actually be of interest to me. I rose from my desk, grabbed a secretarial pad and two sharpened pencils, and went to Ernie's office. Ernie glanced up and frowned at me, but he didn't shoo me away.

"Don't know what to do about it," said Ernie. "Do you think he's bolted? Why would he do that?"

I could hear Phil's voice, but not the words he spoke, dagnabbit.

"You don't think Madison's murdered him, do you?" Ernie sounded incredulous.

Appalled, I stared at him as he listened to Phil. I tried to listen harder, but I still couldn't make out any words from Phil's end of the wire.

"Cripes," said Ernie at last. "I don't know either, Phil. You can hire me to look for him, but since he's a copper, you'd probably be better off using some of your fellow officers."

A drone on Phil's end of the wire.

"Yeah, but Two-Gun Davis doesn't like private dicks snooping into his territory."

I knew "Two-Gun Davis" to be the Los Angeles Police Chief. According to Ernie, Chief Davis preferred to shoot bootleggers rather than bring them in to face arrest and trial. Ernie might have been correct. I had little to no first-hand information about bootleggers. I'd gone to a speakeasy once, but I'd never do it again. At the time, I'd been too innocent to be afraid. Silly me.

"Yeah," said Ernie. "You too." He hung up his receiver and stared at me.

"What's going on?" I asked.

"Phil just told me that his pal in the department who wanted to invest in that gold mine seems to have disappeared."

"He's a policeman, right?"

"Phil's friend? Yes. Name is Gerald Royce."

"How does Phil know he's disappeared? Has he not been to work or something?"

"Right. And Phil hasn't been able to reach him by telephone. Royce wasn't home when Phil checked on him, either."

"Is there a Mrs. Royce or any little Royces?"

"Nope."

"What does Phil expect you to do about it?"

With a shrug, Ernie said, "Don't know. He's just worried, is all. I can snoop around, but I don't do jobs unless someone pays me."

With a cheeky grin, he withdrew a flask from his vest pocket and took a sip. When I'd first met him, Ernie's flask had outraged me. Much to Ernie's irritation, one of his friends let on that he only kept apple cider in the flask.

"Talk to Mr. Horshank," I suggested.

Looking at me squint-eyed, Ernie said, "Why?"

"He keeps turning up at the dance studio. On the day we went to that meeting about the gold mine, Mr. Horshank nearly ran me down outside the dance studio. Then he denied doing it."

"Ah, so that's what you were asking about, was it?"

"Yes. He didn't apologize, either. In fact, he told me to watch where I was going. Rude man. He's also as stupid as a rock if he's paid Mr. Madison any more money. I've heard Charles and Marian Murray squabble about some investment scheme Charles wants to get in on. Marian doesn't want to waste her money."

"And you're sure the gold mine is a sucker's bet, right?"

"Of course it is!" Annoyed, I said, "I told you why. I doubt there's surface gold anywhere in the world any longer; people have been greedy for it for so long."

"Did…what did you say his name was? Charles Murray?"

"Yes."

"Did he mention a gold mine?"

"No, but I've seen Mr. Horshank there or nearby at least twice now. He's hard to miss; he looks so much like a weasel."

"Unkind, Mercy Allcutt," said Ernie, laughing.

"Perhaps, but true. Besides, he deserves no kindness from me. He was *rude* to me."

"Maybe I should call Rob. See if he knows anything about Mr. Royce. I'm not even sure Horshank is still using Rob, for that matter."

"I don't know why Mr. Horshank hired him in the first

place," I said. "What does a lawyer know about nonexistent gold mines?"

"Horshank was going to sue Madison if Rob decided the scheme was bogus."

"And it turned out to be bogus, so why isn't he still with Rob?"

"He didn't believe you."

I allowed my head to fall back, and I gazed at the ceiling of Ernie's room. "What about Rob? Does he believe me?"

"Oh, yes. Your arguments were cogent and believable. That's what Rob said. 'Cogent and believable.'" He grinned. "Of course, I believed you instantly. But Rob went back to his office and did the research you'd already done. Mr. Horshank didn't like the conclusion Rob came up with."

Why was I noticing prepositions all of a sudden?

Never mind.

"The man sounds like an idiot to me," I told my boss. "I can almost understand why a Neanderthal like Mr. Horshank wouldn't believe *me*, but why wouldn't he believe the man he hired to find out precisely what he found out?"

With a nonchalant shrug, Ernie said, "Probably because he didn't want to. He wants the gold mine to be real."

I shook my head. "That's stupid, Ernie."

"Yeah, I know."

"Anyway, I don't like it that I keep seeing Mr. Horshank near the dance academy, and I hope he's not urging Charles Murray to invest in the lousy gold mine."

"Why don't you ask Mr. Murray?"

"I don't want him to know I eavesdropped on his and Marian's conversation."

Ernie laughed. "But let me call Rob. Maybe he knows what Horshank has been up to."

"Is it okay if I stay here while you do that?"

"Sure."

Ernie called Rob. As I listened to the two men chat, I got the impression that Mr. Horshank and Rob had parted company none too congenially. After a few minutes, Ernie hung up his receiver.

"You and I were both right. Rob researched gold mines, discovered what you already knew, and Horshank didn't want to hear it. According to Rob, he stormed out of his office, in fact."

"Hmmm," I said. "I don't believe I've ever seen an enraged weasel. Bet his face turned red. Wonder if his whiskers sizzled."

"His what?" Ernie stared at me.

"Don't weasels have whiskers?"

Shaking his head, Ernie said, "I have no idea."

TEN

Shortly after Ernie entered the office, he left again. A woman had hired him to find out if her husband was cheating on her. I hate to admit that many aspects of a private investigator's work are rather sordid. As Ernie kept telling me, however, no job is exciting all the time.

That morning turned out to be quite busy, telephone-wise. Phil called at least three more times before noon. I also fielded a call from a former client, Mrs. Richard Swale. Mrs. Swale lived in the swanky Hancock Park area and owned two enormous mastiffs. She used to be married to a man who had attempted to kill Ernie and me and who had died before she could divorce him. Her dogs, Caesar and Augustus, foiled his plans. She wasn't an agreeable woman, but she wanted to hire Ernie, so I was polite to her.

"May I tell him what you'd like him to do for you?"

"I generally have no use for underlings," said Mrs. Swale, true to form. "In this case, however, please tell him I am most concerned about one of my friends in the dog world."

"Very well. I'll certainly tell him that. Um, would you like to explain your concerns to me or wait until you can see Mr. Templeton?" Given her attitude about underlings, I figured she'd say a curt "no" and hang up. She surprised me.

"You might as well tell him that I believe Miss Padgett—you recall Miss Padgett?"

I cast my mind back a few months. "Yes. Miss Padgett has a Russian wolfhound and an Irish wolfhound, right?"

"Boris and Bevan. Right," said Mrs. Swale. "I believe Miss Padgett is being taken advantage of by a man—he's certainly no gentleman—whom she and I met at a recent dog show in Pasadena."

So why did Mrs. Swale care? There had been a time when Mrs. Swale had actually threatened the lives of Miss Padgett's dogs. She hadn't meant to carry out her threats, and ultimately it was discovered that the friction between the two ladies—well, women—had been caused by a simple misunderstanding. "Has Miss Padgett deputized you to intervene with the person whom you believe to be taking advantage of her?"

Did that sentence even make sense?

"Of course she hasn't," snapped Mrs. Swale. "I'm concerned for her welfare. I've spoken to her, but I can't seem to get through to her."

I remained baffled but game. "In what way is Miss Padgett being taken advantage of?" Curses! Another preposition at the end of a sentence. I'm sorry.

"A fellow who attends A.K.C. dog shows is attempting to lure her into investing in what I *know* is a fraudulent scheme."

"Oh."

Not a brilliant response. But why the heck were so many people being drawn into so many fraudulent investments these days?

"So make an appointment for me to see Mr. Templeton," Mrs. Swale demanded. "I'll consult with him, and perhaps he can think of a way to warn Miss Padgett away from the man and his suspicious plot."

"Very well," I said. "What time would you like to come in? We have an appointment opening today at one-thirty."

"One-thirty will be fine."

And she hung up without another word. As mentioned earlier, she wasn't a pleasant person. I'm surprised she and Miss Padgett became friends, although I imagine the dog-show world is a limited one.

As soon as I'd written Mrs. Swale's appointment on my desk calendar, the telephone rang again.

"Is Ernie in?" asked Phil Bigelow.

"He went out on a job, Phil. He's still out."

"Damn. Well, have him call me as soon as he gets in."

"I shall," I said primly, not appreciating his curt tone.

The front door opened and Ernie strolled in.

"But wait, Phil," I said into the receiver. "Ernie just walked in."

"Good. Let me talk to him."

"Very well, your majesty."

"What?" said Phil, sounding vexed.

"Nothing." To Ernie, I said, "Phil wants to talk to you. This is the third time he's called this morning."

"Okay," said Ernie. He reached for the receiver in my hand, so I gave it to him. "Why are you harassing my secretary, Phil?"

I heard Phil's voice coming scratchily from the receiver. "Dammit, Royce is dead!"

Both Ernie and I were startled by this news. Ernie plunked himself onto one of the chairs in front of my desk. "He's dead?" He pulled the receiver away from his ear so that I could hear Phil's words more clearly.

"His body was found in Griffith Park by a dog-walker earlier today."

"Yeah? Natural or unnatural death?"

"He was shot," said Phil concisely.

"Murdered then," said Ernie.

"Yeah," said Phil. "I don't know if this has anything to do with Madison and his gold mine, but it's worth thinking about."

"I don't think about anything until someone pays me to do it," said Ernie, telling a grubby truth.

"Yeah, I know," said Phil. "Unfortunately, I *have* to think about this. Someone murdered a Los Angeles police officer, Ern. That's big. The press will be all over the department."

"As well they should be. After all, it's not nice to shoot people, and I suspect the public will be upset that the L.A.P.D. can't even protect its own."

"Cripes. Don't say things like that," muttered Phil.

"Sorry. Just saying what the press will be printing."

"Cripes," Phil repeated. Then he hung up without another word. Just like Mrs. Swale.

Which reminded me. I waved a message at Ernie as he replaced the receiver on the switch-hook. "Remember Mrs. Swale?"

Taking the message and squinting at it, Ernie said, "No. Who's Mrs. Swale?"

"Mastiffs? Caesar and Augustus? Her husband tried to kill us?"

"Oh," said Ernie. "Her."

"Yes. Her. She thinks someone is leading Miss Padgett astray. Or at least into a phony investment opportunity."

"Miss Who?"

"Padgett," I snarled, annoyed that my employer seemed to have such a lousy memory. "Boris and Bevan? Russian wolfhound and Irish wolfhound? Cried all over you? Miss Padgett, not her dogs. You must remember her."

"Oh, yeah. Her. I'd forgotten her on purpose. Why does Mrs. Swale care if Miss Padgett is being led astray?"

"I have no idea, but she's worried. And she's coming in at one-thirty this afternoon."

Ernie cast a glance at the clock on my office wall. "Is she bringing those monster dogs with her?"

"I have no idea and didn't dare ask. She doesn't like dealing with underlings."

"Who's an underling?"

"According to Mrs. Swale, I'm an underling. She only wants to deal with the top brass."

"I'm surprised you haven't set her straight yet," said Ernie, grinning at me.

"I am your private, confidential secretary, Ernest Templeton. It's not my place to set clients straight regarding the importance of my job. If you recommend I do so, I'll tell her to jump in the nearest lake."

"You say she wants to hire me for something?"

"Evidently."

"Eh, then, let's go to lunch and worry about Mrs. Swale and her dogs and Miss What's Her Name when she gets here."

"Fine by me," I said.

"Good. Let's go to Charley Wu's place."

"Oh, good. I love Chinese. Does Charley's mother still give you free food?"

"Sometimes," said my boss, who had been credited by most of the population in Los Angeles's Chinatown with saving Charley Wu from a murder charge. Never mind that it was I who nagged and prodded and ultimately forced him to get involved in the problem he later was credited with solving. Not that I'm bitter or anything.

"Shall we see if Lulu wants to join us?"

"Sure. Why not?"

We took the elevator to the lobby floor. Lulu did want to join us, so Ernie drove all three of us the short few blocks to Chinatown, where he found a handy parking spot nearly in front of Charley's. After climbing up onto the tall seats at the lunch counter, we dined (as usual) on pork and noodles. Also as usual, they were delicious. I'd long since overcome my aversion to picking up my bowl in order to get the last dregs of lunch.

When we returned to the Figueroa Building, Mr. Buck opened the door for us, Lulu resumed her seat behind the reception desk, tucked away her OUT TO LUNCH sign, and Ernie and I went back to the third floor, where we found Detective Phil Bigelow pacing back and forth in front of Ernie's office.

He spotted us and marched from the office door to the elevator cage, which Ernie opened for me. After making sure the floor of the cage was level with the hall, I preceded Ernie from the elevator.

"Where the devil have you two been?" barked Phil.

"Having lunch," said Ernie. "What's eating you?"

"Cripes," said Phil. "Sorry I snapped. But Royce's murder is getting complicated."

"Not your everyday cop killing?" Ernie may have sounded the slightest bit sarcastic.

Phil, Ernie and I walked down the hallway once more. When we got to Ernie's office, Ernie unlocked the door and gestured for Phil and me to enter. The telephone was ringing when the door opened, so I hurried to answer it. Stupid telephone. Because I answered the 'phone in my room, Ernie and Phil walked into his and shut the door! Darn it, I wanted to know what was going on regarding the dastardly murder of a Los Angeles police officer.

Too bad for Mercy Allcutt, huh?

At approximately one-twenty p.m. Mrs. Swale appeared at the office's front door without Caesar and Augustus. She frowned at the closed door of Ernie's office. "I thought you said he had free time at one-thirty." Her tone scolded me.

"He has," I said. "Detective Phil Bigelow of the Los Angeles Police Department came to him with an emergency." Sort of.

"Well, I don't appreciate my time being wasted on others."

"Of course not. I'll let Mr. Templeton know you've arrived for your appointment"—I glanced at my pagoda-shaped clock—"a few minutes early."

"Hmph," said Mrs. Swale.

After rising from my chair, I walked to Ernie's door and knocked softly. As I did so, I turned the knob and opened the door a crack. "Mrs. Swale is here for her one-thirty appointment, Mr. Templeton."

"Ah. Thanks," said Ernie. To Phil, he said, "Let me know what you find out."

Standing, Phil said, "Will do."

Ernie stood as well and walked Phil to the door of his office. I stepped aside and Phil strode to the front office door.

Ernie smiled and said, "Mrs. Swale?"

"Yes," said Mrs. Swale, sounding indignant for no reason I could fathom.

"Miss Allcutt, will you please join us and take minutes?"

Would I? You bet I would! "Of course, Mr. Templeton," I said demurely.

I followed Mrs. Swale and Ernie into Ernie's office. Because I thought it better to be inconspicuous whilst taking notes during client interviews, I sat in a chair in the corner of the room. Mrs. Swale plopped herself down into one of the chairs facing Ernie's desk and said, "I'm sure you recall Eleanor. Miss Eleanor Padgett."

"Yes," Ernie lied. "I recall her. She has two large dogs."

"Her hounds are tall. They aren't as massive as my dogs." Mrs. Swale sounded as though she considered being massive a good thing in a dog. Buttercup might object. I know I did. Mrs. Swale probably liked her massive dogs because they resembled her in the massiveness department.

"Right," said Ernie. "What about Miss Padgett?"

"She's being urged to invest in a fraudulent gold mine in Colorado."

Although I'd almost expected her words, they startled me so much I nearly dropped my pencil.

ELEVEN

After exchanging a glance with me, Ernie said, "Do you know the name of the person who is trying to lure Miss Padgett into investing in what you believe is a fraudulent scheme?"

"Yes. Mr. Frederick Lewiston."

Ernie and I swapped another startled glance.

"And what does Mr. Lewiston do for a living?" asked Ernie.

"Why do you need to know that?" barked Mrs. Swale.

"I need to gather as much information as possible in order to help people with their problems. If you don't know Mr. Lewiston's profession, fine. If you do, then the information might assist me in my investigation."

"Hmph. I think he's a stockbroker or a banker or something of the like."

"In what city?"

"Los Angeles."

Even though I'd sat in the corner in order to become invisible, I couldn't keep my mouth shut. "What breed of dog did he show?"

Mrs. Swale turned her head to frown at me. Ernie didn't have to turn his head. He just frowned at me from his desk.

"What difference does *that* make?" snarled Mrs. Swale. "And why are you using the past tense?"

Bless Ernie's heart (assuming he had one), he jumped into the conversational morass to support me. "As I just said, Mrs. Swale. The more we know about an individual, the greater our chances of solving the case." I could tell he didn't mean it about dog breeds, but Mrs. Swale couldn't.

"He shows Afghan hounds and salukis. That's how he and Eleanor met. They both show hounds."

I'd never in my life heard of a saluki. A trip to the library might be indicated.

"The saluki isn't recognized yet by the American Kennel Club (A.K.C.), although its origins are ancient," went on Mrs. Swale. "Some clubs are allowing the dogs to compete in spite of them not being a recognized breed."

What the heck did that mean? Given the reaction the first time I asked a question, I decided not to risk banishment from Ernie's office and kept silent. Fortunately for me, Ernie decided to ask the question for me.

"What does that mean? To be recognized by the A.K.C.?"

Mrs. Swale huffed as if such a question was so silly as to be outrageous. "A certain number of people need to want to show specific breeds of dogs in order for the breed to be formally recognized by the A.K.C.. The A.K.C. has exacting standards for entry into its club books."

"Ah," said Ernie, who still seemed a trifle baffled by the A.K.C. and its rules.

So was I.

"And Mr. Frederick Lewiston met Miss Padgett when they were both showing their dogs at a show in... Where was it?"

"Pasadena," said Mrs. Swale as if Ernie should have remembered that.

If I'd been as efficient a secretary as I like to claim I am, I'd have written down that information on the message slip. Oh dear. I silently vowed to do better next time.

"I see," said Ernie. He sat back in his swivel chair and pondered something for a few seconds.

Impatient, Mrs. Swale huffed once more and said, "Well? What do you aim to do about this problem?"

After another moment or two of thought, Ernie looked straight at Mrs. Swale. "I'm not sure what I *can* do, Mrs. Swale. Mr. Frederick Lewiston died several days ago. Defenestration."

"He's *dead?*" I couldn't tell if Mrs. Swale was surprised or offended that Mr. Lewiston might have popped off before she could interfere in his life.

"Yes. Mr. Frederick Lewiston is no longer with us," said Ernie.

"What did he die of?" asked Mrs. Swale, although Ernie had already told her.

"He fell out of a window at the Ambassador Hotel."

After a moment of silence, Mrs. Swale said, "That's ridiculous. Is this some kind of joke?"

"No ma'am. I'm surprised you haven't read about his demise in the newspapers."

"I don't read those types of articles," said Mrs. Swale in a snooty voice. Maybe I should introduce her to my mother. They'd probably hit it off nicely.

"If your aim was to keep Miss Padgett and Mr. Lewiston away from each other, it looks as if your problem is already taken care of."

"That's not funny, Mr. Templeton," growled Mrs. Swale.

"I wasn't attempting humor, Mrs. Swale," said Ernie.

A few more seconds of silence ensued. Then, abruptly, Mrs.

Swale rose from her chair. "Well, then, I suppose I don't need your services," she said.

"I suppose not," agreed Ernie. "Let me see you to the door." He rose and skillfully slithered around his desk to take Mrs. Swale's arm. I got up from my chair too and followed the pair into the outer office. There, Ernie gallantly showed the horrid woman to the door and actually bowed her out. Then he turned and gave me a puzzled look.

"I don't know what the devil is going on," he said. "Is the entire world investing in a cursed gold mine that doesn't exist in Colorado?"

"Seems like it," I said.

"And you say the folks at that dance place are investing in it? Or something else sketchy?"

With a shrug I said, "Marian thinks it's sketchy. Charles doesn't. I don't know what Lucille thinks about it, because I've only overheard Marian and Charles talking. I don't know what the so-called investment opportunity is, but I've seen Mr. Horse-feathers there a couple of times now, so maybe it's a gold mine. The investment, I mean. There was another fellow talking to Charles too, but I haven't seen him since that first day."

"What's the name of the fellow who runs the hat shop down the street?" Ernie asked.

Although it sounds as if that question was totally irrelevant, it wasn't really. "Mr. Gallagher," I said promptly. "Shows Italian greyhounds. And he's a big man!"

"And Italian greyhounds aren't big?"

"No. They're tiny and delicate."

"Interesting," said Ernie.

"Well, not that Mr. Gallagher being big means he should show big dogs. It's just somewhat incongruous."

"What's a saluki look like?" Ernie asked then.

"I have no idea."

"Cripes. Guess we don't really need to know."

"No, although now I'm curious."

"But it's not a case we're working on, so there's no need to find out about them," Ernie opined.

"If you say so. I have a grim foreboding that we're going to be knee deep in dogs and phony gold mines before this case is over."

"What case?"

"The fake gold mine case."

"What's with this grim foreboding thing? You've never mentioned forebodings before."

"I haven't had any before. There's just something about the fake gold mine that keeps expanding. Like a...what are those creatures that are blobs and just spread out and engulf other things?"

"I have absolutely no idea."

"Well, the fake gold mine case seems to be something like that, whatever it is. Maybe like a lava flow?"

"I don't have a single clue what you're talking about," said Ernie.

It figured.

"Never mind." I wasn't easy in my mind though. Although it sounds dramatic, my innards actually *did* quiver with apprehension. The gold mine, the dance studio, the dogs, Mrs. Swale, and Miss Padgett were going to get together one of these days and explode. Or possibly merely rain all over the rest of us.

Or maybe I'd just gone 'round the bend. Wouldn't surprise me, especially since I kept mentally seeing my poor lonely manuscript sitting in a pile in some editor's office in New York City, abandoned, alone, unloved, and almost certainly to be thrown out if anyone ever looked at it.

Ernie left the office shortly after Mrs. Swale went away, and I was stuck with nothing to do. Maybe I should begin writing another book.

The notion scared the daylights out of me. Then I recalled Marian Murray's wise words about getting better by practicing. So I sat in my office chair and tried to envision another plot for a murder mystery, only without much gore and grimness. Oddly enough, a plot regarding a criminal banker appeared in my brain almost instantly. Imagine that. Guess my father was good for something after all.

Shortly before quitting time that Monday, Ernie returned. Darned if he didn't have Mr. Gallagher, the haberdasher and Italian greyhound maven, with him! Although considerably surprised, I managed to lay a blank piece of paper over the one in my typewriter and produced a welcoming smile for the two men.

"Miss Allcutt, will you join us in my room, please?" said Ernie pleasantly.

"Good afternoon, Miss Allcutt," said Mr. Gallagher with what appeared to be a pleasant smile. The first time I'd met him, I'd believed him to be a murderous villain, but I guess he didn't need to know that.

"Good afternoon. Yes, I'll join you, Mr. Templeton."

I carefully removed the manuscript page from the typewriter, frustrated because Ernie and Mr. G. had interrupted me in the middle of a spate of words. Nevertheless, I grabbed my pad and a couple of pencils and followed the two men into Ernie's office. At a gesture from Ernie, I shut the door behind me.

Mr. Gallagher politely pulled out one of the chairs in front of Ernie's desk and indicated I should sit in it, so I did. He took the other chair. The corner chair remained vacant. Guess Ernie didn't care if Mr. Gallagher knew our business.

"Miss Allcutt," Ernie said after he'd sat in his swivel chair in front of the window, "Mr. Gallagher is acquainted with both Mrs. Swale and Miss Padgett. He also knew Mr. Lewiston and can tell us all about"—he stopped speaking as if he were searching for the proper word—"those dogs Mr. Lewiston had."

"Salukis?" I asked, having recalled the word, although no doggie images sprang to mind.

"Yeah," said Ernie. "Those dogs."

"I've taken in Mr. Lewiston's dogs, as a matter of fact," said Mr. Gallagher.

Although I'm pretty sure no one cares, the first time I'd seen Mr. Gallagher, not only did I believe him to be a villain of the worst sort (a murderer), but he'd also been perusing a pink racing form. I know: who cares? Just thought it might be interesting for others to know that dog people and horse-racing fans can sometimes occupy the same human body.

"Are salukis anything like Italian greyhounds?" I asked before I could stop myself. After all, I was there to take notes, not question the man.

Ernie shot me a quick frown. "Exactly what I was going to ask."

"Well," said Mr. Gallagher in a musing tone of voice, "Salukis and Italian greyhounds are both in the hound group. Salukis, however, are sighthounds and much larger than my babies."

His babies? Ah. His Italian greyhounds. That's fair. I often thought of Buttercup as my baby.

"I see," said Ernie. "Did you show your dogs at a show in Pasadena not too long ago?"

"Yes, I did. Mr. Lewiston was there, as were Mrs. Swale and Miss Padgett." Mr. G. wrinkled his nose when he spoke Mrs. Swale's name. "I don't know how Mrs. Swale hasn't been reprimanded by the Beverly Hills Kennel Club before now. Miss Padgett is a nice woman, if gullible."

"In what way is Miss Padgett gullible?" asked Ernie.

"She's easily led," said Mr. Gallagher, tenting his fingers under his chin. "I'm sure you know that Mrs. Swale was threatening to harm Miss Padgett's dogs. She wouldn't have gone through with her threat, but she also bribed judges. Terrible woman."

"But Miss Padgett and she became friends in the long run, didn't they?" Ernie again.

Shaking his head as if he didn't understand females, Mr. G. said, "Yes."

"And do you know anything about the investment opportunity in which Mr. Lewiston was attempting to interest Miss Padgett?"

After squinting for a second as if trying to decipher Ernie's sentence, Mr. G. said, "Yes. It was some kind of gold mine in Colorado. I thought it was a risky venture and tried to dissuade her, but Eleanor is a trusting soul."

"Have you any idea who the ringleaders of the gold mine scheme are?" asked Ernie.

Good question! I hadn't even thought about who might have conceived of the idea.

After musing for a couple of seconds, Mr. Gallagher said, "I'm not sure. I know there's a fellow named Madison who came poking around at the show. He had a pal named Mr. Autley—"

I nearly jumped out of my chair. Both Ernie and Mr. Gallagher stared at me. I shook my head and said, "Sorry. Go on."

"Very well. There were Madison, Autley, and a skinny rat-faced man who seemed to be harassing Eleanor in Pasadena. Fred—Mr. Lewiston, that is—ultimately warned him away from her, although he'd invested in the scheme too. I can't remember his name."

"Mr. Horshank?" I asked, forgetting my proper place in the office universe once more.

"Yes, I believe his name was Horshank." Mr. Gallagher shook his head and looked troubled. "But I don't think either Madison or Horshank is the inventor of the scheme. Might be Autley, and I heard Fred and Madison talking about a fellow named Royce. They both sounded as though they were afraid of Royce, but that might have been my imagination."

"Royce?" Ernie sounded incredulous.

"I'm pretty sure his name was Royce," said Mr. Gallagher.

I raised my hand as if I were a student in elementary school. Tilting his head, Ernie said, "Yes, Miss Allcutt?"

"You mentioned a man named Autley?" I asked Mr. Gallagher. "He was one of the gold mine people?"

"Yes," said Mr. G. "He and Madison seemed to be together."

"There's a boy named Lenny Autley who takes tap lessons at the Murray Dance Academy," I said.

"Shoot, Mercy," said Ernie. "You didn't tell me that."

"I didn't know it was important until right this minute. Nobody mentioned an Autley before now."

"Huh," said Mr. G. "Autley is kind of a tough-guy-type."

"So's his son," I muttered.

"Interesting," said Ernie. "Well, thanks, Mr. Gallagher. Appreciate your time."

"Happy to help," said Mr. Gallagher. "Fred Lewiston was a friend, and he was an asset to the Los Angeles dog-show scene."

"I see," said Ernie. "Thank you very much, Mr. Gallagher."

"Happy to help," said Mr. Gallagher, who actually sounded happy. "And I hope you like your new hat."

New hat? I'd ask later.

"I'm sure I will. Thank you," said Ernie.

So Mr. Gallagher left the office, and I pounced on the hat issue.

"What hat?"

"I bought a new fedora. Thought you'd be pleased. You were always disparaging my old one."

"Well, it was kind of a mess after Phil stepped on it, even though Mr. Gallagher attempted to repair it," I pointed out.

"Yeah, yeah, but there's no reason to give up on a garment when there's life left in it."

"If you say so."

"I think you and your pals should steer clear of that dance place until we figure out who's who in the gold mine scheme."

"Fiddlesticks," I said. "I think I'll become an investor. That way I can get the skinny on everything."

"You're not getting anywhere *near* the gold mine scheme. Anyhow, Horshank already knows who you are, so you can't be an investor."

"Fiddlesticks. That's true, although he probably won't remember me. He seems the type."

"The type who doesn't remember lovely women?" Ernie squinted at me.

Did he just call me a lovely woman? I didn't ask, but my heart warmed up. I fear my cheeks did too. Blushing can be *so* embarrassing. I left Ernie's room and went back to my desk before I could do anything awkward. Anything *else* awkward. Bother.

Quitting time on that Monday arrived at last. Ernie came to Mercy's Manor for dinner yet again. Nobody minded. Mrs. Buck positively adored Ernie, and she loved the way he cleaned his plate. Sometimes more than once. I swear, the way that man ate, I don't know how he didn't weigh a ton.

Ah well.

Tuesday at E. Templeton, P.I.'s office was boring. Ernie left shortly after arriving in order to catch straying spouses (spice?) in the act. Well, not *the* act, but in the act of stepping out with people to whom they weren't married.

I swear, a private detective's lot is really ignoble sometimes.

Most of the time.

Fiddlesticks.

Lulu, Sue, and I had a great time at our tap-dance class on Tuesday night, however. Our time spent at the Murray Dance Academy also proved enlightening.

When the class ended and the three of us sat in the folding chairs against the wall and changed our shoes, I decided to snoop out loud. Marian had come over to chat with us, so my question, when I asked it, wasn't totally out of the blue.

"Say, Marian, I overheard you and Mr. Murray talking about an investment the other day. There seems to be no end of investment opportunities floating around these days."

"Bah," said Marian, her usually sunny expression clouding over. "Charles is an idiot."

"Good heavens," said Sue, sounding shocked, probably because she was.

Shaking her head and resuming her smile, Marian said, "I'm sorry, girls, but honestly. Everyone seems to be selling some get-rich-quick scheme these days. Charles thinks this stupid gold mine in Colorado is going to be our stairway to fathomless riches."

How poetic. I didn't say so. What I said was, "Oh, is that why that silly man, Mr. Horshank, comes here so often? And is Mr. Autley also involved in the mine?"

"You know Mr. Horshank and Mr. Autley?" Marian's surprise was unfeigned. At least I'm pretty sure it was.

"Not to say *know* them," I answered, tying my right shoelace. "I had to attend and take minutes at a meeting about a gold mine in Colorado, though, and Horshank was there. The only time I ever saw Mr. Autley was here at the studio. He was talking to Charles. That so-called gold mine is definitely a shady venture. You might want to talk Charles out of spending his money."

"Really?" Marian's eyes widened. "How do you know that?"

"Mercy's smart," said Sue.

"She reads all the time too," said Lulu.

Embarrassed, I said, "I don't know how smart I am, but my boss is a private investigator, and his best friend is a police detective. Two people involved in that gold mine scheme have been murdered, so it's also dangerous."

"Good heavens!" said Marian. "That's terrible."

"You didn't tell us that," said Sue.

"No, you didn't," agreed Lulu.

"I'm not supposed to gab about my job," I said in my own defense. "And I had no idea Mr. Murray was involved until today."

"My goodness," said Marian. "It sounds as though things are becoming downright dangerous in the gold mine investment business."

"They are," I agreed. "The man who explained the scheme in the meeting I was forced to attend was lying through his hat too, although his audience seemed to be eating up his words like candy."

"Holy moly," said Sue.

"There's no gold just lying around on the ground anywhere anymore, either," I told Marian. "It's all been carted away."

"Ha!" said Marian. "I knew it! Thanks, Mercy. I'm going to tell Charles what you found out right this minute. He might drive Lucille and me crazy sometimes, but he's our brother, and we love him." And off she marched, clicking across the floor and to the outer reception room.

"Good for you, Mercy," said Lulu with a laugh. "You might eavesdrop, but you also might have saved the Murrays a bunch of money."

With a sigh, I tied my left shoelace. "I guess I've learned a lot about snoopery from Ernie. I'd hate to see the Murrays taken advantage of. I don't want their studio to close either."

"No! They can't close," declared Sue. "I *love* this class!"

Lulu and I exchanged a glance over Sue's head. Neither Lulu nor I precisely loathed our tap-dance lessons by this time, but we definitely hadn't been gifted with Sue's knack for grace and choreography retention. In other words, Lulu and I still sort of lumbered around, as opposed to Sue's graceful execution of the steps Marian Murray taught—or tried to—teach us.

TWELVE

As the days chugged by, however, Lulu and I gradually began to feel less like ice-skating hippopotami and more like honest-to-goodness tap-dancers.

When I informed Ernie about the Murrays' involvement in the phony gold mine, he squinted at me and said, "I really think you should quit that class."

Startled, I said, "Why?"

He shook his head. "I don't know. It's just that people who invest in that racket are being bumped off right and left. Even you must see it might be dangerous to be around potential investors."

"What do you mean by that? *Even* me? Precisely what do you mean, Ernest Templeton?"

Holding up his hands as if to ward off a blow, Ernie said, "Crumb, never mind. But you said you see that Horshank chump there, right?"

"Right. And Mr. Autley."

"Him too," said Ernie.

"But all we do there is tap dance. Or try to."

"True, but the studio owner is involved with Horshank, Autley and the gold mine," Ernie reminded me.

"Only one of the owners," I said, my excuse sounding feeble even to my own ears.

"Both Lewiston and Royce have been murdered, don't forget."

"Yes, but they were both involved in the gold mine. Lulu, Sue and I aren't investors. We just take tap-dancing classes."

"Huh. I still don't like it."

"Well then, it's a good thing I don't care what you like, isn't it?"

Ernie pressed a palm to his chest. "Ow. That hurt."

Grinning, I said, "Good," and flounced off to my desk.

At our next Tuesday evening class, Marian said, "Very well, ladies, I think it's time to teach you a choreographed routine."

"A what?" Lulu appeared puzzled.

"A little dance routine," Sue gushed, excitement fairly bubbling in the air around her.

"Are we ready for that?" Skeptical was I. I mean, none of us fell over whilst chop-sueying any longer, and even Lulu kept her balance through most of our classes, but still... Occasionally, Lulu'd wobble sideways. This was particularly true when Marian had us practice the three-count riff walk.

"I'm the teacher, and I say you are." Marian gave us one of her silvery laughs.

"Maybe I should stand in the back." Lulu sounded even more doubtful than I.

"Nonsense," said Marian. "However, I will ask Sue to come to the front of the room. Lulu and Mercy, I have other plans for you."

Even though said in humor, her words sounded ominous. At once, my brain flew to New York City, where my manuscript likely now lay, unread and unloved, among a pile of other manuscripts, most of which were destined for the rubbish heap. I feared my own paltry effort would join them there, and my mood drifted downward.

"Whatever is the matter, Mercy?" asked Lulu. She grabbed my arm and hauled me to the back of the small room. "All of a sudden, you look as if somebody kicked your dog."

With a jolt, I returned to the here and now. "Buttercup?" I said. "Why would anyone kick Buttercup?"

"Nobody would." Lulu heaved a sigh. "But you seemed to go away for a second or two. Let's see what Marian is teaching Sue to do. I hope we can just stand back here. Sue's a lot better at this tap-dancing stuff than I am."

Giving myself a hard mental shake, I agreed. "She's better than I am too. That's probably why she loves these lessons so much."

"Probably," said Lulu.

Marian lifted her voice and said, "Mercy and Lulu, watch and learn. I'm teaching an important lesson now."

"Sure," said Lulu.

"All right," I said.

"I'm going to teach you, Sue, to do a paddle turn step." Marian glanced at Lulu and me. "Be sure to follow my instructions, especially the first one, because it's the most important thing to learn if you plan to spin or turn as you dance. You have to *spot*. That means you keep your attention focused on one object—in this case, you'll be spotting on your reflection in the mirror as you turn, then whip your head around when you complete the turn. You need to spot in order to keep your balance. Watch me."

We watched her. My goodness, but she tapped and turned fast. "Oh," I said at last. "I see what you're doing!"

"That's more than I can see," muttered Lulu.

"Watch her," I said. "She keeps her attention fixed on her

114

reflection in the mirror, then turns her head around when she completes her revolution."

"Her what?" said Lulu as if she didn't know that "revolution" could refer to things other than political upheavals.

"Her revolution. Her rotation. You know. See how she rotates—or revolves—in a circle?"

"Oh, I think I understand," said Lulu skeptically.

Marian came to a sudden tappy stop and smiled beatifically at her students. "Very well, now you do it. Just turn. Don't try any steps. Just turn around, keeping your attention on your reflections in the mirror. Keep turning. As you turn, try to stay in one place and don't wander."

I turned, attempting as I did so to keep my attention focused on my reflection in the mirror and then whipping my head around when I finished. Then I did it a little faster. By golly, this was actually feasible if not precisely fun.

With a loud, "Whoops!" Lulu careened off to her right and bumped into the chairs on which our handbags and hats resided.

"Oh dear." Marian rushed over to Lulu, who seemed undamaged but embarrassed. "Here, Lulu, let me help you."

"I'm all right. I'm just no good at this." Lulu sounded despondent.

"Nonsense. You only need to understand what I'm talking about. Nobody is born knowing how to dance."

That was an excellent observation and one I intended to take in and keep close to my heart. "Truer words were never spoken," I said and joined Lulu and Marian. I helped show Lulu how to spot. She caught on! No dim bulb, our Lulu. She couldn't be faulted for not having been born or brought up listening to music or taking mind-numbingly boring ballroom dance classes in Boston with a bunch of boys and girls she wouldn't have spoken to if she hadn't had to.

Oh dear. I seem to have veered off topic. Back to the dance studio.

"There you go!" Marian applauded after Lulu turned three whole times while spotting herself in the mirror.

"I get it now," a triumphant Lulu exclaimed.

"Very good." Marian looked at Lulu as if looking at her own baby after it took its first step. She was an excellent teacher. Wish I'd had her as a teacher when I was growing up in Boston.

"Now," said Marian, returning to Sue in the front. "While I teach Sue the paddle turn step, you two keep practicing your turns. If you want to do a tap, heel, ball and then turn, feel free. Be sure to keep spotting."

"Thanks." To Lulu, I said, "Let's just turn a few times first. If we get good at turning without falling over, maybe we can try a tap step or two as we turn."

"Maybe you can. I'm just going to try to stay upright." She smiled though, so I knew she'd weather this lesson.

By Jupiter, by the end of the class, at nine p.m., Sue was tapping and spinning like a top. Lulu and I learned to tap sideways one way and then the other as a background to Sue's more complicated routine.

It was an exhausted but exhilarated trio of beginning tap-dancers who were actually sorry to see the end of our class that evening. We straggled to the chairs at the side of the room and sat to put on our street shoes.

"You all did very well this evening," said Marian, encouraging as all get-out.

"We have a great teacher," I said in return.

Marian smiled, grabbed the towel she kept flung over a chair at the front of the classroom, wiped her shimmering brow with it, and left the room. We heard her shoes tap across the larger room, and then nothing as she went out to the lobby.

"That was so much fun!" said Sue.

"It actually was, once I figured out how not to fall over," Lulu contributed.

"I think we should put on a show for Ernie and Rob. And maybe the Bucks," I said.

Silence followed this suggestion. Oh well. One couldn't hit the bullseye every single time one shot an arrow, could one?

"After I get a little better," said Lulu. "It might be okay."

"I think so," said Sue. "I mean, we're learning this for our own amusement, but when we get better, we might want to perform in front of real people."

"Instead of in front of a mirror?" asked Lulu.

With a laugh, Sue said, "Yes."

Guess my arrow hadn't landed so far off-target as I'd thought. We gathered our handbags and shoes, clapped our hats on our heads, and walked through the large studio to the lobby, trailing the lean and fit Marian by several minutes. The three of us were getting fitter if not leaner, by golly. A heated exchange seemed to be going on at the front desk.

Was that man leaving the studio as we arrived the weasel-faced Mr. Horshank? I squinted at his back, but I couldn't tell for sure who it was. I returned my attention to the front desk.

"Marian, will you stop harassing me?" I heard Charles say. "Everything's going to be all right, and we'll be able to save this place. Hell, we'll be able to expand."

"I don't believe it, Charles. It's like I told you before, that gold mine isn't even there!"

"Nonsense," said Charles. "I've seen blueprints."

"Faked blueprints, I'll bet. That man is a confidence trickster, and—" Both Murrays spied us walking up to the front desk and stopped talking. Both then pasted friendly smiles on their faces.

"Thanks for the great class," said Sue.

"You all did very well," said Marian.

"It was fun," I declared.

"See you on Thursday," said Charles.

"You bet," Sue declared.

"Wonder if they were beefing about that phony gold mine," said Lulu as we walked to my little Roadster. We no longer limped or felt bedraggled, but strode easily. I was so proud of us!

"I expect they were," I told my companions. "Whoever's in charge of the swindle has convinced Charles to spend his money. Marian doesn't want her and Lucille's money to be used because she has more gray cells than Charles does. And a man seldom, if ever, listens to a woman, even when she knows more than he does about the investment in question."

"That's too bad. I hope the studio doesn't have to close because Charles throws their money away." Sue was bouncier than either Lulu or me, but she deserved to be.

"Same here. These classes are fun, even if I'm never going to be a professional dancer." I shrugged as I opened the back door of the Roadster. We tossed our shoes onto the backseat.

"How come everybody's yakking about investments these days?" asked Lulu. "Rob and Ernie looked into that fake gold mine, and now Charles wants to sink the academy's money in the same gold mine."

"Yes. And it gets worse. Two people have already been killed because of that phony gold mine," I said.

Lulu and Sue squished themselves into the passenger seat of the Roadster, and I walked around to get into the driver's seat. These days, I always parked the automobile under a streetlamp.

"What?" queried a shocked Sue. "People are being *killed*?"

"Really? That's awful," said Lulu.

"I agree. And I could swear the man who left the studio right as we got to the lobby was Mr. Horshank. He's the man who hired Rob to investigate the gold mine venture. Then he refused to believe it was a fake scheme. He's also the guy who plowed into me the day we signed up to take classes. He denied it when I asked him." With a probably evil grin, I added, "I even asked him if he had a rude twin brother."

"Mercy, you didn't!" exclaimed Sue upon a burst of laughter.

"Good for you," said Lulu.

"Didn't do any good," I reported. "He denied having a rude twin or bumping into me himself. But I'm *certain* it was he." I pressed the starter button, and my Moon's engine rumbled to life. It all but purred as I pulled out into the street. Thank heaven traffic was light. Although driving still frightened me a bit, especially at night or when traffic was heavy, I was becoming more and more fond of my little Moon Roadster.

"And you're sure it's the same investment scheme Charles is interested in?" asked Sue.

"If that man I saw leaving really was Mr. Horshank, yes. And Mr. Autley is also involved in the scheme."

"Who's Mr. Autley?" asked Lulu.

"He's Lenny Autley's father, and he's involved in the fake gold mine too."

"Who's Lenny Autley?" asked Lulu.

"He's the nasty little bully who plowed into a kid the first time we went to the studio," I said.

"Crumb, that's right," said Sue. "I remember that kid."

"I don't," said Lulu. Neither Sue nor I was surprised.

"But really," said Sue. "I don't want the Murrays to go broke."

"Or get killed," added Lulu.

"Terrible thought," I said, although Lulu's words haunted me for the rest of the drive home.

THIRTEEN

To our considerable astonishment, both Ernie and Rob were at Mercy's Manor when I pulled into the drive. Because I didn't want to have to back my Roadster out onto the street again in order to allow Ernie to exit the premises—backing up was harder for me than driving forward—I managed to edge past Ernie's almost-new Packard and pull up to the back entrance of the house. Buttercup, of course, had heard our plans as they took place, and she was right there at the back door to greet us when we entered.

"Buttercup, you're adorable," said Sue.

"She's my precious baby," I cooed, lifting Buttercup into my arms and reminding myself of Mrs. Swale, which was moderately disgusting. Buttercup kissed my chin to tell me she appreciated my words, though, so I didn't dwell on the Swale blot.

"I want to have a dog someday," said Lulu wistfully. "I've always loved dogs. We had dogs on the farm. And barn cats. Lots of barn cats."

"Why do you call them barn cats?" asked Sue.

"They kept down the rodent population," Lulu explained.

"When you live on a farm, mice and rats will get into the stored grain and stuff like that. The cats killed the vermin. I'm not much of a cat-lover, but they're useful to have around when you live on a farm."

"What are you good for, Buttercup?" I asked my darling poodle.

She didn't answer, but it didn't matter. I already knew the answer. She was good at making me happy.

When we ambled into the kitchen, it was to find Mrs. Buck feeding sandwiches to the two men seated at the kitchen table. Mr. and Mrs. Buck lived in an apartment off the breakfast room of my home. Rob rose when we three—four, if you count Buttercup—females entered the kitchen. Ernie made a stab at rising, but was too busy stuffing food into his mouth to make it all the way onto his feet.

"There they are!" said Ernie after he'd swallowed. He sounded as though Lulu, Sue, and I had been on an expedition to darkest Africa and had only come back after several years abroad.

"It's us, all right," said Lulu, smiling at Rob, who smiled back. They were absolutely darling together.

Knowing Ernie was a lost cause and would only attempt to look innocent if I pointed out his laissez-faire attitude toward the accepted rules of decorum, I asked. "Want us to show you what we learned tonight?" I only realized I should have consulted my friends before offering when Lulu groaned under her breath. I persevered. "We learned how to spot when we're turning."

"Sounds like you're learning a new language too," said Ernie, grinning. "What is this spot to which you refer?"

"You girls rest now," said Mrs. Buck. "I was just feeding Mr. Ernie and Mr. Rob some sandwiches from the roast I served you ladies tonight. They say they've been too busy working to eat supper yet."

"A likely story," I said, putting Buttercup on the kitchen floor. Naturally, she padded over to Ernie. This was only partially because he was her friend; he also had *food*.

"We'll rest in a minute," I told Mrs. Buck. "But this is a nice linoleum floor, and we can tap on it. Come on, Sue."

"Think I'll sit this one out," said Lulu. She pulled out a chair and plunked herself next to Rob, who instantly put an arm around her and pulled her closer to him. Aw, how sweet. Did that sound bitter? I honestly didn't mean it to. Much.

"Of the three of us, Sue's learning the best and fastest," I said. "Sue, why don't you show the paddle turn step, and I'll just chop suey behind you."

Sue's cheeks were already rosy, probably from dancing so much, but her color deepened at my request.

"You really *are* learning a new language," Ernie muttered before cramming his face with more of the sandwich.

"Take a sip of lemonade before you show off your steps."

Because Mrs. Buck sounded so stern, Sue and I—and Lulu, even though she didn't plan to dance—each sipped from the glasses Mrs. Buck set out for us. Then I gave the introduction, clapping as I did so.

"All right, Sue. Here we go. What are you going to be spotting on?" Was that grammatically correct? Probably not. Does anyone care?

"Um, I'll use the lemonade pitcher," said Sue.

"Very well then. And-a one, and-a two, and-a three, and-a four."

Sue and I started tap-dancing on the kitchen floor. Good thing the kitchen was a large room. We were doing quite well, considering we'd only been to a few weeks' worth of lessons. Then Ernie picked up the lemonade pitcher and began pouring more lemonade into his glass.

Sue came to a graceful stop with a loud tap. I bumped into a wall and nearly fell over. "Ernest Templeton, why did you move that lemonade pitcher?" I demanded. "You heard Sue say she was going to use it to spot herself." This behavior was worse than merely casual; it was downright disrespectful and rude!

"Crumb, I guess I didn't understand what you meant by spotting," said Ernie. "I'm sorry, Sue. Didn't mean to mess up your routine." He sounded and appeared genuinely contrite, and I almost forgave him.

Rob and Lulu applauded.

"Yeah, Ernie. Until you mucked everything up, they were doing swell," said Rob.

"Yeah, Ernie," said Lulu. "What did you do that for?"

Reaching out an arm, Ernie hooked me around the waist and pulled me in to sit on his lap. "I'm sorry, Mercy and Sue. I honestly didn't know you needed the pitcher to stay in one place."

I didn't resist his gesture. Once I was plunked on his lap, I said, "What do you think, Sue? Should we forgive him?"

"Oh, why not?" said Sue. She laughed and drank some more lemonade. Then she left the kitchen and went upstairs to bed.

I could feel heat creep up my neck and decorate my cheeks with red. By the time Sue bade us all adieu and went up to her room, my face must have glowed because I was so embarrassed.

"What were you doing that you were so busy you didn't get to eat dinner?" I asked, attempting to divert everyone's attention from my blushing face.

"Rob had something important he needed help with," said Ernie.

His sentence proved I wasn't the only person in the world who ended sentences with prepositions. Dollars to doughnuts, nobody cares about that either.

"Oh," I said. "What was that?"

"I'll let Rob tell you," said Ernie.

Shifting off of Ernie's lap, I sat on a nearby chair and lifted my lemonade glass. Not only was I embarrassed, but my mouth also felt parched.

"Do you need privacy?" I asked Rob.

Rob lifted his head, shut his eyes, and seemed to contemplate my—extremely easy—question for a second or two. Then he opened his eyes and said, "No."

I shrugged. So did Ernie. Lulu drank some lemonade. Mrs. Buck busied herself by cleaning up the kitchen as we sluggards sat at the table, slurping and munching.

Then darned if the man—Rob, not Ernie—didn't dig around in his coat pocket, retrieve a small blue box, get down on one knee and say, "Miss Lulu Mullins, will you marry me?"

Lulu slapped a hand over her mouth and stared down at Rob as if she'd suddenly been turned into a block of cement. I'd never seen her pretty hazel eyes open so wide. Rob took her left hand from where it covered her mouth and slipped a beautiful white-gold ring onto its fourth finger. The ring slid on as if Rob had known precisely what size ring Lulu would require.

As soon as he stood up again, Lulu threw her arms around him and started sobbing. In between sobs, she said, "Yes, yes, yes, I'll marry you!"

"Glad we got that settled," said Ernie caustically.

As I was leaking tears too, I whapped him on his nearest shoulder.

"Congratulations to both of you," I said, sniffling.

"Yes indeed," said Mrs. Buck in a curiously thick voice. "How sweet."

"Yeah," said Ernie. "Good luck to you both."

"Thanks, Ern," said Rob, smiling up a storm over Lulu's stylishly bobbed head. "And you too, Mercy."

Suddenly, Lulu let go of Rob, swirled around and pulled me into a bear hug.

"Mercy, if it weren't for you, I'd never have met Rob! And I love him so much!"

"Actually, I'm the one who knew Rob first," said Ernie, a smile in his voice.

Lulu let go of me and attached herself to Ernie. I saw Ernie roll his eyes. So I whapped him again.

Lulu and I were the first residents of Mercy's Manor to get to the dining room on Wednesday morning. Lulu was fairly floating on a cloud of ecstasy and couldn't seem to stop staring at her beautiful engagement ring. Caroline and Sue entered the room not long after we did.

Showing her two fellow boarders her ring, she cried, "Look! Look! *Look!*" And she fluttered the fingers of her left hand in front of them. I saw Sue's eyes try to follow their path and pulled out a chair for her to grab in case she lost her balance. "Rob asked me to marry him! And I said yes!"

"How lovely," said Caroline with a prim smile.

"It's beautiful!" said Sue, not prim at all. "Oh, Lulu, I'm so happy for you."

The two of them shared a hug, and then we all sat down to a delicious breakfast prepared for us by the multi-talented Mrs. Buck. I swear, if she were a man—and white—people would call her a chef, she'd wear one of those tall white hats, and she'd run a first-class restaurant. I'm glad we had her, and I paid her well, if not as well as the chief chef in a fancy restaurant might be paid.

Lulu pretty much drifted to Angels Flight that morning. I kept hold of her arm so she wouldn't accidentally wander out into the street and get hit by a car. Sue and I shared many grins at her expense. Caroline, being proper and ladylike, didn't participate in our fun. Lulu didn't care, being lost in a sea of bliss.

Just to clarify matters, we decided we didn't need to walk up and down that steep, steep block from Olive to Hill because three of us were getting plenty of exercise in tap-dancing class. Besides, Caroline was a more delicate creature than the rest of us, and she wouldn't have walked up and down that hill anyhow. We didn't want her to feel left out.

Oh, very well. The truth was that we didn't *want* to walk up and down that incredibly steep street.

When I left Lulu at the reception desk in the Figueroa Building, I hoped she'd come down to earth long enough to answer the telephone. I walked up the three flights and trod to Ernie's office, did my usual morning chores, and thought about Lulu and Rob. Ernie hadn't followed Rob's example and proposed to me. Not that I'd expected him to; then again, I hadn't expected Rob to propose to Lulu.

Bother. This was a futile line of thinking, so I decided to think about something else. Instantly, my mind whizzed to New York City and the publishing house of Halliday, Smith & Ransom. Piffle. That wasn't a topic I wanted to dwell on either. I had a sinking notion that I'd discover a rejection letter in my mailbox any old day now. It had been several weeks since I'd sent my manuscript in, after all.

According to everything I'd read about the publishing industry, I'd gained the impression it didn't move awfully fast. I tried, therefore, to possess my soul in patience. Didn't work.

Fortunately, Ernie strolled into the office shortly after I started thinking.

"Morning," I said.

"Morning," he said.

Heck, it was early. We hadn't had time to become creative yet.

"Is Lulu happy today?"

"Happy? I'll say she's happy! She can't stop looking at her engagement ring."

"It's a nice ring," Ernie commented.

"It is. It's very pretty. Did you go with Rob when he picked it out?"

"I did indeed. I'm also the one who managed to figure out Lulu's ring size."

"How'd you do that?"

"Do you recall a couple of months ago when Junior went around the building asking everyone to try on cigar bands?"

"Yes. I thought it was an odd request at the time."

"I'm sure you did. But Junior came back to me with the one that fitted Lulu's ring finger, so that's how Rob knew what size to buy."

"Interesting." I wondered if Ernie had tucked my own ring size in his pocket. I didn't ask. "Say, Ernie, I swear I keep seeing that fool, Mr. Horshank of the fake gold mine, every time we go to a dance class."

"Yeah? What about the guy named... What was his name?"

"Autley," I said.

"Yeah. Do you see Mr. Autley there too?"

"Only once. The first time we went to a class there. His son takes tap lessons there."

"Yeah?"

"Yeah. I mean, yes, I do. Marian Murray told us she was going to inform Mr. Charles Murray that the scheme was phony, but I don't think Mr. Murray believed her."

"Huh," said Ernie. Helpful comment, that.

"Well?" I said sharply. "Don't you think you should look into the matter?"

"Why?"

127

"Because I don't want the Murrays to be cheated out of their money!"

"I don't either, but nobody's hired me to look into the matter, so I'm not looking into it."

"You're a money-mad man, Ernest Templeton."

"Says my secretary, who has never had to work a day in her life."

"Darn you, Ernie! I work for *you*! I'm a good confidential secretary, curse it!"

"Yes. You are. But you don't *have* to work."

"Bother. One of these days, all these easy-money schemes are going to crash the economy. You just wait and see."

"Guess I'll have to, won't I?"

"You drive me nuts, Ernie Templeton, do you know that?"

"I don't mean to, honest."

"Applesauce. You have fun being mean to me."

"I'm not mean to you."

"You are too! If Buttercup had any sense, she'd bite you the next time you show up."

Drat! I did it again. Prepositions just find their way to the ends of sentences. They're sneaky like that.

"Buttercup wouldn't bite me," said Ernie, frowning slightly. "But why are you so upset about the dancing folks? Does it matter if Mr. Murray's an idiot?"

"Yes, it matters! Charles Murray may well be a chump, but his sisters shouldn't have to suffer for his foolishness. The Murrays might lose their dance academy. I don't think they should suffer such losses along with the mousy Mr. Horshank."

"Mousy?"

"He has a ferret face."

"Unkind, Mercy." Ernie laughed. "Although it's true. He does look kind of like a rat or a ferret, doesn't he?"

"Yes."

Shaking his head, Ernie said, "Whatever you think, *I* think you and I make a great team, kiddo."

"Don't call me kiddo."

Ernie rolled his eyes. "Whoops. Sorry. I think we make a good team, Mercy."

Smiling at my boss, I gave up being annoyed and said, "I think we do too."

FOURTEEN

O n Thursday evening, when Lulu, Sue, and I walked into the Murray Dance Academy, none of the Murrays appeared to be present. As the door had been unlocked, we walked up to the counter anyway.

"Hello?" I said tentatively. "Anyone here?"

Nothing.

Sue said, "Marian, we're here for our tap lessons!"

"Darn it, I finally don't hate this any longer, and here we are without a teacher," grumbled Lulu.

"Maybe they're in one of the studios," I posited.

"Might as well look," said Sue.

"Yeah." Lulu agreed with us.

So we walked to the big studio. Nobody. Not even hordes of bratty children and their appalling mothers.

"This is strange," I said, as we exited the large studio. I pushed on the door to the small room. It wouldn't budge. "Well, heck, the door's stuck."

"Where is everybody?" asked Lulu. She gave the door a shove too.

Nothing.

"Is the door locked?" asked Sue.

I turned the doorknob, and it worked fine. But the door still wouldn't open.

"What's that?" asked Lulu.

As she had her attention fixed on the floor right underneath the door, Sue and I looked too.

"What *is* that?" asked Sue.

I knelt on the floor and grasped the piece of fabric we saw there. I could yank it out a little farther, but then it snagged on something and wouldn't let me pull more of it. Glancing up at my companions, I said, "I don't like this."

"What do you mean?" asked Sue.

"Oh, my gar, is that piece of cloth from Lucille or Marian Murray's gym bloomers?" Lulu clapped a hand to her mouth.

I peered harder.

Oh my lord! I shoved myself backward on the floor and held out the hand I'd used to tug on the fabric. It was covered in a red substance. Not bothering to dig out a hankie, I wiped my hand on my skirt.

I knew what the substance was.

"That's blood!" cried Lulu.

"What?" said Sue.

"We've got to get this door open," I said, pushing myself to my feet and putting a shoulder to the door.

With Lulu and Sue helping, we gradually managed to shove the door open wide enough for me to squeeze through the small gap. The sight that met my eyes was one I wish I could forget, but I'm sure I won't.

"Call the police," I said to my companions. "Call them right now."

"What is it?" asked Sue, sounding scared.

As well she might.

131

"It's Miss Murray. Miss Lucille Murray," I said, my voice sounding odd. "At least, I think it's Lucille. And she's been murdered."

"No!" squeaked Lulu.

"I'm afraid so," I said. I wriggled myself out through the open space again, only to find Lulu and Sue, eyes wide as saucers, staring at me. "The police," I said. "We have to call the police."

"Wh-where?" said Sue. "How?"

"I'll go outside and try to find a copper on the street." Lulu dashed to the front door of the academy and hurtled out onto the street. Sue and I heard her screech, "Help! Murder! *Police!*"

While Lulu screamed on the street, I rushed to the counter and grabbed the receiver of the telephone, a candlestick-style item with a dial plate, closer to me. I dialed "O" for the operator.

"Operator," came a voice almost instantly.

"Police. It's an emergency."

"One moment, please."

I heard clicking sounds as the operator connected my call to a police station. I hoped it was the one where Phil worked, but I'd been too rattled to specify which police station I wanted.

"Los Angeles Police Department," said a crisp voice on the end of the wire.

To the person at the police department, the operator said, "Emergency." To me, she said, "Your party is on the line."

"Hello?" I said, feeling panicky and wanting to get out of the Murray Dance Academy. Fast.

"Los Angeles Police Department," the voice said again. "May I help you?"

My brain registered the correct use of the word "May" before it switched into a useful gear. "We're at the Murray Dance Academy on Figueroa. Miss Lucille Murray is dead. Unless it's

Marian, but I'm pretty sure it's Lucille. I think she's been murdered."

"Who is calling, please?"

"Miss Allcutt. My friends and I came for our dance lesson. Nobody seemed to be here. When we looked around, we found Miss Murray's body."

"I see. Do you have the address?"

"Yes." I rattled off the address.

"I'll have officers dispatched at once," said the voice.

"Thank you," I said. I hung the receiver on the switch-hook.

"Let's go outside with Lulu," said Sue. "I don't want to hang around a dead body. Poor Lucille! Are you sure it was her, Mercy?"

"It was she, all right," I said, correcting Sue's grammar, although grammar was the last thing on my mind just then. "Yes, let's go outside. I don't want to be here either."

Sue and I joined Lulu on the street in front of the Murray Dance Academy. A sick feeling invaded my innards. Lucille Murray murdered! At least…

"I'm almost positive it was Lucille," I said as we waited. I hugged myself. The evening was warm, but I felt chilled to the bone.

"What do you mean by 'almost positive'?" asked Sue. "You mean you don't know?"

"She and Marian look a lot alike. I saw a mop of blond hair and her dancing costume, and I…" My words trailed off.

"Want to go back in and find out for sure?" Lulu sounded skeptical.

"No." I shuddered.

Suddenly, Charles Murray ran up to us, out of breath and panting. He also had a big smile on his face, which I found disconcerting.

"Ladies! I'm so sorry to be late," he said, still smiling at us. "But didn't Lucille let you in? I'm sure she—"

The hand attached to a uniformed arm caught Charles's hand before he could use it to open the door.

"Stop right there, you," said the man wearing the uniform. "What do you think you're doing?"

The smile on Charles's face vanished. He scowled at the policeman who'd impeded his progress.

"Oh dear," said Sue.

"Crumb," said Lulu.

"Mr. Murray," I said, stepping up. "I fear there's been a... a..." Nertz. A murder? I couldn't say that.

"Miss Allcutt?" said Charles. "What's going on?"

"An accident," I blurted out. "There's been an accident in the studio."

"What?"

"All right now," said another policeman, striding up to our little group. "We got a call about a dead body. And this bim here"—he hooked a thumb at Lulu—"was screaming fit to bust about a murder."

"I was not," declared Lulu. "And I'm *not* a bim!"

"An accident?" said Charles, sounding and looking befuddled. "A *murder?* What the devil is going on here?"

"We'll ask the questions," said the second officer. "Who are you?"

"Charles Murray," said Charles. "My sisters and I run this dance academy. What happened?"

"Never you mind asking questions," the first policeman said. He nodded at me. "You the lady who called in the murder?"

"*Murder?*" screeched Charles. In that instant, he reminded me of one of Chloe's good friends, a gentleman named Francis Easthope.

"I'm so sorry, Mr. Murray," I said, feeling about as low as a garden slug.

"Never you mind being sorry," said one of the coppers. "Show me the dead lady."

"There's no need to be rude," I snapped.

"Show me the body," growled the same copper.

"She's in there," I said, gesturing to the studio.

"Well, then, show it to me."

"For heaven's sake," I said. "This man is Miss Murray's brother! Why are you being so boorish?"

"Never mind me being boorish, whatever that is," said the copper, although he seemed a trifle abashed, unless it was my imagination. "Now show me the body." Very well, it had been my imagination.

"It's in here," I said, turning and twisting the door handle, using my skirt to do so. Didn't want to leave fingerprints, although I suppose it was far too late to think about that. Anyhow, I pushed the door open, and we all traipsed inside.

Charles entered the lobby and attempted to race to the counter.

"Stop right there, you," said the uncouth policeman. Unless it was the other uncouth policeman.

"But—" Charles looked at me, a pleading expression on his face. "Miss Allcutt, did you say you found a body in here?"

I nodded. "I'm afraid I did."

Charles gasped. "And it's…Lucille?"

"Be quiet, you two," snapped a copper. One was as bad as the other, so I'll stop attempting to differentiate between them. They were horrid men, both of them. "Now, you show me what you claim is a dead body," a copper said to me.

"This way," I said, trying to convey my sympathy and regret to poor Charles. "She's in here."

The group of people, including the two offensive policemen, Charles Murray, Lulu, and Sue, followed me to the large studio and then to the smaller room. A swath of Lucille's dance costume was still there, as if it were some kind of liquid leaking under the door. I gestured to the fabric. "The body is up against the door on the other side."

"Oh my God," whispered Charles. "I can't believe this. Are you sure?"

One of the miserable coppers pushed the door. It didn't budge. "Hey, Jim, give me a hand here," he said to his equally miserable cohort.

With both of the burly men pushing, the door slowly opened, revealing a patch of dark red liquid on the floor. I shut my eyes. I'd seen the dead body once; I didn't want to see it again. Both policemen had to suck in their tummies and slide sideways through the opening. Fat pigs.

Sue put a hand on my right shoulder. Lulu put her hand on my left shoulder. "I can't believe this," whispered Lulu.

"I can't either," said Sue.

I could, but I didn't want to. Glancing at Charles, I saw his eyes wide with horror. "I'm so sorry, Mr. Murray."

"Is it...? Is it...?" Charles clamped both of his hands to his head, as if he were trying to keep it from rolling off his neck. "Is it...?"

A policeman stuck his ugly head through the opening and said to Charles, "Come in here."

With his hands still cupping his head, Charles took a couple of tentative steps toward the door opening, from which the policeman withdrew his head. "I...I..." Squaring his shoulders and dropping his hands, Charles went to the door and peeked into the room.

Then he fainted.

Lulu, Sue, and I rushed to his side. I glared at the policeman who stuck his head out to see what had happened. "Cripes," he said. "Damn fairies are all over the place these days."

"You are absolutely *obnoxious*!" I snapped to his face.

"You get in here then," said the policeman. "I need you to identify this body."

First glancing at Lulu and Sue and getting a couple of nods from them, I left poor Charles on the floor, rose to my feet and walked to the door. Because I didn't spend my days eating doughnuts and drinking coffee, I didn't have to squish myself between the doorframe and the wall. Blasted policemen.

Before glancing again at the body, I examined each policeman's badge. One of them was named Cooper and the other was Singleton. I didn't bother fixing names to the faces. They were both awful. Good. I'd report the two of them to Phil as soon as I could. If they couldn't be civil, they had no business dealing with the public. Then I took a deep breath and peeked once more at the body on the floor.

She was Lucille, all right. And it looked to me as if she'd been stabbed, although I didn't see a knife. I shut my eyes. "The woman's name is Lucille Murray," I told Cooper and Singleton.

"What's that on your dress?" asked one of them.

"What?" I didn't open my eyes.

"You got blood on the front of your dress," said C or S. "Why's that?"

"Oh, for pity's sake," I said before attempting to leave the room. I wanted to be with Lulu and Sue, not these uniformed thugs. One of them caught my arm and yanked me back.

"Not so fast, lady. Why d'you have blood on your dress?"

"I knelt to see what the swatch of fabric was that showed from under the door. There must have been blood on the fabric, because I got some on my hand. I wiped it on my skirt. Now let me out of this room. *Instantly*!"

I will never, in a million, trillion years *ever* tell my mother this, but when I exert myself and try, I can sound just like her. Both Cooper and Singleton snapped to attention, and I left them with Lucille's body.

FIFTEEN

"If you ever go back to that place, I'll kidnap you and lock you in a closet!"

Ernie had never hollered at me like this before. I didn't like it one bit. I could tell he was mad as fire. His startlingly blue eyes practically shot flames, his fists were clenched, and his face wore the colors of a fiery sunset. That was no excuse for yelling at me.

"You have no right to tell me what to do!" I hollered back, my own fists clenched and planted on my hips. I suspect my cheeks were also red and my not-as-beautiful-as-Ernie's blue eyes blazed. "You're my boss, not my father!"

"Cripes," said Ernie, lowering his voice slightly. "Not even your father can tell you what to do and be obeyed. But that dancing studio is off limits! If you think I'm spewing applesauce, go back one more time. I'll fire you!"

"You can't fire me for something I do outside the office!"

"Try me!"

Very well, this wasn't getting either of us anywhere. I made an effort to unclench my fists and calm down but didn't succeed.

Nevertheless, I made a stab at sounding reasonable when I said, "Ernie, it isn't my fault that somebody killed Lucille Murray."

"I never said it was!" he roared. "But you're not hanging around another murder scene, dammit! Can't you *ever* stay out of trouble?"

"I'm not *in* trouble! Poor Lucille Murray was murdered, Ernie! I should think you'd want to find out who did it and *why*!"

"I'll look into what happened and why when somebody hires me to do it!" His volume had decreased slightly.

"Good!" I snarled. Then I marched out of Ernie's office and into my own. There I opened the right bottom drawer of my desk and plucked out my handbag. I opened the purse in my handbag and withdrew three twenty-dollar bills. I know, I know. It's not my fault that I was born with a silver spoon in my mouth. Ever since I'd moved from Boston to Los Angeles, I'd been attempting to fit in amongst the worker proletariat with mixed success.

Tromping back to Ernie's office, I held out the three twenties and snapped, "Here! *I'm* hiring you to bring Lucille Murray's killer to justice!"

"*I'm not going to take your money!*" Ernie went so far as to stamp his foot. He'd also resumed bellowing.

"Whoa," came a voice from my office. "I could hear you two from the elevator."

This time it was I who stamped my foot.

The voice belonged to Phil Bigelow, who was, according to Ernie, the only incorruptible copper in the entire Los Angeles Police Department. I'd begun to wonder about his assessment of Phil after slightly more than a year's exposure to Detective Bigelow. Compared to Officers Cooper and Singleton, however, Phil was a prince.

"Phil," I said in a colorless tone.

"Dammit, Phil, tell this woman it isn't safe to look into murders by herself!"

"Who said anything about doing it myself?" I barked in a no-longer-colorless tone. I pointed at Ernie and whirled around to face Phil, who most likely wouldn't be on my side but what the heck. "I asked *him* to find the murderer! I even tried to give him money. I never said I'd do it on my own."

"You did too!" hollered Ernie. "You said you were going back to that damned dance studio!"

"To take *lessons*, darn it!" I bellowed back. "Lulu, Sue, and I are taking *tap-dance lessons* there! If we want to continue taking lessons, where else can we go? Anyhow, why shouldn't we?"

"Because people get *murdered* there, you idiot!"

"I'm *not* an idiot!"

Raising his hands as if to ward off a blow, Phil said loudly, "Hey, kids. Take a powder and calm down."

I was about to tell him to mind his own business when Ernie, upon whom I'd turned my back—big mistake, that—clamped his hands on my shoulders. "Shut up, Mercy. I think Phil has some information for us."

"Who precisely is this *us* of whom you speak?" I said, trying and failing to free myself from his hands. Couldn't do it. "And now you're using physical *restraint* on me? Officer, arrest this man! He just attacked me," I shrieked at Phil.

Another voice joined the chorus, this one high and piping. "Holy cow! What's goin' on in there?"

Junior.

I sagged under Ernie's hands. Perhaps we had been a bit noisy. Junior was only a lad who did odd jobs in the Figueroa Building. I didn't want to set a bad example, no matter how furious I was with my boss.

"You better now?" asked Ernie in his normal speaking voice.

I flared up again and almost shouted that I hadn't been

141

unwell and therefore couldn't get *better*, but I didn't. In fact, I didn't speak at all. I was still irate. Then I took a gander at the front office door, which stood open. It wasn't unoccupied, though. Not only was Junior standing there, but he had in his two hands two leashes. One leash was attached to the collar of a tiny, hound-like creature; the other leash was attached to a large, skinny dog shaped like the little one, but hairier. My anger fled, replaced by curiosity.

"Whose dogs are those, Junior?" With one gigantic jerk that nearly dislocated both of my shoulders, I wrenched myself from Ernie's grip and walked to the dogs. And Junior.

"Mr. Gallagher's. Well, the little one's his. He says he's taken in the big one because its owner died. He called the big one a sal…sal…I can't remember."

"A saluki?" I asked, kneeling and holding out the back of my hand to the larger dog. It sniffed my hand. So did the little one. "And this is an Italian greyhound, right?"

With a shrug, Junior said, "I guess so. I think that's what Mr. Gallagher said. It don't look like a greyhound to me. When I went to the dog races, the greyhounds were a whole lot taller. In fact, they looked like this sal…whatever you called it, only they didn't have long hair."

"Yes. The larger greyhounds are the ones that run races," I said, appalled by human behavior not for the first time. "And this little thing is shaped like a greyhound."

"Yeah," said Junior. "Why was you and Mr. Ernie fighting?"

"We just had a little disagreement," I said, embarrassed.

"Sounded like a big one to me," said Junior.

"Yes. I suppose it was."

"So that's what Lewiston's dogs look like, eh?" said Ernie, joining me at the front office door. He knelt and held out a hand for the dogs to sniff. "And the little one is Gallagher's?"

"Yeah," said Junior. "He's got more of 'em in the store. He hired me to walk them 'cause he don't have time to do it."

Suddenly thinking of my own poor dear Buttercup, whose daily walks had been changed to every-other-day walks, I said, "That's a brilliant idea! How'd you like to walk a poodle, Junior?"

"What's a poodle?" said Junior.

"A little dog with fluffy hair."

Another shrug. "Sure. Why not? I've gotta get these guys back to Mr. Gallagher and pick up another two. I'll walk 'em up here if you want to see them too."

"No, don't bother," said Ernie. "Now that we know what they look like, we don't need to see more of them."

"We didn't need to see these two, actually," I said. When I observed Junior's hurt expression, I amended my statement. "But I'm really glad you brought them up here. I wondered what Italian greyhounds and salukis looked like." I endeavored to smile benevolently upon Junior, although my nerves still twanged from my recent shouting match with Ernie. "Thanks, Junior."

"Sure, Miss Mercy. Want me to walk your dog too?"

"Yes, but not today. Today she's at home, but I can bring her to the office tomorrow."

"No, you can't," said Ernie, grumpy again.

"Botheration. If I can't bring Buttercup, I'll just stay home with her," I said. "You were going to fire me anyway, weren't you?"

"Damnation, *no!*" said Ernie, his voice rising again. "I don't want you to get killed, for God's sake!"

"Does somebody wanna kill you, Miss Mercy?" asked Junior, his eyes going huge with eagerness. "Maybe we can sic the dogs on 'em."

Standing, Ernie patted Junior on the shoulder. "Hold that thought, Junior. It's a good one, but right now Miss Allcutt and I need to get back to work."

"Yeah?" Junior's disappointment was palpable.

"If you two have finished your...discussion," said Phil, "you might be interested in the case we just got. Involves a murder at a dance studio."

"Oooh, a *murder*?" Junior sounded delighted. Then he must have seen the bills in my hand. "Criminy! Are those *twenties*?" He spoke as if he'd never seen a twenty-dollar bill before in his life.

I sagged a little when I realized he probably hadn't.

Ernie said in a tentative-sounding voice, "You want to talk about the murder at the Murray Dance Academy, Phil?"

"Indeed, I do," said Phil. He eyed Junior askance and said, "Better not to in front of the kid."

The inquisitive smile vanished from Junior's face, and he said, "Aw nertz."

"Say, Junior," said Ernie, reaching into his trouser pocket. "After you finish walking dogs, will you please go across the street to the deli—or around the corner to the Chinese place—and get us some lunch?" He pulled out a ten-dollar bill.

Forestalling Ernie in his attempt to divert Junior's attention, I handed the kid one of my own twenty-dollar bills. He dropped the saluki's leash in order to grab the twenty. The well-trained dog didn't move. I'd never seen a boy's eyes grow as wide as Junior's when he stared at the bill in his hand. Good grief. This was how the "other half" lived, I guess. Only since I'd departed Boston for Los Angeles, it seemed to me that there were a lot more than half of the people in the U.S.A. who lived less pampered lives than mine had been.

Sometimes I got discouraged, thinking I'd never become comfortable living in the middle class. Upper middle class.

Fiddlesticks.

As Junior just said: nertz.

"After you finish walking all the dogs and take them back to Mr. Gallagher, please go to the Canton Palace, Junior," I said.

"Get enough for all four of us, including you. And Mr. Buck, too."

Snatching the dropped leash as if he feared I might take the bill back, Junior turned and ran down the hallway, the dogs loping along with him. Well, the Italian greyhound appeared to be flying low. Quick little doggie. "Sure thing, Miss Mercy!" he hollered. His was a happy holler, unlike those Ernie and I had been flinging at each other.

After he watched Junior and his latest financial enterprise scamper to the elevator, Ernie put a hand—gently—on my shoulder. "Let's hear what Phil has to say, Mercy."

"Very well." I turned and walked back to my desk. "Your room or mine?"

"Might as well stay here." Ernie sounded defeated.

I walked to my desk and sat in my swivel chair, stuffing the remaining twenty-dollar bills in my pocket as I did so. Ernie and Phil both sat in the chairs facing my desk. Phil's brow was furrowed in what I presumed to be thought.

"You're the one who found the body, aren't you, Mercy?" Phil finally asked as if he should have known it all along.

"Yes, and if you have any influence over the behavior of the Los Angeles Police Department's officers who deal with the public during emergencies, you can demote Officers Cooper and Singleton. They were rude and insufferable when they got to the dance studio. They insulted Mr. Charles Murray and were positively vicious to me. And to Lulu and Sue."

Phil pulled a little notebook from his suit coat's inside front pocket and took a pencil from the pencil cup I kept on my desk. "Cooper and...who was the other one?"

"Singleton."

"What did they do that was so rude?" asked Ernie.

I related the two policemen's boorish behavior to my listeners. "They all but accused *me* of committing the crime because I had

145

Miss Murray's blood on my skirt!" I finished, becoming irate once more.

"How'd you get her blood on your skirt?" asked Ernie, shaking his head as if he figured I'd done it on purpose in order to confuse the coppers or something equally stupid.

"I pulled on an article of clothing. The door wouldn't open and when I glanced down, I saw a piece of fabric. Thinking maybe a rag was impeding the door's movement, I knelt to look. I realized it was actually a part of Miss Murray's gym suit. When I pulled on it, I got blood on my fingers and wiped them on my skirt."

"Not on a handkerchief?" asked Phil.

"No," I snapped. "I was horrified, wanted to get the blood off my fingers, and just wiped them as quickly as I could. When I looked more closely at the floor, I realized there was blood on the material. Then Sue, Lulu, and I shoved the door open a little bit so we could see what had happened." I shuddered and wrapped my arms over my chest. "It was Miss Murray. At first I couldn't tell which Miss Murray it was, but I realized it was Lucille after a second or two."

"It's okay, kiddo," said Ernie. "You did the right thing."

I glared at him. "Don't call me kiddo!"

"Right. Sorry." He didn't roll his eyes at me, but I knew he wanted to.

"Huh."

"How long have you known the Murrays?" asked Phil, pencil poised over his notepad.

"Um…I can't honestly remember. We signed up for classes the same day you and Ernie made me take minutes during that boring meeting about the invisible gold mine at the Ambassador."

"Ah." Phil flipped through his notebook. "That was back in April. Let me see here…" He flipped a few more pages. "Ah.

Here. It was on Wednesday, April 14. That was…one, two…it was four weeks ago."

"That long?" I was surprised. "Wow, we've been going to tap lessons for a long time. No wonder we're getting better."

"Brilliant, Mercy," Ernie said under his breath.

"Pooh on you," I said. "I'm glad we're taking tap, although I'm terribly sorry someone killed Miss Murray." I had a sudden thought. I know, how surprising, huh? "Wait! What about Mr. Horshank? He's always showing up at the dance academy. I'll bet *he* killed her because she didn't want to invest in his gold mine that doesn't exist. And Mr. Autley too! They're probably in cahoots."

"Uh…" Phil stared at me. "What?"

"Don't mind her, Phil. She leaps over tall shrubs in order to reach conclusions sometimes."

"I do not," I muttered, thinking it had been four long weeks since I'd taken my poor manuscript to the post office. I hoped it hadn't been lost in the mail. Or maybe I hoped it *had* been.

No. I wanted to be a published author. I wasn't sure how much longer I'd have to wait to find out my first effort had been rejected, however. Good thing I'd started writing another book. Maybe.

"Anyhow," said Phil, glancing once more at his notebook, "we'll investigate Horshank. And who else did you mention?"

"A man whose last name is Autley. His bully of a son is taking tap classes at the Murray Dance Academy."

"You say both Horshank and Autley have been going to the Murray Dance Academy? Do they take classes there?"

Did they?

I had no idea.

"Um, I don't think so. I've seen Horshank there two or three times. I only saw Mr. Autley one time. I got the impression Horshank was urging Mr. Charles Murray to invest in some crackpot scheme. I figured it was the gold mine, and I was ultimately proved to be correct. Neither Marian nor Lucille—they're Mr. Charles Murray's sisters—wanted him to invest in it, but I'm pretty sure he did it anyway."

"You're guessing a whole lot about this matter, Mercy," said Ernie. "You don't actually *know* a single thing about the Murrays, Autley, and Horshank, do you?"

"I know Marian was worried about Charles investing in a gold mine," I said, stung.

"Is it the same gold mine?" asked Phil.

Fiddlesticks. Was it? But yes! Marian had mentioned Horshank!

Lifting my chin, I said, "Yes, it's the same gold mine. Marian Murray mentioned Mr. Horshank. She said he's the one who's been filling Charles's head with guff about a sure-fire, money-making gold mine in Colorado! I'm not sure about Autley, but I wouldn't be surprised if he's in on the scheme too."

"Huh," said Phil.

"Huh," said Ernie. Then he heaved a sigh and said, "I guess the coppers had better interview Horshank and Autley, Phil. It looks as if Mercy's right this time."

"*This* time? What about the time I saved you from the electric chair?" I growled.

Ernie slapped his hands down on my desk. "For gawd's sake, don't bring up *that* again! You nearly got yourself killed then too!"

"What do you mean 'then too'?" I shot back at him.

"*Stop!*" bellowed Phil.

Both Ernie and I ceased griping at each other and turned to glare at Phil.

SIXTEEN

"Listen, you two, I know you love to fight—"

"*I* don't!" I declared hotly. "Ernie's always trying to stop me from doing things!"

"That's only because you get involved in dangerous situations," snarled Ernie.

"I said *stop it!*" roared Phil.

Although I'd opened my mouth in order to refute Ernie's empty claim, I shut it again, realizing that a continued argument wouldn't lead to a conclusion and would only rile both of us. Well, the three of us if you included Phil. As he was there, we pretty much had to include him.

A knock came at the front office door, causing our trio into starts of alarm. I slapped a hand to my chest.

"Cripes," said Ernie, shoving himself out of his chair and walking to the door. As soon as he opened it, he jumped back a foot or so.

"Oh, Mr. Templeton!" cried (literally) Miss Eleanor Padgett. "I'm so sorry to have startled you."

"Good lord," muttered Phil. "Are those dogs?"

I rose from my swivel chair, having met the dogs in question a few months back. "Yes," I told Phil. "These beautiful hounds are Boris and Bevan. Boris is a Russian wolfhound, and Bevan is an Irish wolfhound."

"Miss Allcutt!" snuffled Miss Padgett. "I didn't mean to startle anyone!"

Ernie recovered himself almost instantly and held the door open for the threesome to enter the outer office. Phil stood like the gentleman he pretended to be in the presence of Miss Padgett.

"Miss Padgett, it's good to see you again," I said, not really meaning it but being polite.

"I'm afraid I need Mr. Templeton's services again, Miss Allcutt."

Now, see? How hard would it have been for Mrs. Swale, the mastiff lady, to be nice to a so-called underling? Miss Padgett didn't seem to have any trouble being civil to secretaries. Underling, my foot.

"Please come in, Miss Padgett," said Ernie. "Are you here about Mr. Lewiston and the gold mine?"

Shocked, Miss Padgett dropped both of her dogs' leads and clapped her hands to her tear-stained cheeks. "Oh, my! However did you *know*?"

I stood, walked around my desk, shoved Phil—gently— aside, and went to Miss Padgett. Laying a hand on her shoulder, I said, "Please don't cry, Miss Padgett. Mr. Templeton will help you."

Standing behind Miss Padgett, Ernie scowled at me.

I didn't care. Much.

"Come over here and take a seat," I said. "Mr. Templeton, will you please bring Boris and Bevan?"

Shaking his head in what I think was irritation, Ernie did as I'd asked of him and retrieved the dropped leashes. Then he stood in the middle of the outer office and didn't seem to know what to do.

I led Miss Padgett into Ernie's room and up to one of the chairs arranged before his desk. "I'll get you a handkerchief," I told the weeping woman. She'd wept at us the last time she'd been here too. Opening Ernie's top desk drawer, I grabbed one of the clean hankies he always kept there in case of sobbing clients.

"Th-thank you," whimpered Miss Padgett.

"Would you like a glass of water?" I asked her.

"N-no, thank you. There's no need for that."

"Very well."

Leaving her in the chair, I strode to the outer office and glared at Ernie and Phil. Well, and Boris and Bevan too, but they didn't deserve it. "Get in here, you two," I whispered. "This might be your chance to solve the crime, Phil. That's what you want, isn't it?"

"Huh?" said Phil.

Transferring both leashes to his left hand, Ernie clapped Phil on the shoulder with his right one. "Just humor her, Phil."

I'd have hollered at him except that I didn't want Miss Padgett to think Ernie and I were at odds with each other. Even though we were, in a way.

"Thank you, gentlemen," I told Phil and Ernie as they entered Ernie's office. I grabbed my secretarial pad and a couple of pencils, zipped back to Ernie's room and said, "I'll just take notes." I sat in the corner chair once more and poised my pencil over my pad.

Ernie handed the dog leads to Phil, who wasn't prepared for them. Boris and Bevan stood beside Phil and stared up at him. Phil, in return, looked to have been turned to stone. Petrified, poor guy.

"Oh, dear, I'm so sorry," said Miss Padgett when she noticed the expression on Phil's face. "Here, let me take my babies." She held out the hand not clutching the hankie, and Phil gave her the leashes. I saw Ernie mouth the word, *babies*? But he didn't comment aloud. A good thing, or I'd have had to yell some more. After Miss Padgett's departure, of course.

"Miss Padgett," Ernie began. "Thank you for coming here today. I have been given to understand through another person that you and the late Mr. Lewiston were friends. Is that correct?"

After a big sniff and a swipe at her eyes with Ernie's hankie, Miss Padgett said with a trace of bitterness in her words, "Mrs. Swale, right? That woman..." She stopped speaking and gulped. After putting her hankie to use once more, she said, "Mrs. Swale means well, believe it or not. She isn't an amiable woman, but we're friends in the dog world. She kept telling me that Mr. Lewiston was leading me astray regarding an investment opportunity. But then Mr. Lewiston died under strange circumstances. Dear Mr. Gallagher took in his Afghans and salukis"—

A pause here to be astonished at Miss Padgett's use of the word "dear" to describe Mr. Gallagher. Not that I knew any ill of him—well, except that he once hired a murderer to work in his haberdashery—but he seemed a far cry from "dear" to me. Back to Miss Padgett.

—"and they're getting along splendidly with his darling Italian greyhounds. But perhaps Mrs. Swale was correct in attempting to steer me away from the gold mine in which Mr. Lewiston wanted me to invest."

"Yes," said Ernie. "It was Mrs. Swale who informed us of your interest in the gold mine venture. I fear she was correct in that the scheme seems fraudulent."

"Oh my," sniffled Miss Padgett. "There's a dreadful man who looks like a weasel who came to our local club meeting a couple of days ago. His name begins with an H, I believe..." She used her hankie once more.

"Mr. Horshank?" asked Phil.

"Yes, I think his name was Horshank," said Miss Padget after another sniffle or two. "He's an extremely annoying person, and he's all but forcing people to invest in the gold mine Mr. Lewiston was backing."

Ernie's and my gazes met for an instant. I gave him a quick nod. He returned my nod with a "God save us all" roll of his eyes, which I didn't appreciate.

"I've met Mr. Horshank too, Miss Padgett," said Ernie. "He seems quite fervent about the gold mine plan."

"Fervent is one word for it," muttered Miss Padgett, again surprising me. I hadn't anticipated acerbity from her.

And then, by Jupiter, I had another brilliant idea! Or maybe it wasn't, but I decided to voice it. If everyone hated it, I'd attempt not to take their disapproval personally.

"May I speak for a moment?" I asked, raising my hand as if back in the schoolroom in Boston.

"Please do, Miss Allcutt," said Miss Padgett. "Do you have a suggestion on how to solve the riddle of Mr. Lewiston's death and the gold mine venture?"

After a quick glance at Ernie, whose countenance displayed no encouragement, I forged ahead anyway.

"I think we should set up a meeting with Miss Padgett, Mrs. Swalc, Mr. Horshank, Mr. Gallagher, Mr. Autley, the Murrays—"

"Who are the Murrays?" asked Miss Padgett.

"Charles and Marian Murray run the Murray Dance Academy up the street from this building," I told her. "Miss Lucille Murray, Charles and Marian's sister, was killed last evening."

"Oh my heavens!" cried Miss Padgett. "How horrid!"

"It was horrid, all right," I said.

Silence filled Ernie's room for several seconds. Then we

heard the front office door open, and the fragrance of Chinese food wafted into Ernie's room.

"Lunch is here!" called out a cheerful Junior. "I just ordered everything because you give me so much money, Miss Mercy! You guys in Mr. Ernie's room?"

"Cripes," grumbled Ernie. "Just what we need."

"Oh my, did I interrupt you at lunchtime? I'm so sorry!" said Miss Padgett, looking as if she aimed to start crying again.

A grinning Junior appeared in Ernie's open doorway, Mr. Buck at his back. Both fellows held paper bags full of little white boxes. Those clever little boxes were a splendid invention by someone. Ernie actually knew who invented them and when, but the information had managed to slide out of my brain. Far from an unusual circumstance, unfortunately.

"Not at all," I said to Miss Padgett, believing it my duty to smooth over an awkward social situation. "Please, there's plenty of food for all of us if you'd care to join us."

Only then did I notice that Boris and Bevan seemed to have perked up considerably. They'd been drooping between Miss Padgett's chair and Phil's. As soon as the scent of food entered Ernie's room, both hounds stood to attention. They gazed at Junior in what appeared to be rapture.

"Holy moley," said Junior, backing up and bumping into Mr. Buck. "Are those dogs?"

"Yes, they are," I said, deciding it was time for action. Therefore, I rose from my chair and gestured for Junior to take Mr. Buck and the sacks of food into the front office. "Please just put the food on my desk. We can sort it out there."

"Will do, Miss Mercy," said Mr. Buck. He'd met Boris and Bevan before, so he wasn't afraid of them. "Come on, Junior. Those dogs are nice. They won't hurt you."

"No, they won't," said Miss Padgett, standing with her dogs

once more. "They're very gentle. Would you like to meet them?" She smiled sweetly at Junior.

Junior wasn't easily charmed, but he was interested in the dogs. As he and Mr. Buck set the food on my desk, therefore, he said, "Yes, ma'am. What kind of dogs are they? They're sure big."

"They're very big," agreed Miss Padgett. "Boris here"—she gave her Russian wolfhound's leash a slight tug, and he stepped smartly forward—"Is a Russian wolfhound. Would you like to shake hands with Boris?"

"Shake hands?" said Junior. "He don't have hands."

"Shake hands with the boy, Boris," commanded Miss Padgett in her soft voice.

Instantly, Boris sat and lifted a paw.

"Wow!" cried Junior. "He's really gonna shake my hand?"

"Approach him slowly," I cautioned the boy. My advice was unnecessary, probably because Junior wasn't sure Boris wouldn't try to eat him if he got too close. He therefore inched up to him with his hand held out.

I think Boris got bored because before Junior could grab his paw, the dog slapped his outstretched paw onto Junior's open palm. Junior smiled and shook the dog's paw.

"And this," said Miss Padgett, "is Bevan. Bevan is an Irish wolfhound. Irish wolfhounds are the tallest dog breed, according to the American Kennel Club. Shake hands, Bevan."

Bevan, too, sat and held out a paw. Delighted, Junior shook Bevan's paw. "Gee, I never shook hands with a dog before."

"Today is your special day then," I said, wishing the kid would leave the office. "You got to shake hands with two dogs."

"Yeah," said Junior, beaming. "They're the *berries*!"

"All right, Junior, let's leave the ladies and gentlemen to their meal," said Mr. Buck, giving me a wink. I swear, both Bucks could read my mind.

"Okay," said Junior.

Mr. Buck gave him a shoulder nudge, and Junior said, "Oh, yeah. Almost forgot. Thanks, Miss Mercy!"

"You're welcome, Junior. Thank you and Mr. Buck for bringing our lunch to us."

"Sure. See ya!" said Junior, bouncing to the front office door and waving at us. Mr. Buck followed him more sedately, smiling.

"Would you care to have lunch with us, Miss Padgett?" I asked again.

"What?" Miss Padgett stared after the retreating forms of the two caterers, then gave a slight start. I guess she didn't take in the meaning of my question, although I thought I'd spoken clearly. However, after a second or two, she said, "Oh, thank you, Miss Allcutt, but I don't believe I'd better dine with you. I would like to hire you, Mr. Templeton, to look into the death of Mr. Frederick Lewiston. I don't believe he merely fell out of that window at the Ambassador. No more do I believe he committed suicide. He was a fine gentleman who loved his dogs and his life." She sniffled again. "We were quite close, actually."

"I'm so sorry for your loss," I said. Poor Miss Padgett.

"Miss Allcutt," said Ernie in his boss's voice. "Will you please draw up a contract for Miss Padgett?"

"Certainly, Mr. Templeton."

"Oh, no!" said Miss Padgett. "I came today without an appointment, and you were kind enough to meet with me. May I return later and sign the contract? I don't want to take up your luncheon hour."

In spite of my best effort, my nose wrinkled. It had taken me almost a year to stop calling my mid-day meal *luncheon*. That word belonged to Boston. What we ate here in Los Angeles was *lunch*, darn it!

"That would be fine, Miss Padgett," said Ernie. "Miss Allcutt, will you make an appointment for Miss Padgett for this afternoon? Will you be able to return this afternoon, Miss Padgett?"

Ernie sounded so professional. I almost forgot we'd been hollering at each other only a short while earlier.

"This afternoon will be fine," said Miss Padgett. "Is two o'clock free for you?"

I almost expected Ernie to tell her his work couldn't be had for free, but he didn't. Rather, he said, "Miss Allcutt?"

After shoving a couple of paper bags full of small white boxes aside, I glanced at my desk calendar. Ernie could have discovered the same information by looking at his *own* desk calendar, but never mind that.

"Yes," I said. "Two o'clock will be fine."

"Good. Thank you. Thank you, all of you. I know it wasn't kind of me to barge in on you, but I do *so* appreciate your willingness to help in this distressing time."

"Of course," said Ernie. If a person didn't know him, that person would have thought he meant it.

SEVENTEEN

After Miss Padgett left the office, Ernie locked the front door. The food was already on my desk, so I said, "Let's just eat out here. I'll set up my desk."

"Sounds good, Mercy," said Ernie, shrugging out of his suit coat and hanging it on the coat tree near the front door.

"Yeah. Thanks," said Phil.

I cleared inedible items from my desk and spread out the Chinese feast. The little white boxes had wire handles, making them easy to pluck out of the paper sack. The clever cardboard inventions also opened out to create paper plates when they weren't full of food. Junior, smart kid, had brought three empty white boxes along with the filled ones.

Because I knew how to do it, I unfolded the three empties, spread them open to make plates, gave one to Ernie, one to Phil, and set the third one at my place. "All right, gentlemen, take a seat and eat." How about that? I just rhymed.

"Thanks, Mercy," said Phil, sitting on the chair to my right. He removed his suit coat too, but he just draped it over the back of his chair.

"Yeah. Thanks," said Ernie, plunking himself on the chair to my left.

"Get out your fancy knife, Ernie," I told him. "You need to open the root-beer bottles."

"No sooner said than done." He pulled a multi-purpose knife from his trouser pocket and, in slightly more time than it took me to tell him what to do, he did it.

"Wish you'd do that all the time," I muttered.

"Do what?" asked Ernie.

"Do what I tell you to do."

Ernie gave me a hideous frown, so I didn't press the issue. Besides, I was hungry.

After filling our flat white cardboard plates with piles of Chinese food, we dug in. With tacit approval among the three of us, we discussed how to solve the various crimes connected with the phony Colorado gold mine as we lunched.

"Your idea of getting everyone involved to attend a meeting to talk about the problem and what to do about it is a good one, Mercy," said Ernie.

He spoke without an eyeroll or a speck of sarcasm. I had to swallow before I could respond.

Phil swallowed first. "Yeah, I think it's a good idea too. You say you know the Murrays, right?"

"Yes. Lulu, Sue, and I take tap-dancing lessons on Tuesday, Thursday, and Saturday. Unless they close the academy because of Lucille's murder, the three of us will be there tomorrow evening."

"And I expect Rob has Horshank's telephone number," Ernie mused, holding up a Chinese sparerib and eyeing it hungrily. He chomped on it as soon as the words were out of his mouth.

"Do we need Horshank?" asked Phil. "He's a pain in the neck."

"Mercy's seen him at the dance place a few times now. I want to know what he's up to. Maybe he's behind everything."

"I doubt it," said Phil right before he stuck a shrimp in his mouth.

"Why?" I asked him, stabbing my own shrimp with a little wooden fork the Canton Palace had provided along with the food.

"He seemed too eager," said Phil with a shrug as he scooped up some chow mein noodles. "And didn't you say he fired Rob after Rob verified Mercy's report on the mine?"

"Yeah, he did," said Ernie, taking a sip of the root beer Junior had brought us along with the bags of food.

"It's almost as if he thinks if he can get more people to invest, the mine will turn out to be real after all," said Phil. He stuffed noodles into his mouth.

"That doesn't make any sense," said Ernie, scooping up some chicken with cashews.

"He always seems nervous to me," I reported. "I don't believe he's in charge of a single thing."

"That doesn't mean anything," said Ernie after another swallow of root beer. "He could be acting."

"I don't think he's acting," I said. "I think he's a chump who's got the willies. He's a chump who doesn't want to be the *only* chump."

"It probably means he's not the man behind the gold mine and the murders," said Phil. "Nervous people are more liable to be killed than to kill."

"How do you figure that?" I asked, curious.

"You claim to have met grifters like Mr. Madison before," said Phil. "Did any of them seem nervous types to you?"

After chewing, mulling, and ultimately swallowing, I answered Phil's question. "You're right. They weren't nervous. If anything, the Madisons I met in Boston were too self-assured. If

Horshank asked any of them for money, they'd probably laugh in his face."

"What I don't understand," said Ernie, shoving some chicken and rice onto his little wooden spoon, "is why Horshank is still so eager to get people to invest in the gold mine when he's been told by two reliable sources that the mine doesn't exist."

"Men seldom believe anything a woman says," I opined.

"Probably true," agreed Ernie, his spoon held aloft, "but Rob told him the same thing after doing his own research."

"Some men are more stupid than others," I murmured. Then I picked up another sparerib. We were all friends; nobody cared if people picked up their food. With the exception of rice, of course. Maybe noodles. "And what about Mr. Autley?"

"Hmm," said Ernie. "We don't really know Mr. Autley's involved, do we?"

I shrugged. "He was at the studio talking to Charles once."

"Well, his kid's taking lessons at the studio, isn't he?"

"Yes."

"Unless you can figure out a way to get in touch with Autley, let's leave him out of the meeting."

"All right," I said.

"I think we ought to make the meeting official," said Phil. "If Horshank and the others know the police are looking into the murders, they'll be more likely to show up."

"And tell the truth," said Ernie.

"Want me to talk to the Murrays tomorrow evening if they're open?" I asked after swallowing some rib meat.

"If they're open, I'll take you to your class tomorrow," said Ernie.

This statement startled me so much, I swallowed wrong. Ended up coughing as if I had some dread inflammation of the lungs.

Rising and patting me on the back, Phil said, "Take it easy, Mercy. You all right?"

Clutching my root beer bottle, I brought the opening to my mouth and sipped some of the liquid. Then I nodded.

"I'd really feel more comfortable if you'd let me drive you guys to your class tomorrow night," Ernie clarified. He rose, too, and also gave me a few back-pats. His were harder than Phil's.

I chugged a little more root beer—not my favorite beverage, but who cares?—and finally managed to clear my throat. "Really?" Another coughing fit rendered me speechless again.

"Of course I mean it," said a grumpy Ernie. "For god's sake, Mercy! A woman got killed there last night. If the place is open, I don't want you to go there alone."

"There are three of us," I gasped. "I wouldn't be alone."

"You know good and well what I mean, dammit. I'll take the three of you to your class tomorrow night. I want to talk to those people." He trained his gaze on Phil. "You should probably come with us. Then it will be an official request to meet."

"All right with me," said Phil. "Pauline might be interested in sending Rosie to tap classes."

"Oh no, don't inflict those awful children on your poor daughter!" I cried, appalled at the notion of Phil's sweet daughter, Rosie, being bullied by Lenny Autley and his ilk.

"What awful children?" Phil sounded confused.

"Mercy met some of the mothers who want their darlings to be in the flickers," Ernie explained.

"And they weren't nice?" asked Phil.

"The kids were awful, and their mothers were worse," I said. "What did you call the mothers, Ernie?"

"Stage mothers," said Ernie. He nodded sagely.

"Well, Rosie doesn't have to be in the class with the other kids, does she?" Phil frowned.

"You'll have to ask the Murrays," I said. "They've just lost a family member who was also one of their teachers, so I don't know what's going to happen to their business."

"What's their telephone number?" Ernie plucked the receiver from where it rested on my candlestick phone, and his fingers hovered over the dialing plate.

"I don't know offhand. Ask the operator. It's the Murray Dance Academy on Figueroa," I told him. "You just got Chinese sauce on my telephone receiver, Ernie."

"Oh. Sorry," said Ernie, wrinkling his nose as he replaced the receiver on the switch-hook. He withdrew a handkerchief from his pocket and wiped his fingers and the receiver.

"Finish your lunch. Then call them," suggested Phil.

"Great idea." Ernie dumped some more fried rice onto his plate.

"Do either of you know how to get in touch with Mr. Madison?" I asked.

"Wasn't there a number on some of the papers he handed out at the meeting?" asked Phil.

"Don't know," I said. "They're filed in my desk drawer."

"Is there room in that drawer, what with the books you keep writing?"

My heart gave a huge spasm, and I gasped in shock. Not sure why. I know Ernie had read part of my first manuscript, which was undoubtedly languishing in a pile of manuscripts on the floor of some underling's room, waiting to be read and tossed aside. An underling, and one who wielded *much* greater power than I.

"What books?" Phil appeared interested.

"Nothing I care to talk about at the moment," I said frigidly.

"Did I make a mistake?" Ernie actually appeared troubled.

I didn't trust the expression on his face, so I scowled at him in an attempt to appear ferocious. Through gritted teeth, I managed to spit out, "Yes."

"Whoops. Sorry. No books here, Phil," said Ernie.

Sheesh.

A loud rap came at the front office door. My nerves were already twanging thanks to Ernie's reference to my book, and I do believe I set a record for the sitting high jump.

Slapping a hand to my chest, I said, "I'll see who it is."

"I'm closer than you are," said Ernie, telling the truth. He was, after all, sitting in front of my desk while I sat behind it. "I'll go."

After swallowing, he rose, walked to the door, and pulled on his suit coat. As soon as he unlocked and opened the door, he executed a quick step backward. "Mrs. Swale," he said in a far from welcoming tone. "I don't believe we have a scheduled appointment."

I popped another shrimp into my mouth and rose from my chair to see not merely Mrs. Swale, but Caesar and Augustus as well. "You brought the dogs," I said stupidly. After, of course, swallowing.

"Yes, well I was in the neighborhood and didn't have time to take them home first," said Mrs. Swale. Ernie had stepped back but hadn't stepped aside, so she remained at the open door. Because they were so huge, I could see her dogs, one on either side of Ernie. They both looked bored.

"Holy Moses, are those dogs?" whispered Phil.

Cranky, I snapped, "You've met them before. You know they're dogs."

"Of course, they're dogs," said Mrs. Swale. "Step aside, Mr. Templeton. I need to talk to you."

"You don't have an appointment scheduled," I told her from my perch behind my desk. "You've interrupted a luncheon meeting between Mr. Templeton and Detective Bigelow." I pitched my voice to achieve a Boston-Brahmin snooty tone. I could out-snoot Mrs. Swale any day of the week if it proved necessary. Perhaps it wasn't necessary, but my nerves hadn't yet recovered from Ernie's mention of my book. Besides, Mrs. Swale was a rude, pushy woman and didn't deserve courtesy.

"That's right," said Ernie.

"Oh, for heaven's sake! I apologize for interrupting your meeting," said Mrs. Swale. She didn't come across as particularly sorry for her misdeed.

"Mr. Templeton has an open appointment at three o'clock this afternoon," I told the horrid woman.

"I need to speak to him *now*. It's terribly important."

"Will your dogs eat our lunch?" asked Ernie.

"Of course they won't," barked Mrs. Swale as if Ernie's question had been silly.

"Just tell me what you want to tell me then," said Ernie, still standing in front of her. "If you sic either of those monster dogs on me, the detective will arrest you."

"Caesar and Augustus are *not* monster dogs!"

"You want to tell me why you came here, or do you want to return at three?" asked Ernie.

"For heaven's sake! It's Eleanor. Eleanor Padgett! I'm terribly worried about her."

"We've been in touch with Miss Padgett," I said, still speaking from behind my desk. I pretty much trusted Caesar and Augustus, but I didn't trust Mrs. Swale not to order them to do something ultimately painful to Ernie, Phil, or me.

"True," said Ernie. "Miss Padget doesn't need you to speak for her. She can speak for herself. She left here less than an hour ago, in fact."

"Oh."

By golly, I do believe Mrs. Swale sagged on her throne. I could barely see her because Ernie is a tall man, but I noticed her shoulders slump.

"Hold on for a minute though," said Phil, rising from his chair and not bothering to put on his suit coat. Walking to the front door, he said, "Are you interested in attending a meeting for people who have invested in the scheme Mr. Lewiston was peddling?"

"Peddling! I wouldn't call it peddling. Mr. Lewiston was a true gentleman."

"And now he's a dead one," Ernie said brutally. "If you're interested in finding out who killed him—and two other mine investors we know of—you're welcome to attend the meeting. If you're not, please make an appointment if you still need to talk to me."

"I...I..." I think I heard Mrs. Swale gulp. "*Three* deaths?" she squeaked.

"Three," Ernie confirmed, his voice still hard.

"Then yes. I do wish to attend," said Mrs. Swale, sounding almost like a regular human being for the first time since I'd met her over a year prior.

"In that case," said Ernie, "my secretary will telephone you and give you the time and place of the meeting as soon as the details are confirmed."

"Well, but..."

Ernie took another step back and began shutting the door. An alarmed Mrs. Swale said, "Yes! Yes. I'll go to the meeting. Let me know as soon as it's arranged."

"Very well," I said haughtily. "I'll telephone you with the details."

"Thank you."

Ernie shut the door.

I banged my fist on my desk and said, "That's the first time I've ever heard her thank anybody for anything!"

Either Caesar or Augustus gave a loud, rumbling bark.

Mrs. Swale said, "Quiet!"

Ernie and Phil walked back to my desk, and we resumed dining.

EIGHTEEN

When we finally finished our delicious lunch, Ernie called the operator and got the telephone number for the Murray Dance Academy while I packed away the leftover food-stuffs in their little white containers. Then I called Lulu at the Figueroa Building's reception desk.

"Mercy! Did that lady with those two big dogs go to see Ernie? Those dogs are *gigantic*!"

"Yes," I said. "The dogs are big, but they're a lot nicer than she is."

Lulu laughed.

"Say Lulu, the next time you see Junior, will you send him up to Ernie's office? I want to give him the leftovers from our lunch today."

"That kid brought enough Chinese food into the Figueroa Building to feed the entire place," said Lulu. "He even gave me some."

"Good."

"You paid for it, right?"

Lulu knew me so well. "Yes, but he did the hard work. I'm glad you got some."

"I took it to one of the meeting rooms in the building because I'm not supposed to eat at my desk."

"Brilliant idea. I'm glad you got to eat."

"Thanks, Mercy," said Lulu. "Here's Junior. I'll send him right up."

"Thanks!" I hung up just as Ernie called my name.

When I scurried to his office, he held the telephone receiver in his hand. Both he and Phil appeared unhappy.

"What's the matter?" I asked.

"The coppers just arrested Charles Murray for the murder of his sister, Lucille Murray," said Ernie, with a frown for Phil.

"*What*? That's crazy!" I frowned at Phil too.

Phil held up his hands. "Not my fault. I wasn't even there."

"You're supposed to be in charge," I snarled.

Speaking into the mouthpiece, Ernie said, "Miss Murray? Miss Allcutt is here. Will you please tell her what you just told me?" He handed me the 'phone.

"Marian?"

"Yes." Her voice was thick with tears.

"I'm so sorry about the dimwitted policemen," I told her. "Mr. Templeton and I are arranging a meeting for all of the people who've been suckered into the gold mine venture Charles invested in." Another preposition! Those blasted things are everywhere.

"Really?" I heard Marian sniffle.

"Yes. So, do you know if they're going to set bail for Charles?"

"I don't know," Marian gave a sob. "I'm sorry!"

"You have nothing to be sorry for! Please don't apologize. You're grieving, you've been through the wringer, and the police are numbskulls."

I heard Phil grumble something, but I paid him no mind.

"Even if the police do set bail, I don't think we have enough money to get Charles out," said Marian after clearing her throat. I could tell she was trying hard to control her emotions.

"Hold on one moment, Marian," I said. "Do you mind? Just for a couple of seconds?"

"I don't mind," said Marian. I heard defeat in her voice, and it riled me.

So, I put my hand over the mouthpiece and growled at Phil, "What the heck are your underlings doing, arresting Charles? He wasn't even there when Marian was murdered!"

"Don't blame me," griped Phil. "All I know is that there was a murder at the dance place last night. I only found out you and your pals were taking lessons there when I came in to talk to Ernie today."

"Well, I'll bail Charles out of the clink. I'll bet you anything—well, almost anything—that the coppers don't have a single whit of real evidence against him. They just don't like him because he's a man and a dancer."

"They think he's a fairy," said Ernie bluntly. "Being a fairy, however, doesn't make him a killer."

"Cripes," said Phil. "I'll go back to the station and straighten it out. I'll call you, all right, Ernie?"

"Yeah. Do it quickly, or your station is apt to be invaded by a bunch of infuriated dancers. And their mothers."

"And dogs," I added. "Don't forget all the dogs."

"Cripes," Phil said again. "All right, all right. I'm going."

Phil headed to the front office door. As soon as he was out of earshot, I whispered, "Ernie, we have to spring Charles. He didn't do it, and if the coppers focus on him, the real murderer will get away. Don't forget that there are, so far, three dead bodies."

"How can I forget?" muttered Ernie.

"You and I need to go and talk to Marian Murray now. I'd ask her to come here, but the poor thing is probably about to collapse, what with her sister dead and her brother locked up. We should go to her."

"All right. I'll go with you."

Before I took my hand from the mouthpiece, I got on my tiptoes and gave Ernie a kiss on the cheek. "Thank you!"

To Marian I said, "My boss Mr. Templeton and I will be right there, Marian. Please lock the door to the academy. We're just a few buildings away from your studio."

"Thank you, Mercy. I just don't know what to *do*!" The poor thing resumed weeping.

"Try to calm down if you can. Ernie and I will be there in less than five minutes."

I was correct. Even though I paused to get a pad and pencils, fetch my handbag and put on my hat, Ernie and I arrived at the Murray Dance Academy about four and a half minutes after Marian and I disconnected our respective wires.

Marian told us that the Murray Dance Academy wouldn't be open for a while at least, what with Lucille dead and Charles charged with her murder. She feared the business would fold because of the crisis. With Phil's approval, therefore, she agreed to attend a meeting at 7:00 p.m. Sunday evening to be held at my very own house on Bunker Hill.

Then I had another one of my brilliant ideas. Have I mentioned how difficult it is to tell if ideas are really brilliant? Well, it is. But I blurted it out before thinking about it. "Say, Marian, why don't you stay at my place for a while? Lulu, Sue, and I all live there, and we'd love to have you."

She blinked swollen eyelids at me. "Really?"

"I'm sure you don't want to go home to an empty...wherever you live," I said.

Squinching her puffy eyes together and attempting to

smother more sobs, Marian nodded. After a second or two, she swallowed and said, "Our apartment. Yes, I don't want to go back there. Lucille, Charles, and I live in a one-bedroom apartment on First Street. It's pretty crowded with all of us there, but without Lucille and Charles—" She couldn't continue but began weeping again. I patted her on the shoulder.

"Mr. Templeton and I will take you to my house now. My housekeeper, Mrs. Buck, is a wonderful woman, and she'll fix up a bedroom for you. And one for Charles too. I'm sure the police won't keep him long."

"I wish I were as sure as you are," said Marian, wiping her cheeks with her hands.

So Ernie and I walked Marian to Ernie's Packard, and Ernie drove us to my house. As I'm sure both Ernie and I had expected, Marian was too astonished to be weepy when he pulled the Packard up the drive. Even I have to admit that my home was impressive.

"Oh my," Marian said. Again and again. And again.

When I explained to Mrs. Buck why Marian was visiting, the kindhearted woman took charge instantly. "Never you mind, Miss Mercy. We'll fix up a room for Miss Marian and another one for her brother. Charles, is it?"

"Yes," whispered Marian.

"You just come with me, child," said Mrs. Buck.

Naturally, Buttercup was excited to meet a new person. Well, she was also excited about seeing Ernie and me, but we had to leave her with Mrs. Buck and Marian. I don't think Buttercup was too upset. Marian nearly melted and gushed all over Buttercup.

"I can't believe you just up and invited the Murrays to live at your place," Ernie said as he drove us back to the Figueroa Building.

I opened my mouth to say something, but he lifted a hand

from the steering wheel and said, "No, I'm not. I should have expected you to do it."

"Yes," I agreed. "You should have."

Ernie only grinned.

Ernie and I stayed late at the office that Friday night. I had to call people and attempt to set up a meeting, and Ernie had to remain in his office until Phil called him about setting bail for Charles Murray.

"Please tell Mrs. Buck I'm sorry," I told Lulu when I called the front desk. "I'd rather be eating at home than calling all these stupid people."

"Will Ernie drive you home?" asked Lulu.

"He'd better," I said. "If he doesn't, we're going to have to have a serious chat about my future employment at Ernest Templeton, P.I." Okay, so it was a fib. I might find my job boring sometimes. Often, even. But when it wasn't boring, it was fascinating. Also, I was increasingly fond of my infuriating boss.

"I'm sure Mrs. Buck will be happy to heat up dinner for you when you get here."

"I don't want to put her to the bother. I already dropped Marian into her hands, and she'll fix a room for Charles too, if the coppers set bail for him. Ernie and I will forage. Besides, I'm still full from lunch."

"Yeah, I am too. Guess I'll see you when you get here then."

"Yes, I suppose so. Please pet Buttercup for me."

"I'll even take her for a walk."

"Lulu, you're wonderful. Thank you!"

"Not a problem, Mercy. I swear, you feed the world, then you're surprised when people appreciate you for it."

Her words gave me pause, but not for long. "Nertz," I said. "I was born with a silver spoon in my mouth. Not everyone is as lucky as I."

"You've made up for it, believe me."

"If you say so." I didn't believe her. "But I need to call more people. See you later, Lulu."

"Bye, Mercy."

It took a *whole* lot of telephoning and re-telephoning to set up a meeting of Mr. Madison's fake gold mine investors. Naturally, the most difficult invitee was the miserable, mousy Mr. Horshank. He flatly refused to attend a meeting when I called him, being the woman-hating imbecile he was. Finally, Detective Phil Bigelow telephoned him and told him to appear at my own personal house at 7:00 p.m. on Sunday evening, or he'd be apprehended for obstruction of justice.

"Golly, really?" I asked Ernie when Phil called to tell him.

"If he doesn't show, he *will* be obstructing a police investigation. This matter isn't just about the gold mine any longer. Three investors are dead, and one of them was a police officer. The L.A.P.D. doesn't approve of people murdering their own."

"And they didn't have a handy Negro or Chinese person to pin it on this time. I understand," I snarled. Very well, so sarcasm was my pal that day. I sometimes manage to keep my opinions under wraps, but the inequities in the world were proving particularly annoying that day.

"Mercy, Mercy, Mercy," said Ernie. "Whatever will I do with you?"

"Nothing if you're smart. Don't forget that I had to call Mrs. Swale about eighty times today. And she was rude and officious every time."

"Thought she had underlings to answer telephones for her," said Ernie with a teasing grin.

"She does, but I needed to talk with Mrs. Whale herself. An underling couldn't agree to attend a meeting for her."

"But Mrs. …Whale, did you call her? Anyhow, she finally did agree to be there?"

"Yes, after I called on my mother's authoritarian vocal reserves. I hate having to do that." I hesitated for a moment before admitting, "Although that tone gets results. But I think people should be reasonable without having to be threatened or bullied first."

"You live in dreamland, Mercy." Sarcasm was Ernie's pal too.

"I'm gaining more understanding of that fact daily."

We also invited Mr. Gallagher, as he had agreed to take Mr. Lewiston's salukis after Mr. L's death. He was happy to oblige, as was Rob Gabriel. Because Lulu, Sue, and I would have been attending tap lessons at the Murray Academy were it not for the recent problems there, I figured we'd attend the meeting as well. I was nominated by both Phil and Ernie to take notes.

There had been a time when I'd believed—or at least hoped—I'd be a published novelist. Now it looked as if my main role in life was destined to be taking minutes at meetings. At least the one on Sunday evening probably wouldn't be boring.

Finally, *long* after our usual five p.m. closing time, Phil called the office to tell Ernie that bail had been set for Charles Murray.

"They must know they don't have any evidence against him," said Ernie, stretching after he hung up his receiver. "They set the bail low. Five hundred bucks."

"For a suspected murderer?"

Even though I knew Charles Murray to be innocent of his sister's murder, I figured the coppers were…um… Honestly, I'm not sure what word to use here. The coppers weren't all stupid. And they weren't all crooked. They did, however, harbor prejudices. In fact, the main reason Officers Cooper and Singleton arrested Charles Murray was that they perceived him as being unmanly. Unmanly men—or "fairies," as Ernie called them—

175

were generally disliked by the male population of the nation. Perhaps other nations, too.

"They don't suspect him awfully hard," said Ernie, caustically.

"They don't like him because he's… Well, you know."

"Yeah," said Ernie. "I know."

"Idiots."

"Who?"

"The police."

"Aw, they're not all idiots," said Ernie. "Just most of them."

"If you say so."

"Come on, kid…I mean Mercy. Let's go spring Charles Murray from the clink."

So we did.

For the record, it had been Detective Phil Bigelow who decided it would be a great idea to use my home as a meeting place rather than a room at the First Street Station where he worked.

"One of the victims was a police officer," he said sententiously, as if we didn't already know that. "If the culprit turns out to be another member of the L.A.P.D., I don't want to give him any hints about actions we plan to take."

"I'm sure that will make Mrs. Buck feel a whole lot better about her home being taken over by a bunch of nitwitted gold mine investors," I growled. "I also don't want Mr. Horshank to know where I live."

"We don't have to tell anyone it's your house," said Phil.

"Right," said Ernie. "That'll do a whole lot of good."

"I'll just tell my tenants and friends to pretend the house belongs to… Oh, I don't know. Yes I do! *Ernie*! We'll tell everyone the house belongs to Ernie." My suggestion wasn't serious. In fact, it was said using words that might have been dipped in alum before they left my lips.

"Great idea!" said Ernie.

I gave him a good hot scowl and then caved. What the heck. I kind of wished Ernie *did* own the place. With me.

Please don't tell anyone.

NINETEEN

Saturday wasn't precisely a fun-filled day. Mrs. Buck claimed she didn't mind losing her day off, although I wasn't sure I believed her. I aimed to give her a big bonus along with a week's holiday if this case ever ended.

At any rate, thanks to Phil deciding to use my house as a meeting place, Mrs. Buck, Lulu, Sue, Caroline, and I frantically prepared edibles for the people who would gather the following evening. Mrs. Buck also declared that we tenants of Mercy's Manor weren't in her way, but I didn't believe that either.

Lulu, Sue, and Caroline even managed to prepare cheese straws. I attempted to do likewise and ended up with cheese all over my hands and fingers, flour on the floor, and Buttercup gulping pounds of butter. Well, and cheese too. Ernie finally suggested I leave the kitchen and consult with him, Rob, Phil, and the Murray siblings in the living room. I think I heard Mrs. Buck mutter a barely audible, "Thank God."

Because I knew when I wasn't wanted—and why—I left the kitchen feeling crushed. I really wanted Mrs. Buck to teach me how to cook, but she was too busy to do it.

When I joined the group in the living room, it became clear that the two remaining Murray siblings alternated between overpowering grief and numb incredulity. That being the case, they also alternated between wanting to kill the killer and shedding tears of sorrow.

I couldn't fault them for either emotion.

Although I was far from being a champ in the kitchen, I was relatively well-organized and compassionate. The remaining Murray siblings, as was only reasonable, focused on the fact of Lucille's death and couldn't see beyond the grim fact. As we sat in the living room, therefore, I asked Marian and Charles, "Would you like me to help you make plans for Lucille's...burial? Funeral? Well, you know what I mean."

Marian and Charles first gaped at me and then at each other. "A f-funeral?" said Charles.

"Arrangements?" said Marian.

Thank the good lord Ernie was there with us. "Mercy's an expert at coordinating things. Do you two have any other siblings or relatives who need to be told about Lucille's passing? And do you believe they would care to attend a ceremony?"

I joined Marian and Charles in gaping at Ernie. I hadn't realized until then that he could be tactful.

Eyeing me with what could only be called an evil grin, Ernie said, "What?"

"Uh...nothing," I said, changing conversational gears more quickly than I could change the gears in my little Moon Roadster. "Yes, I'll be happy to help you organize a funeral for Lucille. Or...well, if you need to have her...remains shipped to a different city or state, we can make plans for that."

Now Marian and Charles—and Ernie, for pity's sake—gaped at *me*.

"A f-funeral?" whispered Marian.

"Golly, I hadn't even thought about a funeral," said Charles, sounding stunned. "Poor Lucille. We should do something for her."

"If we had any money, we could bury her properly," said Marian with a hint of accusation in her voice.

"Oh, God." Charles buried his face in his hands.

Marian kept up her stony facade for a second or two, then pretty much melted into her brother and put her arms around him. "I'm sorry, Charles. It isn't your fault."

Actually, it was (according to me), but I didn't say so. Rather I said, "Don't fret about money."

And then I didn't know where to go from there. If I said I'd pay for a funeral, it would look as though I were flaunting my wealth. I'd already done that, which was why Marian and Charles were staying in my home. I feared offering more mazuma would be perceived as me rubbing the Murrays' noses in their relative poverty and flaunting my own relative wealth. They might refuse my offer if only out of wounded pride.

Fortunately, Ernie picked up my dropped stitch and resumed knitting in my stead. "Miss Allcutt means that you're entitled to some funds. There's an organization in Los Angeles that helps with...final expenses in cases like yours."

Bless Ernie's heart, if he had one! "That's right," I said, nodding vigorously. "I'll be happy to get in touch with the"— what had he called it? Oh, yes—"the organization for you. I understand how upset you are right now."

"Oh, could you?" said Marian. "That would be so kind."

"What's the name of the organization?" asked Charles. He would. Numbskull.

I'm sorry. I didn't mean that.

Very well, I did mean it, but it was unkind of me.

After Ernie and I exchanged a quick glance, Ernie again took the lead. "I can't remember the official name of it, but the Los

Angeles Police Department has funds available for final expenses in these types of cases."

These types of cases? Cases of murdered dance teachers? I didn't ask.

"That's wonderful." Marian broke down and sobbed.

Charles put his arms around her and said, "It'll be all right, Marian. The gold mine will pay off any day now."

He shouldn't have mentioned the gold mine. Marian pulled out of his arms and screeched, "Don't you *dare* talk to me about that gold mine, Charles Murray! That stupid mine is why Lucille is dead!"

Looking hurt and baffled—I concluded Charles wasn't the sharpest tack in the Murray clan's toolkit—Charles said, "But no, Marian. That can't be."

I opened my mouth, but Ernie held up a hand, quelling my verbosity. When I glanced at Phil and Rob, I saw they too were interested in the Murray siblings' spat.

"It is, Charles! Don't you understand yet? Horshank is just a tool of Autley, and Autley and Madison are flimflam artists!"

Aha! Autley again! Once more, I opened my mouth, but this time Phil's lifted hand stopped me.

"Excuse me," Phil said, effectively interrupting the siblings' argument and me too.

Marian and Charles turned to look at Phil. Brother and sister appeared ravaged, poor things.

"I'm sorry, Officer," said Marian, pressing a palm to her head. "I have *such* a headache. I didn't mean to start a quarrel in front of you. You've been awfully good to us."

"Would you like a powder, Marian?" I asked solicitously, figuring none of the men in the room could object to this offer.

I was wrong. All four males in the room frowned at me. Honestly! Men.

"Yes, please," Marian whimpered.

"Go get Miss Murray a powder and some water, Mercy," Ernie suggested, giving me a tight smile. "Perhaps Miss Murray can tell us who Mr. Autley is and what part he plays in the gold mine investment group."

"I'd like to know the answer to the Autley question too," I said, deciding no one, not even Ernie, was going to ban me from my own living room. "Is Mr. Autley related to the Autley boy who disrupted your tap class the day we signed up for classes?"

Marian blinked at me. So did Charles. The rest of the room's inhabitants continued frowning.

After several seconds, Marian said, "Lenny Autley?" She sounded tentative.

I nodded.

"I…I don't know. Charles?" She glanced at her brother.

"Yes, Lenny's father is Mr. Leonard Autley," said Charles, picking up from where Marian had left off. "He and a fellow named Madison are in charge of the gold mine."

"This is the gold mine in Colorado?" Ernie.

"The same one in which Mr. Frederick Lewiston invested?" Phil.

"And Mr. Horshank?" Rob.

"Yes." Charles.

Now that we had the gold mine issue settled, I decided it was safe to leave the room. "I'll fetch some aspirin and water for you, Marian," I said.

"Thank you, Miss Allcutt."

"Please call me Mercy," I told her.

"Good name for you," she said. "Thank you."

Marian's comment, while kindly meant, sealed my resolve. Should anyone at Hamilton, Smith and Ransom—or any other publisher—decide to publish one (or more) of my books one day,

I aimed to assume a *nom de plume*. Several authors used their initials. M.L. Allcutt might work. Then again, it might not. People might assume the publisher had accidentally reversed the initials, and that they should refer to Louisa May Alcott. What a lousy name I had!

Guess I'd been staring off into space long enough for people to notice, because Ernie finally said, "Mercy?" he said. "Powders? Aspirin tablets? Water?" thereby goosing me into action.

"Oh. Sorry," I said.

I got up, went to the downstairs bathroom and fetched a bottle of Bayer Aspirin tablets. Tablets, I'd discovered on my own, worked as well as salicylic powders for relieving pain, and they didn't taste horrible. You just gulped them down with some water, and they did their magical job. They even helped when your muscles ached from tap-dancing too hard for too long. I knew it for a fact.

My detour to the kitchen to fetch a glass of water was eye-opening. Mrs. Buck and her assistants had accumulated trays of cheese straws and piles of sandwiches. "Oh, my," I said. "Look at all your great work. People won't starve at tomorrow's meeting anyhow."

"There's more in the Frigidaire," said Caroline, not sounding prim and prudish for once.

"We'll keep them fresh by wrapping them in waxed paper," said Sue happily.

"Waxed paper is *such* a great invention," said Lulu.

"It is indeed," said Mrs. Buck, bestowing a fond smile on her assistants. The woman was a marvel.

"Thank you all so much for doing this," I said.

"What do you need, Miss Mercy?" asked Mrs. Buck.

"Uh…what do I need? Oh, yes! I'm sorry. I need a glass of water for Miss Murray."

Mrs. Buck reached into the cupboard for a glass and filled it from the kitchen tap. "Here you go. Poor Miss Murray must be feeling awfully low."

I nodded. "She is, and now she has a bad headache, so I'm taking her some aspirin tablets. That's why I need the water."

"Poor Marian," said Sue.

"She should probably lie down for a bit," said Caroline, appearing worried. Guess she wasn't starchy and stodgy all the time.

What a killjoy I am, huh? Ah well.

Marian was glad to get the aspirin and water. "Oh, thank you, Mercy," she said when I rejoined the living-room group. She appeared relieved to see me, which was nice. Lately, people seemed happier to watch me leave than arrive.

As Marian downed her aspirin tablets with a gulp of water, Ernie said, "The Murrays have told us that their only relations are in Minneapolis."

"Minneapolis! My goodness, that's so far away," I said and instantly wished I hadn't.

"Boston's farther," said Ernie.

"But we only have an uncle there," said Marian. "And he always dis-dis-disapproved of us." She broke down again.

I laid the box of aspirin tablets on a coffee table and put a hand on Marian's shoulder. "Marian, if these fellows are through asking you questions, would you like to go upstairs? You probably should lie down for a while. It might help your headache."

"Thank you, Mercy," she said weakly. "I'd like to do that."

When she attempted to rise from the sofa, she teetered. Charles instantly leaped to his feet and grabbed her other shoulder. "I'll help you," he said.

And he did. Mrs. Buck had prepared two rooms that had been standing idle for months on the second floor of the house. Traversing the staircase got me to thinking about something other than Ernie, my job, my poor orphaned novel, murdered gold mine investors, and tap-dancing. Maybe I should rent out more rooms to more people. Mrs. Buck might need a helper if she had more mouths to feed, but I could hire one for her.

Then I decided I'd be better off not thinking at all.

So that's what I did.

TWENTY

On Sunday morning, Sue and Caroline went to church like the good Christian girls they were. Charles and Marian Murray remained in their respective rooms. I figured they needed rest. Mr. and Mrs. Buck also went to church on Sundays, but the wonderful Mrs. Buck had prepared cinnamon rolls for those of us requiring breakfast. Lulu cooked bacon and fixed a pot of coffee, and we had a tasty meal to start our day. We also had an icebox positively stuffed with food, so we wouldn't need to worry about lunch or dinner.

Lulu and I bade farewell to our more disciplined friends and then sprawled in the living room. Lulu read the most recent copy of *Motion Picture Magazine*. Stuffier than my pal, I read the *Los Angeles Times*. Almost instantly, I regretted my choice of reading material.

"Oh, my goodness!"

Buttercup, on the sofa beside me, gave a startled woof. Lulu jumped about three feet from her perch on a living room chair and slammed a hand over her heart. "What's wrong?" She sounded as if she expected me to point out a masked intruder.

"I'm sorry, Lulu. I didn't mean to holler. You too, Buttercup."
I gave my pup a reassuring pat, rested the newspaper on my
knees and gazed out the window. The May sky featured a few
clouds. To my mind's eye, those clouds looked like puffs of
meringue floating in a sea of azure. Los Angeles was one lucky
city.

"What's the matter?"

"Nothing here. I was just reading about a school in Michigan.
Some crazy person blew it up. A *school*. Killed more than thirty
children and at least two adults."

"Why would anybody do something like that?" Lulu was at
least as horrified as I. I could tell.

"He was a lunatic, I guess." I lifted the newspaper and shook
it out so I could resume reading the article. "He killed his wife
and then blew up the school." Again, I laid the paper on my
knees. "Kids. He killed *kids*."

Lulu and I stared at each other in disbelief and revulsion.

"I…I can't even imagine something that awful," said Lulu.

"I couldn't either until I read this article. In fact, it would
never have occurred to me that a person might even *think* about
doing such a vile thing. After he blew up the school, he drove
back to the ruins and killed himself and some more school
personnel."

"That's evil," said Lulu.

"It is," I agreed.

"Why do you read stuff like that?" asked Lulu as if she really
wanted to know.

"Stuff like that? Stuff like what's happening in our country?"

"Crazy people killing kids isn't the only thing that's
happening in our country," Lulu demurred. "I mean, it's a
terrible thing, but there are good things happening too."

I thought of Mr. and Mrs. Buck's children, Calvin and
Loretta. Calvin had been accused of murder several months back

because he was a Negro. Honestly, there was no other reason. Loretta had gone to college and was a qualified teacher, but she couldn't teach in most public schools because she too was a Negro. Then there was Charley Wu, accused of a man's murder because he (Charley) was Chinese. So was the victim, so no one much cared.

And now Lucille Murray had been murdered. She was white, so her murder wasn't race-related. Nor was it being completely ignored. Still... "There must be good things happening here, huh?" I lifted the newspaper and tried to find good news. "I guess Mae West is out of jail now. Is that good news?"

"I don't know. She was jailed for corrupting the morals of children, wasn't she?"

"I think so. Let me see if I can find an article." But I couldn't.

"Well, if that's why she was locked up, I think the judge made a mistake. Any parents who let their kid see a show called *Sex* are the ones doing the corrupting."

After mulling over her statement for a second and a half, I agreed with Lulu. "Good point," I said. Then my peepers found another dismal article. "Crumb, they're still looking for bodies of people who drowned in that terrible flood in Mississippi."

"Too bad," said Lulu.

"Oh, that new theater is open! The one Mr. Grauman built on Hollywood Boulevard? I think Chloe and Harvey went to the grand opening on the eighteenth."

"That's the one that looks like a Chinese restaurant?" asked Lulu.

"That's the one, all right." I heaved a tiny sigh. "I miss Chloe and Harvey."

"You talk to Chloe almost every day," Lulu reminded me.

"I know, but it's not the same."

"How's their beautiful daughter?" Lulu gave a larger, more rapturous sigh.

"She's fine," I said.

Confession time here. Ernie and I seemed to be the only two people on the face of the earth who didn't think the Nashes' four-month-old daughter, Heather Rose, was spectacularly gorgeous. The last time I saw her, I thought she looked rather like a pink and wrinkly bulldog puppy, and Ernie agreed with me. According to everyone else in the Los Angeles area, Ernie and I were wrong. I thought her name was lovely though, if that counts.

"Do you want kids?" asked Lulu.

Taken aback by her question, I said, "Children? I'm not even married!"

"I'm talking about *eventually*," said Lulu, a bite to her voice. "Not today or tomorrow, or even next week. Do you want kids?"

"Hmm. I've never even thought about having children," I admitted.

"Ask Ernie if he wants them," Lulu suggested.

"Why should I ask Ernie?"

"The two of you are going to tie the knot eventually. You probably ought to talk about either having children or not having children before you do it."

"You think Ernie and I are going to *marry*? Each *other*?" My question reflected my astonishment.

"Sure! So does Rob." Lulu sounded as if I should think so too.

"Really? So far, Ernie hasn't shown the least inclination to propose to me," I said, telling the dismal truth.

"Applesauce! He adores you," claimed Lulu.

"If you say so," I muttered. Another item in the paper caught my eye. "Oh, this is interesting. The economy in Germany has collapsed."

"What does that mean?"

"I guess it means that Germany went broke. It says here"—I

stabbed at the article with my forefinger—"the stock market in Berlin crashed."

"I still don't know what that means," said Lulu.

"Honestly, I don't either, but I think it means that people who bought stocks on margin or, say, people who invested money in swampland in Florida—"

"I thought you were talking about Germany. Is there a Florida in Germany?"

"No, I don't think so. I was using Florida as an example. Like that nonexistent gold mine people keep getting murdered over. I guess what happened in Germany was that a whole bunch of people bought stocks and shares on margin—that means they paid maybe ten or twenty percent of their own money and borrowed the rest from the banks—and asked the banks for their money back. The banks didn't have their money because they'd depleted their funds by lending them to other people. And I guess people who bought shares of stock tried to cash them in and had the same problem—the money wasn't there. I imagine overproduction can be a factor. If you produce too much stuff, and if people no longer have money, there's no one left to buy your stuff. Prices fall, but regular people can't take advantage of the lowered prices because they've lost all their money."

Silence from my companion. I lowered the paper and saw Lulu's brow furrow as she attempted to make her way through my—grossly flawed—explanation of high finance. At last, I asked, "Did that make sense?"

"I'm not sure."

"I'm not either." I heaved another little sigh. "Actually, I think Germany had problems other than the stock market. After the war, they were assessed huge fines."

"They deserved them," said Lulu.

"The people who started the war deserved fines. The normal,

everyday people of Germany were probably just trying to get by from day to day."

"I guess," said Lulu. I could tell she was unconvinced.

I folded my depressing newspaper and said, "I'm going to take Buttercup for a walk." A rapturous bark sounded from Buttercup next to me on the sofa. "Want to come along?"

First tilting her head one way and then the other, Lulu said, "Yeah. It's a nice day for a walk."

So the three of us went for a long, lovely walk through the neighborhood. The homes on Bunker Hill in Los Angeles were nice for the most part. Some of them had begun to sag here and there, and a couple of huge apartment buildings had been built in recent years, spoiling the cozy nature of the place, but the neighborhood still retained a good deal of its original beauty. Buttercup watered bushes here and there, wagged nonstop, and had a great time. Lulu and I didn't talk for a couple of blocks.

Ultimately, Lulu broke our silence by delivering a blow that nearly knocked me sideways.

"Rob and I are thinking of moving to Pasadena."

"*What?*"

I'd heard her; I just couldn't quite take in the significance of what she'd said.

"No need to holler," said Lulu dryly. "Rob and I are thinking about moving to Pasadena after we get married."

"Oh," I said. "Interesting."

Honestly, I didn't know what to say. Lulu moving? First, my sister moved to Beverly Hills; now, Lulu wanted to go to Pasadena? Next thing you knew, Ernie would be telling me he was moving back to Chicago. For some reason, I felt lonely and bereft—not unlike my poor manuscript being ignored as it sat in a big stack with other orphaned manuscripts in New York City. If it ever even got there.

"Interesting? You think it's interesting?" said Lulu. She sounded exasperated.

"Well, yes, I do. I'm sorry, Lulu. I had no idea you were contemplating a move to anywhere at all. Does Rob have a job waiting for him in Pasadena?"

"He's looking around. He doesn't think it will be difficult to find a law practice in Pasadena that will be happy to hire him."

"Oh. That's nice." It was awful, was what it was. I didn't want Lulu to move!

"Mercy, what's the matter? I mean, Rob and I are getting married, so I'd be moving anyway—"

"Why?" I asked, rudely interrupting Lulu in mid-sentence.

"Why? What do you mean, why? We're getting married! His apartment is too small for both of us, and he can't live in Mercy's Manor with Sue, Caroline, you, and me."

"Why not?" I asked, suddenly envisioning something akin to a happy community of friends.

Silence from Lulu. When I glanced at her, she appeared puzzled. "You started renting rooms to working women who needed a place to stay. No men were allowed."

"I know," I said. "But that was in the beginning. I don't think I'd mind having a married couple—or even two or three married couples—living in my home. God knows, it's big enough."

"True. But do you really mean it, Mercy? It would be a big change, wouldn't it?"

"Would it?" I thought about Lulu's question for a few seconds. Buttercup interrupted my train of thought when she barked hello at what looked like an Italian greyhound standing guard behind the fence of another Bunker Hill mansion.

"Oh look!" said Lulu. "It's one of those itsy-bitsy dogs like the one Junior was walking on Friday. Was it Friday?"

"I think so. Hmm. Wonder if this is where Mr. Gallagher lives."

"Who's Mr. Gallagher?" asked Lulu.

"He owns the menswear store down the street from the Figueroa Building. He shows Italian greyhounds. He took in Mr. Frederick Lewiston's salukis after Mr. Lewiston died."

"I don't know what you're talking about," said Lulu.

So I filled her in on the dog issue and how it might—or might not—relate to the gold mine issue, the tap-dance issue, and the various murders happening all over the place.

"Golly. You mean the two dog ladies are involved with the fake gold mine and the Murrays?"

"They seem to be connected somehow. Not sure how. But I'd never seen an Italian greyhound until Junior brought one of them by the office on Friday. It was Friday, wasn't it?"

"We don't know," said Lulu.

"Anyhow, it seems odd that Italian greyhounds should be popping up all over the place."

"Do the Figueroa Building and Bunker Hill count as all over the place?"

"Good question. I don't know."

Suddenly, a large dog bounded up to the fence and started barking at Buttercup, Lulu, and me. "A saluki!" I cried. "Mr. Gallagher *must* live here! I'd never seen an Italian greyhound and a saluki before in my life. And now they're living in my neighborhood! Good heavens."

"I'm confused," said Lulu.

"That makes two of us."

Then darned if Mr. Gallagher, clad in trousers, shirt and pullover sweater, didn't round the corner of his house to see what the dogs were barking at. Clapping his hands at them, he said, "Quiet, you two!" Then he glanced up and noticed Lulu, Buttercup, and me. "Oh, good morning, Miss Allcutt and Miss LaBelle. Is that your poodle, Miss Allcutt? Junior told me he might be taking your poodle for walks soon."

"Good morning, Mr. Gallagher. Yes, this is Buttercup, my toy poodle. And I talked to Junior about walking her because I don't have as much time to walk her as I used to have. I didn't know you lived around here."

"I do indeed." He walked over to the fence and shook first my hand and then Lulu's as we held them out to him. "The neighborhood's going downhill, though. Not sure how much longer I'll stay here."

"You really think so?" I asked, feeling disappointed that my own observations were validated.

"Mercy!" came another voice. It was one I recognized.

"Francis!" Mr. Francis Easthope lived in a bungalow court on Alvarado Avenue, but he used to visit Chloe and Harvey when they owned my house. Did that make sense? "Are you visiting Mr. Gallagher?"

Francis walked over to the fence and also shook Lulu's and my hand. "I am indeed." He gave us a glorious smile. Mr. Francis Easthope was perhaps the most handsome man on the face of the earth. This was especially true since poor Rudolph Valentino passed away last year.

"I'm trying to talk him into taking over the care and feeding of salukis," said Mr. Gallagher, grinning. "But come into the house! We don't have to stand here and yak. We can go inside where I have refreshments."

"And more dogs," said Francis.

"True, but these ladies don't mind dogs," said Mr. Gallagher. "Miss Allcutt even has a toy poodle."

"Yes. I've met Buttercup several times," said Francis.

Lulu and I exchanged speculative glances, but we didn't get the opportunity to accept or reject Mr. Gallagher's kind offer of refreshments—and I wanted to see what the interior of his house looked like—because an almost-new Packard-Six came to a halt next to the sidewalk upon which Lulu, Buttercup, and I stood.

We all turned to discover Ernie and Rob, who were the Packard's driver and passenger, respectively.

"Good morning, Mr. Templeton," said Mr. Gallagher politely.

"Morning, Gallagher, Easthope," said Ernie.

Ernie used to dislike Mr. Francis Easthope and his ilk because they were what he called "pansies." I personally love pansies— the flowers—and have nothing against men like Mr. Gallagher and Mr. Easthope.

Men are strange creatures, so I've ceased expecting logic from them. But for heaven's sake, why like or dislike someone merely because society has stuck a label on him or her? Besides, what one does in one's own home is nobody else's business—unless one is stockpiling dynamite in order to blow up a school. But most of the fellows of Mr. Easthope's persuasion whom I'd met weren't nearly as belligerent as most so-called "normal" men.

There I go again, being radical. That's according to my mother. I prefer to think of my stance as reasonable.

Never mind.

After all the men had greeted each other, Ernie said, "Come on back to your house, Mercy. Rob and I came bearing foodstuffs."

"Food?" I stared at my boss. "There's already enough food in my house to feed an army."

"But that stuff is for the meeting, right?" said Ernie.

"Right," I said.

"Well, Rob and I went to Philippe's, and we have sandwiches and potato salad for everyone."

"Are we hungry?" I asked Lulu.

"I'm not sure," said Lulu.

With a laugh, Mr. Gallagher said, "I'll let you figure that one out on your own. But I'll be at the meeting tonight."

"Looking forward to it," said Ernie, surprising me. I figured he automatically disliked Mr. Gallagher because he was of Francis Easthope's persuasion. Guess Ernie wasn't as biased as he used to be. Good.

"Want a ride?" asked Rob of Lulu.

After a glance at me—I nodded my approval—Lulu said, "Sure."

"What about you, Mercy?" asked Ernie.

"I think I'll walk Buttercup home. This is the first walk we've taken in several days. Poor baby thought I'd deserted her."

"Right," said Ernie. But he grinned.

Rob opened the front door for Lulu and scooted over so she could fit on the big bench seat. Then Ernie drove to the nearest intersection, made a U-turn, and drove back to where my house sat.

After the car and its occupants left us, I turned to Francis. "Do you think you will take up the care and feeding of salukis?" I glanced at the saluki at present nuzzling Buttercup's nose through the fence slats.

"I don't know," he said. "I can't have pets where I live, so I'll have to think about it."

"Well, if you do decide to take them in, let me know. I'd love to meet more of them." To Mr. Gallagher, I said, "Your Italian greyhounds are adorable."

"Thanks, Miss Allcutt."

"Call me Mercy," I said.

"Only if you call me Bill."

I smiled at him. "Very well, Bill."

When Buttercup and I walked back to my house, Sue and Caroline had returned from their different church services. The Murray siblings had also come out of hiding, if they'd been hiding. Ernie and Rob had taken my tenants and guests into consideration when they'd visited Philippe's, so there were sandwiches and potato salad enough for everyone. And they were really good, too. The sandwiches and potato salad, not my tenants. Well, that is to say my tenants were good too, but…

Oh bother it all.

TWENTY-ONE

That evening, Phil arrived at my house at six on the dot. The Murray siblings were already there. The rest of the invitees started arriving at a little past six-fifteen. The first people to show up were Mrs. Swale and Miss Padgett, who had come in the same automobile. Then came Mr. Gallagher, *sans* dogs.

No one had been able to get in touch with Mr. Madison or Mr. Autley.

Naturally, the straggler was Mr. Horshank, who seemed both peevish and nervous.

"I don't know why I had to come to this stupid meeting," he groused as he walked past Phil, who had opened the door for him. Then Horshank stood still and gazed through the arched entry into the living room. "Who lives here?" he asked querulously. "It's a grand home, but this neighborhood is going to the dogs."

I'd never tell him that he was correct if you took Mr. Gallagher and me into consideration.

"You know why you're here. This meeting is in aid of an official police investigation," said Ernie, who stood behind Phil. "Just come in and be seated."

"I don't know why I have to be here," he whined.

"We'll tell you," said Ernie. "Come in, sit down, and be quiet."

"Well!" said Mr. Horshank. I think he wanted to argue, but Phil had brought two uniformed officers—not Cooper and Singleton—to stand at attention and look menacing. Or maybe they were only meant to look official.

One of the uniforms stalked up to Mr. Horshank and said, "Come this way, sir."

Mr. Horshank went that way.

Ernie, Rob, and Phil had arranged the furniture in my living room so that everyone seated thereon would face the staircase. They'd added folding chairs to supplement the sofas and chairs already there. The two uniforms placed themselves at the entrance to the dining room and the archway leading to the tiled entryway and the front door. Except that the meeting was taking place in my own personal home, which was relatively grand in the overall scheme of things, the meeting seemed quite official.

Shortly after Mr. Horsefeathers arrived, Phil called the meeting to attention by having one of the uniforms blow his police whistle. Hard. Thought my eardrums would burst. Phil himself stood about four or five steps up the staircase. Ernie stood beside the staircase. Rob joined Lulu and sat in the back of the room. They held hands, which I thought was sweet.

Silence ensued. More or less. I don't suppose there's ever been complete silence in a room (or a cave) full of human beings. We're a noisy lot, we people.

"You're here today to discuss increasing violence occurring with regard to a gold mine in Colorado. The existence of the mine is under question—"

"It is not!" squealed Mr. Horshank.

"Quiet!" said one of the uniforms, walking over and placing a hand on Horshank's shoulder.

Mr. H. squeaked and sat still, shooting sideways glances at the owner of the hand. He looked like a terrified vole.

"Hold all questions and comments until after I've explained the purpose of this meeting," commanded Phil. He sounded more official than I'd ever heard him sound. I was impressed. I doubt my mother could have done a better job of lording it over a room full of people. He glared around the room, and everyone sat up straighter.

"Now," he continued, "so far, three people who are interested in the supposed gold mine in Colorado have died. We believe all three deaths were the result of murder."

A collective gasp went up, but not even Mr. Horshank dared speak.

"We need to talk about how to get to the bottom of these crimes, and how to find and stop the perpetrator or perpetrators. As you may note, the mine investment scheme has involved people from different occupations. The deaths included a businessman who was involved in the dog-show world, an L.A.P.D. police officer, and a dance instructor. Completely different walks of life, but they all had an interest in the gold mine offered by Mr. Clive Madison."

"Where is Mr. Madison?" asked Mr. Horshank, breaking Phil's rule as soon as he could.

"We were unable to find him," said Phil. "We've also been unable to get in touch with Mr. Autley."

"But they're the ones who know about the mine," squealed Mr. Horshank.

"Please save your comments until the appropriate time," said Phil sternly.

"I don't know why—" Mr. H. shut up when the copper standing next to his chair squeezed his shoulder. "Ow," he said, glancing at the officer, who gave him an impressive scowl. Mr. H. decided to keep further complaints to himself for the nonce.

Ernie walked up the stairs and stood beside Phil. He held up a hand and said, "I know Detective Bigelow will excuse me if I say a few words."

"Absolutely," said Phil. He didn't even sound sarcastic.

Ernie went on: "Mr. Charles Murray and Miss Marian Murray are here with us this evening for a tragic reason. Their sister, Miss Lucille Murray, was killed last Thursday. We understand from several sources that you, Mr. Horshank, have been attempting to get the Murrays to invest in the gold mine. Is that correct?"

"Well," said Mr. Horshank. "I don't know what you mean by—"

"Yes or no will suffice, Mr. Horshank," said Ernie in his death voice.

"Well…"

Mr. Horshank squeaked again when the officer with a hand on his shoulder squeezed said shoulder. Hard.

"Just answer yes or no, Mr. Horshank," Ernie said, his voice even deadlier than before.

"Y-yes!" shrilled Mr. Horshank. "But I'm not the only one!"

"Do tell," said Ernie, easing up on the deadliness timbre. "Give us names, Mr. Horshank. We need names if we're ever to get to the bottom of the pit."

"What pit?" Horshank sounded angry.

"You know the pit of which I speak as a gold mine," said Ernie, venom fairly dripping from his words. "In Colorado."

"But—ow!" The hand on Mr. Horshank's shoulder dug in again.

"That's not what I asked, Horshank," Ernie said. "We need the names of the people who were in charge of the gold mine investment project. Do you have any names other than those of Mr. Clive Madison and Mr. Leonard Autley?"

"Huh." It wasn't really a word, but a grunt, so I guess the policeman with his hand on Horshank's shoulder didn't squeeze it again.

"Think about it, Mr. Horshank," said Ernie. "We'll ask you again later."

Phil took over. "Mr. Murray, please tell us how you first learned of the gold mine in which you wanted to invest."

"Oh, God," said Charles, hanging his head and looking miserable. "Leonard Autley was the first person to talk to me about it."

"Who precisely is Leonard Autley?" asked Phil.

"He's the father of one of Lucille's…" He choked back a sob.

Marian took over for him. "Mr. Leonard Autley is Lenny Autley's father. Lenny is a bully and a pig, but Charles persuaded Lucille and me not to expel him from our classes. Lenny's mother, Edna Autley, brings him to the studio for lessons. I don't know if she's involved in the gold mine scheme."

"I see," said Phil. He wrote something in the notebook he carried.

"So we have Mr. Clive Madison and Mr. Leonard Autley, is that correct?" Ernie asked.

Charles nodded. So did Marian.

"I understand from witnesses that you, Miss Murray, weren't keen on the gold mine plan," said Ernie. "Is that correct?"

"Yes," Marian whispered. "I urged Charles not to invest. The plan sounded sketchy to me."

"I see," said Ernie. He transferred his attention to Mr. Horshank. "And you, Mr. Horshank, were seen several times at the Murray Dance Academy. Why was that? Were you interested in taking dance lessons?"

After shooting a glance at the hand on his shoulder, Mr.

Horshank opened his mouth. I suspect he wanted to rag on Ernie and Phil, but the presence of that menacing hand quelled his tendency to prolixity. Rather than spouting excuses, he said merely, "No."

"You weren't there to take dance classes?" Ernie pressed.

"No."

"And did you talk to Mr. Charles Murray about the alleged gold mine proffered by Madison and Autley when you visited the academy?"

"It wasn't just Madi— Ow!" Again, Mr. Horshank had his shoulder pinched.

"Yes or no will suffice, Horshank," said Ernie. "Did you attempt to persuade Mr. Murray to invest in the Colorado gold mine?"

After hesitating for a few seconds, Mr. H. said, "Yes."

"Did Mr. Autley join you from time to time in your efforts at persuasion?" asked Ernie.

"I... Ack! Yes."

"Thank you," said Ernie.

"Do you have an address for either Mr. Madison or Mr. Autley?" asked Phil.

"No," said Mr. H.

"Very well." Ernie turned his attention to Miss Padgett. "Miss Padgett, I understand a gentleman named Mr. Frederick Lewiston spoke to you about investing in a gold mine when you were at a dog show. Do I have that right?"

Already holding a hankie for tear-blotting purposes, Miss Padgett said, "Yes. He believed it was a legitimate business venture, and he urged me to invest in it."

"Where and when was this?" asked Phil, pencil poised over his pad.

"The first time was at a dog show in Pasadena. Mr. Lewiston

was enamored of Afghan hounds, and he'd begun to push for salukis to be recognized by the A.K.C."

"Has anyone mentioned Afghan hounds before this meeting, Miss Allcutt?" Ernie's quizzical blue gaze landed on me.

His question surprised me, but I managed (I think) not to show it. "Ah, no. We heard about the salukis, but not the Afghans."

"I thought not," said Ernie. He glanced at Mr. Gallagher. "Mr. Gallagher, did you know about Mr. Lewiston's Afghan hounds?"

"Oh, sure," said Mr. Gallagher. "We folks in the dog world pretty much know each other and what dogs everyone shows. I've taken in one of Fred's Afghans and three of his salukis."

Ernie lifted one of his eyebrows. "Do you expect this to be a permanent condition? That is, will you be keeping all four of the dogs Mr. Lewiston left behind?"

With a slight grimace, Mr. Gallagher said, "I hope not. I'm attempting to find homes for most of them. I have enough dogs of my own, although so far, Fred's aren't any trouble."

"I see," said Ernie.

"Very well," said Phil. "Was anyone in this room acquainted with a police officer named Gerald Royce?"

Again, silence more or less descended upon the folks gathered in my living room.

"Gerald Royce," said Ernie. "Someone must know him. If you ever had any interactions with Officer Gerald Royce, please raise your hand."

It's probably because my nerves were twanging, but I swear nobody spoke for an hour and a half. It was, in fact, more like thirty seconds. After that long, long spate of silence, Mr. Gallagher raised a hand. "I met him a couple of times," he said.

"What was the nature of your interaction?" asked Phil.

I wasn't the only one in the room who gave Phil a puzzled glance.

"Not sure what you mean, Detective," said Mr. Gallagher. "He came into my haberdashery occasionally when he was patrolling the neighborhood."

"Did you ever discuss the gold mine?" asked Phil, clarifying (slightly) his earlier question.

"Oh." Mr. Gallagher tilted his head to one side. "I think he mentioned it the last time he stopped by. I wasn't interested and told him so. He got kind of pushy."

"What do you mean by 'pushy'?" asked Phil.

"He didn't want to take no for an answer, is what I mean by pushy," said Mr. Gallagher. "I got the feeling he was worried about something or someone."

"Interesting," said Phil, writing.

Marian Murray lifted a hand as if she were in a schoolroom.

"Yes, Miss Murray?" said Ernie, as Phil was too busy writing to notice her.

"You say Mr. Royce is a policeman?" Marian's face was white and pinched. I felt terrible for her.

"Yes," said Ernie. "He was a policeman."

"Was," said Marian. "Was he killed too?"

"Yes," said Ernie, not prettifying his answer.

"Then he and Mr. Horshank both came to the academy to pressure Charles into investing in that cursed mine." She wiped a couple of tears from her eyes. "I wish they'd never come near the place."

Charles had pretty much collapsed. His shoulders heaved as he bent over, his head touching his knees. "It's all my fault," he whimpered several times.

Nobody contradicted him.

To be fair to Charles, I don't suppose it was his fault he'd been born a man and, therefore, believed himself superior in all

205

ways to his sisters. Women who had brains and talent were ignored by society unless they were remarkably pretty.

I'll stop there. Nobody needs to hear more of my rants.

Did I just hear a cheer?

Giving Charles a squinty side-eye, Ernie said, "Why were you so convinced of the soundness of the gold mine scheme, Mr. Murray?"

Sobbing uncontrollably, Charles tried to answer but couldn't. Rather, it was Marian who once more picked up the dangling plot left by her brother. "He believed Mr. Horshank and Mr. Autley," she said simply.

"And you didn't?" said Ernie.

"I was…skeptical," said Marian. "The one solid fact I've learned so far in my life is that nothing is easy unless you're born rich. Those of us who weren't have to scrape and fight and struggle to get past our origins."

Heat slithered up my neck and assaulted my cheeks. Darn it, I hated blushing! Anyhow, it wasn't my fault that I was born into a rich family. I'm sure my blush deepened when I glanced at Ernie and saw him grinning at me.

TWENTY-TWO

The rest of the meeting passed, and I discovered I'd been wrong about it. This meeting, except for one or two interesting exchanges, was as boring as the meeting at the Ambassador Hotel.

Mr. Gallagher proved himself to be twice the man Mr. Horshank was, which I thought was funny. Horshank sniveled and whined and kept getting his shoulder pinched by the policeman who never left his side. I'm sure Mr. H. had bruises.

A plan, however, had been adopted by the end of the meeting. This was primarily due to Miss Murray, Mr. Gallagher, the two dog ladies (Padgett and Swale), Sue, Ernie, and me. Phil wasn't altogether sure it would work. Neither was Rob nor Lulu.

The suggested plan didn't start out as a huge spectacle. I merely suggested we hold a fundraising event to benefit the Murray Dance Academy.

"How many people will want to do that?" asked Mrs. Swale. Her voice was as snobby as ever, but her question was valid.

"Nobody," said Marian in a despairing tone.

"Can't we announce something larger than that?" asked Mr. Gallagher. "I mean, I'll be happy to donate to the dance academy, but if you want to draw crowds, you might want to broaden the base of your fundraiser."

"Do we want to draw crowds?" I asked.

"If you want to get Madison and Autley to crawl out of the woodwork and attend, it would be a good idea to make it worth their while," said Ernie.

"And helping out neighbors isn't worthwhile enough?" Very well, my tone was rather biting.

"I certainly don't give a care about your dance studio," sniped Mr. Hornswoggle.

"You cared about it when you pressured Charles into investing in the stupid gold mine," Marian reminded him.

"Well, but that mine is a golden opportunity!" said Mr. Horshank. He got a pinch for his efforts. "Ow!"

"That gold mine is a dud, Horshank. Why don't you keep your mouth shut for the time being?" said Phil.

"Well, I don't see why— Ow!"

"Wait a minute," said Miss Padgett. She spoke so seldom that we all turned to stare at her. Unused to attention, she turned bright pink, but she said her piece anyhow. "Why don't we put on a little dance act, show some of our dogs, and make it a benefit for the Society for the Prevention of Cruelty to Animals? The S.P.C.A. has been working in Los Angeles for seventy-five years or more."

A stunned silence greeted her words. She chewed on her lower lip, probably because we thought her idea stank. We didn't. At least *I* didn't.

"That's the best idea anybody's had so far!" I said. Loudly.

Miss Padgett's blush deepened. "It is?" she squeaked.

"Yes, by gad it is," said Mr. Gallagher. "Brilliant suggestion, Eleanor."

Her cheeks on fire, Miss P. batted his words away as if she didn't believe them.

"My nephew has a printshop," said Mrs. Swale, surprising me. That's partially because it was the first thing she'd said that evening, but mostly because I couldn't imagine her with any living relations. Not any who spoke to her, anyhow. "I'm sure he'll be happy to provide signage for us. We can post signs all over the city."

"Not *all* over the city," said Phil repressively. "But we can blanket the few streets near Chinatown and the dance studio."

"That's still plenty of signs," I said.

"My goodness," said Marian faintly.

"No," said Mr. Horshank, his voice a fairly firm squeal. "Ow!" Wrenching his shoulder away from the policeman, he went on. "You don't know Madison and Autley. Well, Madison's probably all right, but if Autley sees signs advertising an event that includes dogs and dancing, he'll get suspicious. He might kill *me* next!" His little bulgy eyes nearly popped out of their sockets.

"Aha," I said with a considerable note of triumph in my tone. "So you *do* know the gold mine purveyors are crooked. Yet you kept trying to get people to invest in it."

His nose wrinkling and his eyes crinkling, Mr. Horshank sniffled and said, "I had to."

"Why did you have to?" asked Phil, his voice like granite.

"H-he threatened me." Horshank.

"Who threatened you?" Phil.

"With what?" Ernie.

"Huh?" Horsefeathers.

"Who threatened you, and did he threaten your life?" Me.

Another sniffle. "Y-yes."

"And who did the threatening?" I pursued.

"M-Mr. Autley," sniveled Horshank.

"So rather than go to the police, who might have been able to help you, you chose to embroil even more people into Autley and Madison's phony scheme." Me again.

"It's *not* phony!" Horsefeathers. "*Ow!*"

The policeman must have rendered a prodigious squeeze, because Horshank's last "Ow" was considerably louder than the others.

"Let me get this straight," said Ernie, walking down the stairs and up to Horshank's chair. Watching Ernie with horror writ large on his features, Mr. Horshank withdrew his body parts until he looked as if he were attempting to become one with the chair cushion. "You've been pestering people to invest in a mining project you know to be fake—"

"*No! Ow!*" The poor policeman had to straddle the chair back to reach Mr. H's shoulder in order to pinch it.

"Why else are you afraid for your life?" asked Ernie.

"I-I-I don't know. But"—he shot a scared glance at the police person, who refrained from hurting him, this time at least. "But three people who have invested have been killed. I-I'm scared."

"We'll keep you safe," Phil said with a smile that looked downright wicked.

"Mercy?" said Ernie.

"What?" I gaped at my boss when it dawned on me what he wanted to ask me. "No! I won't have that ghastly man taking up space in my home!"

"We can keep him safe at the station," said Phil.

"Great idea," I said with a whoosh of relief.

"I'm *not* a ghastly— *Ow!*"

"Keep quiet," I told him in my mother's voice. He frowned at me, but he didn't squeak again.

"Very well," said Phil. "I think most of you can leave now. Miss Allcutt, Mr. Templeton, Miss Krekeler, and I can work out the details. Miss Allcutt can telephone you with final plans tomorrow."

"When do you want to do this?" asked Ernie.

"The sooner, the better."

"Maybe, but we've got dancers and dogs to shape up, you know."

"True, true." Phil appeared unhappy.

"Mrs. Swale and Miss Padgett, do you have any dog shows coming up in the next couple of weeks?"

The two women peered at each other. Miss Padgett shook her head. Mrs. Swale did likewise. Mrs. Swale said, "No, not in the next couple of weeks. But weekends are usually busy."

"How about doing it on a Wednesday afternoon?" I suggested. "I'm sure the folks in Chinatown won't want their businesses shuttered on a weekend."

"Probably true," said Ernie.

"The Wednesday after next weekend," said Phil. "Anybody object?"

"Yes!" squealed Mr. Horshank. Then darned if he didn't stand up and hit his guard-dog policeman in the face. It was more of a slap than a blow.

"Assault on an officer of the law!" cried Rob with great pleasure.

"Lock him up!" said a gleeful Ernie.

"He hit me first," whined Mr. Horshank.

"All right, take the man away," Phil said to the guardian police person. To Mr. Horshank, he said, "You'll be safe in police custody."

"But I haven't— *Ow!*"

"You haven't done anything illegal?" said Ernie. "Was that what you were going to say?"

After shooting a frightened glance at his policeman, Horshank whispered, "Yes."

"I think you'll discover you're incorrect," said Ernie. "Fleecing people out of their money is illegal."

"But I didn't—"

"Yes, you did. You got my sister killed, too."

Another county heard from, by Jupiter. It was the first whole sentence—well, two whole sentences—Charles had uttered since he sat in the chair next to Marian.

And thus, our plan to nab the gold mine bandits/killers was created. After most of our guests had stuffed themselves with the edibles that Mrs. Buck and my tenants had created for them, they left my house. The Murray siblings retired to bed, and Lulu and Sue helped Mrs. Buck clean up after the meeting. As they cleaned, Ernie, Phil, and I talked a little bit. I know none of us was completely happy with the plan we'd come up with.

"Might as well try it," said Ernie. "We'll probably never be able to get everyone together in the same place otherwise."

"But it might be dangerous," cautioned Phil.

"When has that ever stopped my intrepid secretary?" Ernie's mouth twisted into a wry grin.

Rolling his eyes, Phil said, "Never."

"That's not true," I said to both men. "At least we're doing something positive. Besides, it will benefit Marian and Charles."

"Not sure I want to benefit Charles," muttered Ernie.

"He's weak, not vicious," I reminded him. "If he'd been a woman, we'd never be in this situation because no one would have listened to him. Her. You know what I mean."

"Unfair, Miss Allcutt," said Ernie, laughing. "I listen to you all the time."

"Good thing, too." I gave him what I hoped was a hideous scowl.

At any rate, our plan was to stage a special event for the benefit of the Society for the Prevention of Cruelty to Animals, which was raising money to build a shelter to house animals in need. William S. Hart had donated the Society's first gas-powered horse ambulance several years earlier. Mrs. Swale, Miss Padgett, and Mr. Gallagher all said a shelter to house abused animals—including, believe it or not, women and children who were technically animals—was necessary. Los Angeles, they said, was growing too fast to accommodate those in need.

TWENTY-THREE

T he following week was a busy one.

First thing on Monday morning, Phil Bigelow called to confirm to Ernie that Mr. Autley's fingerprints were found at the scene of Lucille Murray's murder. According to Ernie, Mr. Autley's fingerprints had also been found in Mr. Lewiston's hotel room and Officer Gerald Royce's home.

"Good grief. He killed all three of them?" I was appalled.

"Looks like it," said Ernie. "They also found Madison's prints in Lewiston's room."

"Gracious sakes."

"I guess," said Ernie in a semi-grumpy voice.

"We're going to have to work up a dance routine," I told Ernie then. "We'll have to involve those horrible children, or Autley won't show up. And poor Marian isn't in any shape to choreograph anything. Her sister was just murdered."

"I agree. If we're going to put on a show, *somebody's* going to have to work up a dance routine," said Ernie, frowning at me. His frown didn't express displeasure with me, *per se*, but at the facts staring us in the face.

"Who's going to do it? I'm no dancer. Sue's good, but I don't think she has any experience with choreographing dance performances or anything like that. Lulu and I are both duffers."

"You're not a duffer. You're a most competent young lady," said Ernie.

A squint at him told me he wasn't being sarcastic. I still didn't know how to take his words. "Is that so?" I used sarcasm for both of us.

"Yes. Where are the Murray siblings today?"

After giving him a blank stare, I said, "At my house, I guess."

"Do they have a car?"

"I have no idea. You drove them to my place, and I haven't asked them about an auto."

"Hmm. Let me think about this for a second."

"You may have all the seconds you wish," I told him. "But we still have to get somebody to choreograph a dance routine for next Wednesday."

"Yes, I know."

We both stood in Ernie's room at the Figueroa Building. As usual, I'd arrived at work promptly at 7:55 a.m., as my workday was supposed to begin at eight. I'd dusted and polished and dillied and dallied, and Ernie had shown up at around eight-fifteen, which was early for him. He must have been deep in thought, because he actually walked over to the hat rack and put his new fedora on a peg. Then he took off his suit coat, hung it up, loosened his tie, and opened the top buttons on his white shirt.

I blinked at him. While I was accustomed to what I believed to be his eccentric insouciance, he generally kept his office attire on whilst in the office. At the hat stand, he turned and gave me another intense frown. Again, this frown wasn't personal. The man was thinking. I could almost hear the hamster on its wheel inside his head. Ahem. Beg pardon for that one.

"Does Calvin Buck ever visit his parents?" Ernie asked out of the blue.

"Uh…Calvin? I don't know. I haven't seen him since last Christmas."

"If I call your house, will Mrs. Buck answer the 'phone?"

"Yes. She takes messages while I'm at work. But Mr. Buck might be easier to find if you need to talk to a Buck. Mr. Buck is here in the building. I think Mrs. Buck generally does her marketing on Monday mornings."

"Ah. In that case, will you please call Lulu and see if she can direct us to Mr. Buck?"

With a shrug, I said, "Sure." And I went to my desk and called the lobby.

"Mr. Buck?" said Lulu. "Yes, he's right here. Do you want to talk to him?"

"Ernie wants to talk to him," I said.

"Shall I give him the receiver? Wait. What?" I think she put her hand over the receiver because I heard muffled words. When she came back on the line, she said, "He said he'll go up and see what Ernie wants."

"Thank you. Thank you both."

"Not a problem," said Lulu.

Because I heard the crowd of people milling around the lobby, I didn't bother her with more chitchat but just said, "Thanks, Lulu," and hung up my own receiver.

"Mr. Buck's coming up here," I called to Ernie.

"Thanks," he said, startling me because I hadn't seen him exit his room and enter mine.

"Stop sneaking up on me," I said sharply.

Naturally, he rolled his eyes. "Promise," he said. "No more sneaking up on you. Sheesh."

"Thank you," I said. Fortunately—because I didn't know

what to say next—the telephone rang. I answered it as usual. "Mr. Templeton's office; Miss Allcutt speaking."

"Miss Allcutt?" a timid voice said. As I'd just told the caller my name and recognized the voice, I said, "Yes, Miss Padgett. May I help you with something?"

"I just wanted to know what the plans are for the S.P.C.A. benefit?"

It was my turn to roll my eyes. "They haven't been finalized yet, Miss Padgett. I'll telephone everyone as soon as I know what they are."

"Oh. Well, thank you. Please let me know if you need me to do anything."

"We will definitely do that." Then I had yet another brilliant idea. Oh, very well, so it probably wasn't, but it couldn't hurt. "How do your dogs get along with crowds of people?" I asked.

"Crowds of people? There are often crowds of people at dog shows, if that's what you mean."

"Not exactly," I said. "I just wondered if they'd be upset if they were onstage with people dancing and playing music."

"Oh." And she didn't continue.

Peering up at Ernie, I mouthed, "Miss Padgett." He nodded and didn't move.

Silence on the wire nudged me to give Miss P. a prompt. "Do you think they'd object to dancing and music, Miss Padgett?"

"I'm thinking," she said, making one of us. After another, longer spate of silence, she said, "I don't think they'd be upset. I'd have to stay with them and make sure they didn't get startled and run off."

"Of course," I said, because her explanation made sense. "What about Mrs. Swale's mastiffs? Do you think they'd be upset by dancing and music?"

"Caesar and Augustus? Heavens, no. Those dogs are like statues most of the time. The only time I've ever seen them the least bit animated is when Mrs. Swale runs them around the ring."

"She runs them around the ring?" I said, my flabber having been gasted at the mental image of the large, solid, crabby-looking Mrs. Swale doing anything so undignified as running around a ring, mastiffs or no mastiffs. I noticed even Ernie lift an eyebrow or two.

"Yes, we all run our dogs around the ring when we show them. Some people"—I could hear the disparagement in her words—"hire handlers to show their dogs, but both Mrs. Swale and I consider that all but cheating. Well, unless you have to travel to another city in another state or something."

"You show your dogs in other states?" I said, again startled.

"Of course," said Miss P. "The A.K.C. is a national organization. It's based in New York City. I thought you knew that."

"I probably just forgot," I said lamely. "Thank you for the information, Miss Padgett. I'll be sure to call you as soon as arrangements are made for the show."

"We'll have rehearsal time, won't we?" she said hastily, sounding a trifle panicky.

"Yes, we will definitely have to rehearse our show," I said, wondering as I did so where the heck we could hold rehearsals for a dozen—I expected a half-dozen would do—bratty kids, a bunch of dogs, a coterie of tap-dancers, and several dog people.

"Thank you, Miss Allcutt," she said.

"You're welcome. I'll call you soon."

We disconnected our telephones.

And Mr. Buck came into the office, bless his heart! I adored both Bucks. They were kind, generous, thoughtful people who didn't deserve the bias they faced because of the color of their skin. This was especially true because their grandparents—heck, maybe even their parents—had most likely been slaves in some southern state before the end of the Civil War.

"You wanted to see me, Mr. Ernie?" said the obliging Mr. Buck with a big smile.

"Yes," said Ernie, still hatless, coatless, with his tie loosened and his first two shirt buttons unbuttoned. "Have a seat." He gestured at the chairs in front of my desk.

"Thank you," said Mr. Buck, who didn't seem altogether comfortable about sitting in front of Ernie and me.

Made my heart hurt to notice his uneasiness. Nevertheless, he pulled out a chair and sat. Ernie pulled out the other one and sat too.

Ernie started the conversation. "Buck, is your son Calvin still in the Los Angeles area?"

"Calvin?" Mr. Buck's eyes widened.

"Yes," said Ernie. "Does he still live around here?"

"Yes, he does. Near the First A.M.E. Church on Harvard."

"Does he still play the piano?"

"Oh, yes. He plays at church and at...well, some of the night spots in our part of town."

"What a magnificent idea!" I said, suddenly understanding Ernie's interest in Calvin Buck. He played the piano beautifully. I knew it for a fact because he'd played my big grand piano last Christmas.

I saw Mr. Buck shoot me a startled glance.

"I'm sorry, Mr. Buck," I said, smiling at him, "but we need someone to play music for us next Wednesday afternoon."

"You do? How come" His eyes narrowed. Clearly, I hadn't sufficiently explained Ernie's interest in Calvin Buck.

"I'll take it from here, Mercy," said Ernie in a long-suffering voice. Guess I had been slightly precipitate.

Ernie went on to explain to Mr. Buck what we planned to do regarding staging a benefit performance for the Los Angeles S.P.C.A. and why. "There might be some danger involved," admitted Ernie. "But we think the crooks have at least one little kid who will be performing at the benefit, so I don't think there will be any trouble. The L.A.P.D. will be there."

Mr. Buck's skeptical expression made my heart twang again. "They won't harass you or anyone else there, Mr. Buck. Promise. Detective Bigelow aims to have the place well-guarded, and I think it will be in…" I glanced at Ernie. "In Chinatown?" It was a question, and Ernie nodded.

"Yeah. We're going to close off Third and one side of Chinatown and put on a show there. On Third. Where they hold the Chinese New Year's Parade every year."

"Oh?"

I could tell Mr. Buck wasn't totally won over to our side. "You see, Mr. Buck, the reason that Marian and Charles Murray are staying at my house is—"

By golly, Mr. Buck interrupted me! Talk about a startling circumstance. "Because some gentleman named Autley killed their sister. Yes, I know. Loretta told me all about it. But that man was white. The police don't seem to care much about us Black folk as a rule."

My gaze fell from his penetrating stare. He was right.

Ernie picked up the baton and ran with it. "You're right, Buck, but Mercy and I do care. We also have pals in the Chinese community now, and they'll help us keep the peace too. The L.A.P.D. won't be roughing up anyone except the men who murdered Miss Lucille Murray and Officer Gerald Royce. He was one of their own, so they'll care about keeping the peace for once."

"And Mr. Lewiston," I added. "They killed him too."

"That so? I knew Officer Royce a little," said Mr. Buck. "Sorry he was killed. Royce seemed all right, for a copper. He used to visit Mr. Gallagher down the street. I think they played the horses together or something."

"That's right," I said, casting my mind back to the day Mr.

Buck and I had visited Mr. Gallagher's haberdashery and observed him looking through a pink racing form. That's when I thought Mr. Gallagher was a villain. I'd had no earthly idea about his Italian greyhounds or his preference in partners at the time.

"So," said Ernie, "you'll have the L.A.P.D., the citizens of Chinatown, several huge scary-looking dogs—"

"And their scary-looking owners," I plopped in for the heck of it.

"Including Mr. Gallagher?" asked Mr. Buck.

"Yes," said Ernie. "We'll have a multitude of protectors observing the scene. The coppers want to get their hands on a guy named Autley and one named Madison."

"I heard those names last night," observed Mr. Buck. "At Miss Mercy's meeting."

"Right. Do you think Calvin might be able to play the piano for the dancers at that performance?" asked Ernie.

"I can ask him," said Mr. Buck, whom I could tell wasn't entirely won over to our plans. "He works during the day, but it's at my cousin's cigar shop, so I'm sure we can make arrangements."

"We'll be tap-dancing," I told him. "Calvin knows lots of jazz music, doesn't he?"

"Yes," said Mr. Buck. He didn't smile when he spoke the word.

"You don't care for jazz?" asked Ernie.

"Ah, I don't mind it much. Loretta keeps claiming jazz is from the pit."

Ernie and I swapped a startled glance each.

"She does? I'm surprised," I said. "She's the one who gave us the bottle caps in order to create tap shoes."

"Yeah, but that was for you white gals. She don't like Calvin playing jazz because she thinks it'll lead him astray."

"How could it do that?" I honestly wanted to know.

It was Ernie who answered my question. "You're a privileged young lady from Boston, Mercy. According to people who claim to know such things, jazz clubs are havens for drunkards, cocaine fiends, and reefer madness."

Shocked, I said, "You're kidding me!"

"No, he's not," said Mr. Buck. "So far, Calvin hasn't had any trouble with booze and drugs, but Loretta's worried sick that he'll get lured into that low life one of these days."

"But he still goes to church with you, doesn't he? I know he used to, and then he'd do his homework at my place," I said.

"You were generous to allow that, Miss Mercy."

"Fiddlesticks!" I said, perhaps too loudly. "You and Mrs. Buck live there, and you're both friends of mine. My home couldn't function without either of you. Besides, Mrs. Buck is the best cook in Los Angeles."

"Probably the whole state of California," said Ernie, who had taken to grinning at me.

After looking first at Ernie and then at me, Mr. Buck said, "Well, maybe it'd be all right. If you explain to Loretta that Calvin's playing jazz music for you, she might not forbid it."

"It's not just for me," I said. "It's honestly a program to benefit the Los Angeles Society for the Prevention of Cruelty to Animals. And the Murrays. And there will be dogs and kids and stuff there, too. Calvin can play something other than jazz when people are showing off their dogs. I mean, I'm sure that will be all right."

"Aha," said Mr. Buck. "Maybe you can explain that to Loretta tonight, and she won't fuss. She doesn't fuss at you, Miss Mercy, even when you do things she doesn't like."

Fairly stunned, I said, "What do I do that Mrs. Buck doesn't like?"

"I suspect she thinks you should be more careful," said Ernie. "You keep running into danger and begging people to hurt you."

"I do not!" I cried, offended.

I noticed the look Ernie and Mr. Buck exchanged and decided it wasn't worth arguing with them. "Well, I hope Calvin can play for us," is all I said.

Mr. Buck said, "We'll ask him."

Ernie said, "Thanks, Buck."

Mr. Buck left the office and went back to his regular duties.

Ernie and I didn't. Rather, he said, "Let's go to your house, kiddo—I mean Mercy! Sorry about that. Let's go to your house and talk to the Murray siblings. We can ask them about music and choreography and so forth."

"Not sure they'll be thrilled, what with their sister dead and not yet buried."

"The L.A.P.D. has her body on ice. She'll hold for another few days. If this production goes as planned, they should be able to bury her on Thursday or Friday of next week."

Ew. "That's kind of...disgusting, Ernie."

"It's just the way it is." He stood, stuffed his hands into his trouser pockets and bowed his head, I presume in thought. "Maybe you can type up a message and tack it to the outer door. Just have people call your telephone number if they need to get in touch with either of us while we're not here."

"Do I want a bunch of strangers telephoning my house?" I asked without much venom.

"Do you think a bunch of strangers will telephone your house, given our daily workload?"

The man had a valid point. Ergo, I typed up a note and tacked it to the outside of the front office door, hoping the tack wouldn't leave an ugly hole when it was removed. Then Ernie drove himself and me to my house.

TWENTY-FOUR

W hen we arrived at my stately home, we found Marian Murray, a feather duster in her hand, cleaning up the living room. Charles appeared to be following her around, plumping cushions, brushing chairs and sofas with a lint brush, and looking worried.

They both must have glanced up when Buttercup yipped excitedly at the front door, because they seemed surprised when Ernie and I entered the house. I leaned down to pet Buttercup. So did Ernie.

"Oh," said Marian. "You're home so soon. I was hoping we could tidy up while Mrs. Buck was marketing and give you both a break because you're being so kind to us."

"Yes," said Charles. "Thank you."

"Nonsense," I said, embarrassed. "You just lost your sister, and we came here in order to plan the show we want to produce in order to capture her killer."

"Do we know who her killer is?" asked Marian sadly.

Nodding, I said, "The police found fingerprints that they believe identify the killer."

"Who was it?" asked Charles, sounding breathless.

"Mr.—"

I stopped speaking because Ernie clapped a hand over my mouth. I was outraged for only a second. Then he said, "We don't want to spread the word yet. I don't want any of the suspects involved to hear a word about what the cops have discovered." He carefully lifted his hand away from my lips, but I knew he'd cover them again if I said anything remotely indicative of the killer's identity.

"My goodness," said Charles, frowning in clear disapproval. "Do you always treat Miss Allcutt that way?"

"No," said Ernie. "Not usually."

"As much as I hate to say it," I said, "he was correct in silencing me this time, even if he chose a rude way to do it." I peered over my shoulder—and up—and gave Ernie a good, hot scowl.

"Sorry, Mercy. In a hurry," said my annoying boss with a grin. "Anyhow, we thought maybe you two could help us plan a show for next Wednesday. It'll have to include Mercy, Sue, and Lulu; a few kids from your tap classes; and some dogs and dog people. We need the dogs and dog people to make people think it's really a benefit performance for the S.P.C.A."

"Which it is," I said, "We just hope to reap other benefits from it. Like, catching a killer and a few grifters. And assisting you two."

"So, you really think the gold mine is bogus?" Charles asked forlornly.

Rather than say what I was thinking, which was *incredibly* unladylike, I said, "We're sure, Charles. Madison's gold mine doesn't exist."

"And Detective Bigelow's team has wired the police folks in Denver and found the corpses of a few other investors. Madison gets around a lot. Autley appears to be more local."

"You didn't tell me that!" I cried, stung.

"Just learned about it this morning," Ernie said as if that excused his uncalled-for tardiness in passing on vital information. "We were talking about other things, and now we needed to talk to Mrs. Buck."

True, but I still didn't like it.

That, however, was nothing to the purpose. Ernie and I hung up our hats, etc., on the rack beside the front door, and Buttercup dashed away from us, past the Murray siblings, and all the way into the kitchen. I heard her little toenails clicking on the linoleum.

"Good doggie, Buttercup," we heard Mrs. Buck say to my dog. "You just go along with you now. From that Packard in the drive, it looks as if your Uncle Ernie has come to visit."

"Good morning, Mrs. Buck," Ernie called from the living room.

Mrs. Buck appeared in the doorway between the dining room and the living room. She wore a pretty flowered hat. "Good morning. And Miss Mercy! You're home too? What's wrong?"

The poor woman appeared truly worried. Then she must have spotted the feather duster in Marian's hand and the lint brush in Charles's, and she said, "What in the world are you two doing? That's my job!"

"We wanted to be useful," said Marian, looking sorrowfully at the feather duster.

"Yes, we did," Charles agreed.

Because I didn't want to hear more irrelevancies, I said, "Mrs. Buck, may Ernie and I ask you something? We'll go to the kitchen."

Opening her eyes wide, Mrs. Buck said, "Of course! You'll have to talk while I stow away the groceries and start dinner."

"We can do that," said Ernie. "We can even help."

"That's all right," said Mrs. Buck. Was there a dry note to her voice? Hmm. "I don't need help."

With that, Ernie and I left the Murrays to continue dusting the house and trailed Mrs. Buck and Buttercup into the kitchen. Sure enough, a great big shopping basket sat on the kitchen table, overflowing with foodstuffs.

"You two sit right there and I'll deal with this," ordered Mrs. Buck, gesturing at the table.

So Ernie and I sat at the table like good little children while Mrs. Buck emptied the grocery basket. The contents of the basket were a revelation to me. Not only were there vegetables— corn, carrots, green beans, and turnips—but also a watermelon, two cantaloupe melons, and two baskets of strawberries. Also housed at the bottom of the basket were a can of pineapple, what looked like a large cut of meat which I couldn't identify because it was wrapped in butcher's paper and tied with twine, a string of sausages, and a smaller basket packed with straw.

I wanted to ask what she was doing with a basket packed with straw, but then she began delicately removing eggs from the straw, and I didn't have to. A glance at the kitchen clock told me it was only ten-thirty a.m., so it was evident that Mrs. Buck planned well in advance of our household's needs. I decided then and there that she was not merely going to get a bonus and a week's holiday, but I was going to raise her salary.

"Did you have to carry that heavy basket all the way from Angels Flight?" I asked her. Lordy, that was a load!

"Lord bless you, child, no! I pay little Jose Vargas a nickel, and he helps me carry everything from the market."

"You have to pay his fare, too," I said, grieved that I didn't pay the woman more.

"It's not a problem, Miss Mercy."

Maybe not for her, but I felt guilty. "You treat us too well, Mrs. Buck."

"Nonsense," she said, carrying the watermelon over to the sink. "Mr. Buck and I like working for you, Miss Mercy. Best place we've ever worked."

"Well, I'm glad of that, but I still don't like the notion of you having to pay someone to carry *our* groceries."

"Get 'em to deliver," said Ernie.

"Could do that," said Mrs. Buck, "but Miss Mercy will have to pay the delivery man."

"I'll pay the delivery man!" I cried. "I never even thought about how food got into the house."

"Not sure about you, Mrs. Buck, but I'm sure surprised to learn that," said Ernie drily. I whacked his arm. "Ow! Now she's beating me."

"Don't tease the child, Mr. Ernie. It's not her fault she don't know these things."

"I wish you'd told me," I said to both of them, feeling guilty.

"Well, now you know," said Ernie. "So let's ask Mrs. Buck the main question of the day."

"Very well," I said. "But we need to talk about how to get our food delivered, Mrs. Buck. You shouldn't have to carry huge loads of groceries for us."

"That'll be easy to do, sweetie," said Mrs. Buck, sounding cheerful. "But what's this big question you need to ask me. Let me get some water boiling for tea, and I'll set out some of those cheese straws that're left over from yesterday. The gals did a good job on them."

I felt guiltier than ever. All I'd done with the butter, flour, and cheese was create a mess and make my dog fat. Ah well; it appeared that this problem, too, could be solved with money. I honestly don't know how people without a lot of family money live their lives; yet they do. In fact, there are more folks who don't have lots of money than who do. My stupid ivory tower was showing again.

"Cheer up, Mercy," said Ernie, clapping me on the shoulder. "Not your fault that you come from money."

Mrs. Buck laughed. "She's a good girl. She does useful things with her money. She doesn't just order people around, buy raccoon coats, and drink bootleg gin."

While the above was true, it didn't make me feel significantly better.

"Thanks," I said, not meaning it. "Let me get a teapot for you."

"Sure," she said. "And a plate for the food."

So I did at least that. From the pantry, I retrieved a pretty tea service that came complete with four cups and saucers, four small plates, and a larger plate for sandwiches (or cheese straws) to rest on. It had come complete with some little silver tongs that someone (I'm sure it was one of the Bucks) kept polished to a remarkable shine, a cream pitcher, and a sugar bowl. I'd bought the set when I went to Europe. Found it in a shop in Stratford Upon Avon, believe it or not, and had it shipped home to Boston. It might have been the only thing in my life I'd done about which my mother hadn't scolded me. She claimed I was finally acting like the lady I was supposed to be.

Huh.

My short life as a working woman had taught me that most working women didn't have fancy British tea sets. Because I had one and liked it, I took it to the kitchen anyhow.

"That's pretty," said Ernie.

"Thanks," I said.

"That's my favorite of all the China pieces you have, Miss Mercy," said Mrs. Buck, taking the teapot and pouring hot water into it. She swished the water around, emptied the pot into the sink, dumped some tea leaves into the pot, and refilled it with hot water. Then she took the serving plate and deftly tonged cheese straws and finger sandwiches onto it.

"Thank you," I said. I didn't tell Mrs. Buck and Ernie the story of the set's purchase.

I wasn't totally useless. After I brought the set into the kitchen, I poured milk into the cream pitcher, put some sugar cubes into the sugar bowl, and set both items on the kitchen table. I also set out three teacups and saucers. I noticed Ernie watching me closely, and I frowned at him. I wanted to ask him what he was staring at but didn't.

After she deemed the tea had brewed sufficiently, Mrs. Buck poured out two cups, one for Ernie and one for me.

"You have some too, Mrs. Buck," I said.

She gave me what I thought was a somewhat quizzical glance, but she obeyed my suggestion—unless she considered it an order—and poured tea into the third teacup. Then she put the tray of food in the middle of the table and sat with a sigh.

Ernie instantly took a finger sandwich and a couple of cheese straws and set them on his little plate. I did likewise.

"This is kind of you," said Mrs. Buck. "Having me take tea with you and all, but I still have work to do, so maybe you'd better tell me what you wanted to tell me."

"Have some cheese straws," said Ernie.

"Thanks, Mr. Ernie. Don't mind if I do." She served herself two cheese straws.

"And have some of the sandwiches, too," I offered.

"I think these will do me just fine," said Mrs. Buck. "I ate too many o' them sandwiches for breakfast."

"The cheese straws are really good," I said, wishing I'd been able to contribute to their construction. In case you couldn't tell, I actually felt *lower* than a garden slug just then. I put a cube of sugar into my cup, stirred, and sipped. The tea was delicious.

And then I gave myself a hard mental shake, told myself I was at least attempting to learn how to live life as an unprivileged person, and waded into the reason for Ernie's and my intrusion into Mrs. Buck's kitchen. Mrs. Buck eyed us both with concern.

"You want Calvin to play jazz piano for you?"

"Yes. Lulu, Sue, Marian, and I will dance a little bit to his jazz music. Then he can play whatever he wants to play when people and their dogs strut around. So he won't *only* be playing jazz music."

"Dogs, eh?" said Mrs. Buck, plainly not enamored of our project.

"It's for two good causes," said Ernie. "We're hoping to help the Los Angeles S.P.C.A., the Murrays, and catch a murderer."

"That's three causes," muttered Mrs. Buck.

"But they're all good causes," I said, attempting to sound enthusiastic.

After heaving a sigh, she said, "I reckon they are, but I don't know. Where will this show take place?"

"Third Street, where Chinatown is," said Ernie.

"Those Chinese folks don't much like people my color." I'd never heard Mrs. Buck sound acerbic before, but she did a great job then.

"True," said Ernie, shocking me. "They don't like us whities, either."

"They don't mind you as much as they mind us," said Mrs. Buck.

"Poppycock," said Ernie. "In the late 1800s, a bunch of whites and Mexicans massacred a whole community of Chinese people right here in Los Angeles."

Mrs. Buck's eyes grew round. I'm sure mine did too.

"I didn't know that," I said. "That's terrible."

"Yes, it is," said Mrs. Buck. "We Black folks've been lynched for decades, but I never heard about the Chinese before this."

"Human beings carry a whole lot of fear and hate," said Ernie, whom I'd never pegged as a philosopher before. "When they get scared, they tend to get mad and lash out at what scared them."

"Huh," said Mrs. Buck. "I'd like to know what a bunch of slaves could do to a white man that'd scare him."

"Ow," I said, feeling terrible about my country's history. I mean, it wasn't all bad, but there were enough bad things to read about that it made me wonder why my so-called excellent education hadn't taught me about them.

"Don't forget the Tulsa massacre in 1921," said Ernie, clearly having a delightful time exploding my fancies.

"Can't forget that," said Mrs. Buck. "They killed my grandfather, father, and Mr. Buck's brother and sister." With a glance at me, she said, "They were bankers in Tulsa."

"And people killed them?" I whispered, aghast.

"Bombed and burned them out," said Ernie. "But we're not going to let anything bad happen at the show we're producing, Mrs. Buck. Detective Bigelow and officers of the L.A.P.D. will be there."

"Huh," said Mrs. Buck.

"And there will be members of the Chinese community helping keep the peace too," said Ernie. "They still think they owe me, you see."

And if that didn't rankle, I don't know what did. Except for giving Ernie a furious scowl, I didn't react to his words.

"And they won't bother Calvin?" said Mrs. Buck.

"No, they won't bother Calvin."

Then I could honestly *see* Ernie coming up with a helpful idea. All of a sudden, his eyes lit up, and he said, "Besides that, he'll have help with the music. I know some of my pals will be happy to play their instruments with Calvin."

"Oh, yes?" Mrs. Buck was still skeptical.

"You bet."

"Whom do you know who'll play with the junior Mr. Buck?" I asked.

"Kid named Johnny Jackson. He plays the horn at the Ambassador's Cocoanut Grove. Has to come in through the kitchen, but they let him play for the white folks. And Charley Wu's sister Lily plays the flute."

"She *does*?" There went my flabber, being gasted again. Lily Wu had *lived* in my house, for heaven's sake, and I hadn't learned about her musical ability.

"She does. And her sister plays the saxophone. A couple of other kids who play with Johnny Jackson can play on the drums. I'm sure he can pick some talent to work for us."

"Talent is all well and good," said Mrs. Buck, sounding firm and unyielding. "But who's going to supervise the action? You can't take a bunch of kids and dogs and shove them onto a stage and expect them to do what you want them to do. They'll need to rehearse, and somebody has to figure out a program."

Ernie tilted his head to one side and then to the other. He shared a glance between Mrs. Buck and me. Eventually, he spoke to me.

"You remember when I told you I was all tapped out?"

I blinked a couple of times and searched my brain for a memory that ultimately seeped from between several thousand other memories. "Oh. Yes, I remember. I asked if you wanted to take tap lessons, and you said you were all tapped out. I thought it was a bad joke."

"It was," said Ernie. "It was also the truth. I told you I was a copper in Chicago, which was true. What I didn't tell you was that before I joined the force, I helped support my family by being one of my Uncle Charlie's Templetonians. He owned his own vaudeville theater, and my sister Elizabeth and I were the kid stars of the show. We were the *Tiny Templetons*." He shuddered and shook his head. Hard. "Gawd, it was awful."

"You helped support your family by dancing with your sister?" I said, dumbfounded. "You never told me that."

"Oh, yes. We bucked and winged and tapped and waltzed and wore sparkly costumes and acted like dolts for at least eleven or twelve years."

"I had no idea," I whispered.

"There's a good reason for that. I've been trying to forget it ever since I left Chicago." Ernie's voice sounded as if he'd dumped his words in lemon juice before speaking them. Again, he shared a glance between Mrs. Buck and me. "I also never told you my old man was a lousy drunk who beat our mother and us kids. If Uncle Charlie—he's my mom's brother—hadn't taken us in, we'd've been dead when Liz and I were five or six. Our mother tried to help but as you've already noticed, Miss Allcutt, women alone are relatively helpless in this cold, cruel world of ours. Unless, of course," he added with a snide smile, "they have money."

I sat there and stared at my boss incredulously. I suspect my mouth hung open too, but I'm not sure. I know for certain that my brain had gone dry.

"I always knew you were a good man, Mr. Ernie," said Mrs. Buck. Then she wiped tears from her face with her napkin.

TWENTY-FIVE

I t took me a while to reconcile what Ernie had just told us with what he *hadn't* told me in the year and a half I'd been working for him. My mental mayhem, however, didn't negate the fact that we had a murderer to catch, a dance studio to save, and a reputable animal-welfare organization to assist. I probably needed to plan a funeral too, if Lucille Murray were ever to be buried.

Mrs. Buck rose from the table shortly after Ernie's revelation and began preparing our dinner. First, she whacked the watermelon in half. Then she dug out its insides and attempted to remove all the seeds. Using the watermelon's shell as a bowl, she then proceeded to fill it with sliced watermelon pieces, sliced strawberries, and the pineapple rings she took from their can and chopped.

"Fruit salad," she said. "For your dinner tonight. I'll put it in the Frigidaire so it'll be nice and cold."

"Sounds good," said Ernie.

As I remained overwhelmed, I said nothing, although I finished drinking my tea and ate three cheese straws. After a long spate of silence, only interrupted by the sounds of various fruits being cut up, Ernie jogged my shoulder. Darned near fell off my chair, I was so unstrung.

"Careful, Mercy," he said, softly taking my arm and holding me in my chair.

"What?" I said. Then I remembered where we were, why we were there, and the story Ernie had just related. "Oh. Yes. Thank you."

With a furrowed brow and a thin squint, Ernie said, "You all right, kidd—I mean Mercy? Didn't mean to upset you."

"You didn't upset me," I lied. "I'm just surprised, is all. I mean, I'm *really* surprised. You never gave any indication that you'd performed when you were a child."

"Not sure if performed is the right word," he said, still sounding vinegary. Lemony. Either one will do. "Grew up onstage in Chicago. Didn't seem like performing. Seemed like life, and it was a hard one."

"Yes, I'm sure that's so." Then I recalled a certain night a week or so prior. "And you told us you didn't know how to spot! You fibbed!"

Holding up both hands as if I'd pulled a gun on him, he said, "No fib. Uncle Charlie never told us to spot anything. He told us to keep our eyes on the middle footlight or he'd tan our hides."

"Was he mean to you?" I wanted to cry.

"No." Ernie gave at least a good approximation of a chuckle. "Charlie was a great guy. He and my mom were both good people. My mother was what you might call 'led astray' by my father."

"I'm so sorry."

A shrug. "To be fair to the old man, he wasn't a total wastrel when Mom met him. He was a singer in Charlie's vaudeville troupe. Handsome fellow. Started using cocaine and whiskey to calm his nerves after he and Mom were married. Uncle Charlie finally kicked him out of the troupe, and that's when we all began living with Charlie. It was Charlie and Mom who made sure Liz and I went to school.

"They were both happy when I decided not to continue singing and dancing—which is a haphazard way to make a living—and joined the police force. Back then, Chicago wasn't as corrupt as it is now, although it was trying hard to catch up with New York City. Charlie, Mom, and I were all glad when Liz married her husband and moved to Evanston."

"I had no idea," I said, struggling to cope with this new aspect of Ernie and his life.

He'd told me a very little bit about Chicago, and I knew he had a sister in Evanston. He'd also mentioned something about not liking his father, but as my own personal father was something of a stuffy Cronos—Cronos was a cruel Greek god who ate his children so they couldn't dethrone him—not liking his father sounded logical to me. Not that Chloe and I ever wanted to dethrone him. We only wanted to get away from him and our mother, whom we called—for good reason—the Wrath of God.

"Listen, you two," said Mrs. Buck, kindly but firmly. "I have to get your supper started or you won't have any, so maybe you can take your discussion somewhere else? You got a good breakfast room and a good dining room, Miss Mercy—"

"Please just call me Mercy," I said too loudly. "I don't want to be Miss anybody. I just want to be me, and I want you to be my friend."

Then I humiliated myself and burst into tears.

Ernie hauled me away from the kitchen and into the breakfast room. He shut the door to the kitchen and pantry and sat me down on a hard chair. Then he offered me a clean handkerchief.

I already knew he kept clean hankies in his office desk drawer in case of weeping clients, but I didn't know he also carried clean hankies around with him.

"This doesn't change anything, Mercy," he said.

He sounded as if he were attempting to be kindhearted and compassionate, and I reacted negatively. I did so by bawling even harder. What the heck was *wrong* with me?

"Hey," he said more sharply. "Cut it out. I've been trying to get over my childhood my whole life. I didn't want to talk about it ever. Now, however, my personal singing and dancing skills look like they might come in handy. We're hoping to catch a cold-blooded killer, not to mention a shyster who's stealing people's money. And most of those people can't afford to lose their money."

I mopped my face with Ernie's large white (clean) hankie and then blew my nose. As I did so, I took deep breaths and ordered myself to control my emotions. Didn't work well at first.

Ernie spoke once more. "Mercy, please. I had no idea you'd react so strongly to learning this stuff about my childhood. I've been trying to forget it for years."

"But…but you're not who I thought you were." The words came out of my mouth like a wad of crumpled paper, all creased and wrinkly.

"I'm the person you met last year when you strolled into my office and applied for a secretarial job. I haven't changed."

"May…maybe not, but…but… I don't know!"

"Mercy Allcutt, my name is Ernest J. Templeton. The J stands for James. It was my father's name, so I don't use it. I like my father about as much as you like yours, only for different reasons."

"I suppose so." There. Only three words in the sentence, but they didn't crack or wobble. An improvement, that.

"Come on, Mercy. I didn't think you'd care if I didn't talk

about my childhood. It wasn't a deep, dark secret. It's just that I didn't want to remember it. You don't like talking about your childhood either, don't forget."

Blew my nose again. "True."

"So can you forgive me?"

"That's stupid. You have nothing for which to be forgiven." My voice was stronger. Hurrah! "I'm stupid for believing you should have told me more about your youth, especially when we started taking tap lessons. I...I... I don't know. I guess I'd begun to believe we were becoming a couple. I mean, a romantic—not romantic—I don't *know*!"

Darned near bawled again but squared my shoulders and didn't.

"I'm not romantic?" Ernie's mouth pursed into a moue of discontent. "I guess I'm not. My mother, who was a really good, good person, was romantic. Then she was undermined by a stone-cold bastard, and she couldn't do anything about it. "If it helps any, I love you."

A start of surprise almost slid me from the chair. I would have landed on the floor if I hadn't grabbed the chair seat. "You...you love me?"

"Yes. I've never loved a woman before. I love you, and I'm hoping we can get married one of these days."

I gaped at him.

"I was kind of hoping you love me too," he said then.

Not sure how long we sat there in the breakfast room, staring at each other. I'm sure my face was blotchy and swollen, especially my eyes—unfortunately, I'm not one of those ethereal women like my sister Chloe who look beautiful crying. But I stared at him, and he stared at me for what seemed like an hour and a half.

At last, I broke the prolonged, unsettling silence by saying. "I do love you, Ernie!" and flinging myself into his arms.

He hugged me hard and kissed the top of my cropped hair. I heard him take in a deep breath and blow it out slowly.

"Thank God," he whispered. "Thank God."

"I d-didn't mean to cry at you," I said.

"It's all right, kiddo. I mean Mercy."

"Oh, I don't care what you call me," I croaked. "I didn't like it when you called me kiddo because I wanted you to respect me, and it didn't sound respectful. That's probably my mother's influence."

"Respect? I've always respected you. Your efficiency, your hard work, your diligence, and even you writing a book. The only thing I wish you wouldn't do is find dead bodies all the time. I worry about you."

"Thank you." Mortification, thy name was Mercy Allcutt. Not really, but I sure felt stupid. And I have no earthly idea why Ernie's admission had upset me so.

"So, get over it, all right? We've got a benefit performance to plan."

"Let me wash my face, okay?"

"Sure. Want me to wait for you here?"

After thinking about it for a second and a half, I said, "No. Come with me. We can go up the back stairs so nobody sees me."

"Very well," he said. I could tell he was trying not to laugh, which made my heart lurch. I'd made *such* a fool of myself.

Too bad. So sad. Silly Mercy.

I led Ernie to the utility room and up the back staircase. That stairway was intended for servants to use, but I thought I was being "of the people" by not insisting that people who work for me use it. The main staircase was good enough for everyone living in my house. How magnanimous of me, huh?

I opened the door to my suite of rooms, and darned if Buttercup didn't meet us there. Guess she'd been in the living room. I let her in first, then Ernie. "Sit anywhere," I told him.

Then I went to the bathroom and scrubbed my face with soap and water. After I'd dried same, I peered at my reflection in the mirror and didn't like what I saw. Swollen red eyes. Pallid cheeks. Pathetic expression. The face of a blithering idiot.

But Ernie had said he loved me. Would Ernie love an idiot?

Apparently.

Now I felt lower than slug slime. Huh. Listen to me. As if I knew a slug from a peanut. Well, I did now, but I hadn't even heard of slugs (or snails, for that matter) until I moved to California and poked around the back garden with Mr. and Mrs. Buck. Mary Pickford and I. Poor little rich girls.

"Get a grip on your nerves, Mercy Allcutt," I told my reflection. "It really *isn't* your fault you were born with a silver spoon in your mouth. Both you and Ernie are attempting to overcome your origins."

My self didn't buy it. But what the heck. I sucked in a big breath, squared my shoulders, slathered my face with Pond's Face Cream, wished I had some cucumber or strawberry slices to put on my eyelids, and went back to my bedroom. There I found Ernie relaxing on the easy chair with Buttercup on his lap. They both seemed perfectly happy and serene.

"Mrs. Buck brought up some sliced cucumbers," Ernie said. "She said you should lie down, close your eyes, and lay cucumber slices on your eyelids. I think she'd be shocked if you lay on your bed while I'm still here."

"Bother. The woman is a goddess, and I'm going to lie on top of my bed. You can stay there with Buttercup if you want. Thanks," I added when I walked to his chair and reached for the small bowl of cucumber slices. "If you attempt to ravish me, I'll have Buttercup bite you."

"You don't wanna be ravished by me?" Ernie feigned sorrow.

"If we ever get married, I'm sure I'll want you to ravish me.

Actually, if it wouldn't shock everyone in the house, I wouldn't mind being ravished now as long as you're gentle."

"I'll be gentle," promised Ernie. "But we need to plan a show, and ravishment isn't part of it."

Shucking off my shoes, I lay on the bed, which I'd neatly made up that morning. In Boston, our maid Bridget used to make my bed. I didn't have or want a Bridget here in Los Angeles.

"Here you go," said Ernie, placing a cool cucumber slice over each of my shut eyes.

"Thank you. They feel good."

"Excellent. So, what should happen first? Dogs, tap-dance, or what?"

"We need a host."

"A host?"

"Yes. Someone to announce different acts and remind people who benefit from the...well, the benefit performance."

"Ah," said Ernie.

"Actually," I said after thinking for a second and three-quarters, "if you won't kick and scream, I think you should be the host."

"Me?"

"You."

"Why me?"

"Except for the Murray siblings, who will be performing with the kids and Lulu, Sue, and me, you've got more show business experience than any of us."

"There's always Calvin Buck," said Ernie, sounding as if he didn't believe himself.

"Calvin is a Negro, Ernie, or have you forgotten that pertinent fact? He performs at the Cocoanut Grove, and he has to enter through the kitchen."

"Yeah, I know." He heaved a gust of breath. "Very well, I've got my notebook and pencil. I'll host the damn benefit. What should we do first? In the show, I mean."

"You should be the announcer. You can tell people we're trying to raise money for the Los Angeles S.P.C.A."

"Right."

"I'd like the kids to perform next, because they're kids and will get bored if they have to stand around doing nothing. Besides, Lenny Autley might cause trouble."

"Kid takes after his dad, does he?"

"Yes." Then an idea occurred to me. I'm going to stop calling these ideas brilliant, because they seldom are. "After a musical and dancing act, you can then introduce a breed of dog! You know, after the kids dance, Junior can take Buttercup onstage and have her do a few tricks. Then we should have another musical number, and then show more dogs. I think Mr. Gallagher might do well to introduce the audience to Afghan hounds and salukis. He can point out that they're built more or less the same, but there are differences."

"There are?"

"There must be," I said. "Otherwise, why are they called by different names?"

"Beats me," said Ernie. "Hurts, too."

"Mr. Gallagher should show his Italian greyhounds too. It would be swell if he could show a regular greyhound and one of his itsy-bitsy ones."

"You know," said Ernie, sounding somewhat surprised, "this show might turn out to be pretty good. And we can catch a murderer too."

"We hope," I said, bringing negativity into the conversation, which was wrong of me.

"The place will be crawling with cops, Mercy. We'll at least get Autley, and if we get Autley, he'll probably spill the beans on his cohorts so he doesn't get blamed for everything."

243

After contemplating Ernie's statement, I decided he was correct.

"I hope Miss Padgett and Mrs. Swale will talk about their dogs in front of an audience. I expect Mrs. Swale will, but Miss Padget seems rather shy."

"If she's too embarrassed to talk about her dogs, we'll find someone else to do it."

"Makes sense," I said.

We spent more than an hour creating a program for the show we intended to produce the following Wednesday. I think we did a great job. Surprise, surprise!

TWENTY-SIX

Because the Murray Dance Academy was considered by the Los Angeles Police Department to be a crime scene, we couldn't rehearse there.

When Ernie announced this to our participants, most of them were downcast. So was I. But I bit the bullet.

By the way, Ernie told me that expression (bite the bullet) was born in one of the world's many wars. When doctors had to operate on wounded soldiers without ether or any pain medication, the docs told the poor soldiers to "bite the bullet" so as not to scream and move around on the operating table. If they used tables. Sounded like heck to me, and I prayed that, if ever Ernie and I had children, they wouldn't have to fight in any stupid war.

Sorry about the diversion.

"We can hold rehearsals here," I said, attempting to sound happy about it. I wasn't. I didn't want those awful children scuffing up my floors and being rude to the Bucks.

"That would be fine," said Mr. Gallagher. "But my house has a ballroom. It hasn't been used in a quarter of a century or more, but it's there, and I can have my housekeeper dust it and wash the windows."

I cheered up instantly. "What a great idea!" I said.

"Don't know how great it is." Mr. Gallagher appeared some-what startled by my enthusiasm.

"It is," said Ernie. "Trust us."

"Guess I'll have to," said Mr. Gallagher, grinning.

Another thing that cheered me was that the Murrays said, if Lenny Autley were to perform, there shouldn't be any other boy dancers.

"He's a bully with other boys," said Charles.

"He's only disgusting with the girls," said Marian.

I quirked an eyebrow or two at her, and she explained.

"He flips up their skirts so he can see their underwear and other things of a like nature."

"Good heavens, he really is a horrible little monster, isn't he?"

"Yes. But his parents have money," said Marian. "If I kicked Lenny out of the class, they'd probably kill..." Her voice trailed off.

"Do you think that's what Lucille did? Kick the kid out of a class?" asked Phil Bigelow.

"Oh my, I hadn't thought about it before," whispered Marian.

"Lucille had a heck of a time with the little fiend," said Charles. "I know she wanted to chuck him out. She might have done it. Good lord. Maybe her murder wasn't all about the gold mine."

"Maybe," said Ernie, not wanting to let Charles off the hook too soon. "But the classes lured him into your studio so he could persuade you to invest in the nonexistent mine."

"Oh. That might be true," said a morose Charles.

"But if Mr. Autley murdered Lucille, how will you prove it?" asked Marian.

"We're working on that," said Phil.

Hmm. Feeble answer, if you ask me. I know, you didn't.

———

Rehearsals in Mr. Gallagher's huge ballroom were almost fun—except when Lenny Autley was around. And then after a couple of incidents, Ernie had a conversation with the brat. The first time Lenny pulled a stunt—I think he untied one of the little girls' hair ribbon—Ernie grabbed him by his shirt collar and yanked him off his feet.

Mrs. Autley instantly reacted. "How dare you manhandle my child!"

"Because he's ruining the show," said Ernie in a voice that sounded like acid. "If you don't want your kid to participate—"

I took in a breath and held it. We needed that little monster to be in the show. Ernie knew it.

"No! I want him to participate," declared Mrs. Autley.

I released the gust of breath I'd been holding.

"Fine. I'll have a little chat with him." He hauled Lenny into a corner and loomed over him. He spoke softly so none of us could hear him. Lenny however, after first saying, "I'm gonna tell my dad on you," straightened his shoulders, looked scared, and pinched his lips together.

Wish I'd heard their conversation. When it was over, Ernie stood up tall—he stands a little over six feet—glared down at the kid and said, "So do we understand each other now?"

"Y-yes, sir," stammered Lenny.

"Don't forget it." Then he gave the bratty child a terrifying smile.

Lenny's eyes first got huge, then he closed them, then he swallowed hard, and then he said, "Y-yes, s-sir."

From somewhere—perhaps a costume shop—Ernie acquired

247

a black suit with tails. He added a huge red bow tie with white polka-dots on it. Mr. Gallagher found him a black top hat and a pair of shiny black shoes to wear. He even put real taps on them.

Lulu, Sue, and I decided to keep using our bottle caps at least until after the show.

Marian, Charles, and Ernie worked out choreography for the dance numbers. We decided that Mrs. Swale's huge, mean-looking mastiffs should be the closing dog act. "She can sic them on the crooks if they try to run," I said, smiling at the happy image. I'm not generally a cruel person, but darn it, those criminals were fleecing folks of their money, and they killed at least three people. I think justice would be served if the mastiffs tore their throats open.

Ew. Maybe I don't mean that.

Well...maybe I do.

The next seven days were busy, although not in a money-making sense. Both Lulu and Sue had to get permission from their places of employment to take Wednesday off. I aimed to reimburse them for a day's salary if their bosses docked their pay, although I didn't say so. Every now and then, I thought about my manuscript lying alone and forlorn in somebody's office at Halliday, Smith, and Ransom, but preparing for the show took most of my time.

On Tuesday evening, we had a dress rehearsal in Mr. Gallagher's ballroom. Everyone was willing to attend, even Mrs. Swale. The kids squealed like piglets when they saw all the dogs. Ernie, who seemed to be excellent at disciplining children, showed them the error of their ways in no uncertain terms. In fact, Mrs. Autley—Mr. Autley didn't attend—got mad at him. Ernie, not Lenny.

"Your kid's a menace," said Ernie. "If you want to take him home, that will be fine with the rest of us."

My heart almost stopped, and I gasped once more. We *needed* Lenny Autley in order to catch his father.

"No!" cried Lenny. "I wanna do this, Ma! Don't take me home."

"If you want to do this, you have to behave yourself. I saw you lifting Janie's skirt. That's actually a criminal offence." Ernie transferred his glower from Lenny to Lenny's mother. "Would you like me to call the cops, or will you make your kid behave?"

"I'll behave," Lenny hollered.

Mrs. Autley stared at her son as if she'd never seen him before. "Did you really lift that girl's skirt, Leonard Wesley Autley?"

Lenny's gaze fell to the floor. "I-I didn't mean to," he lied.

"How'd it happen if you didn't mean to?" Ernie asked reasonably.

With a shrug, Lenny said, "I dunno."

Then Mrs. Autley gave her son a tremendous slap on the back of his head. He almost ended up face-first on the floor. "You mind your manners, Lenny Autley, or I'll make sure your father will mind them for you. You wouldn't like that, would you?"

"N-no," whimpered Lenny.

Crumb. The kid sounded scared to death. Maybe his father was a bully too. Like father, like son? Who knew at that point?

"Exactly," said Mrs. Autley. "Now you apologize to Mr. Templeton and…that girl, and do what you're supposed to do from now on. Do you understand me?"

"Yes, ma'am," said Lenny.

"Good," said Ernie. He clapped his hands. "All right, folks, let's take it from the top."

"Does that mean from the beginning?" asked Sue.

"Yes," said Ernie. "We'll begin at the beginning and run

through the entire show. I'm hoping it won't take more than forty or forty-five minutes."

By the way, in case you wondered where Mr. Horshank was during this period of time, let me answer your question. He still sat in a jail cell at the L.A. County Jail. He'd been charged with obstruction of a police investigation, and Phil convinced the judge to deny bond for a week or two. Served him right.

Oh, by the way again, I asked Ernie what dire threat he used to make Lenny Autley behave properly. He said he told Lenny that if he didn't shape up, he'd discover both of his legs broken. And maybe an arm. It seems Ernie scared the kid into believing he—Ernie, not Lenny—was a gang boss of one sort or another. In those days, we were always reading articles about gang killings in New York and Chicago. Ernie was from Chicago. He told Lenny that, and Lenny believed him.

I swear, I was already in love with Ernie, but watching him host the show during that dress rehearsal cemented my adoration. He was wonderful! You wouldn't know he had a nerve in his body as he stood in front of the clot of dancers and mothers and ran through the speech he'd written to introduce the show. Guess he'd begun entertaining people before he heard of stage fright.

He could tap-dance like nobody's business too. He used his hat as a prop, found a cane somewhere, and used that too.

As for the little girls, Lulu and I found pink dresses for them. Lenny Autley would wear a suit and tie. He looked almost respectable in it. The band wore formal attire. Lulu, Sue, and I wore loose-fitting, dropped-waist dresses with short sleeves and about a ton and a half of beads. Those dresses were *heavy*. Then there was the fringe. It tickled my calves, darn it, and Marian had to keep reminding me not to scratch.

Calvin Buck and the other musicians were spectacular. Calvin managed to find a young man—he was really just a boy—who played the clarinet. Our opening number was *Rhapsody in Blue*, and the clarinet introduction was so perfect that it nearly made me cry. Then Calvin came in on the piano, Lily Wu on the flute, the kid named Johnny Jackson played the horn, and they sounded magnificent! They were definitely good enough to play at the Cocoanut Grove. Well, some of them already did, even though they had to enter the Ambassador Hotel via the kitchen.

Then came Ernie, who tapped onto the scene as skillfully as Fred Astaire. Perhaps I'm a tiny bit biased, but the man was *good*. He went through his opening speech. I don't think he memorized it, but just explained why we were there doing what we were doing—well, not there in Mr. Gallagher's ballroom, but there in Chinatown, which we weren't yet.

Oh, you know what I mean.

Anyhow, the kids performed next. Lenny Autley didn't mess up once, either on purpose or accidentally. He wasn't a graceful dancer, but at least he didn't collide with anyone. The girls danced much better than he did.

And then came Junior with Buttercup. Junior had Buttercup sit up, shake hands, and dance with him on her back legs. Buttercup didn't know how to dance, but Junior did, so it worked out quite well. As they danced, Calvin Buck played "Honey." I anticipated chuckles and applause from the audience.

Another dancing moment featuring Charles and Marian.

Another dog moment featuring Mr. Gallagher, the Afghan and the saluki.

Another musical moment to the tune of "Crazy Blues." This time, Lulu, Sue, and I tapped. Lulu and I more or less shuffled in the background while Sue did a more complicated routine in front of us. Sue had a whole lot of what they call "stage presence." Her smile looked genuine, and she seemed happy. Lulu and I had to be reminded to smile when we concentrated too heavily on remembering choreography and forgot that we were supposed to smile and look happy too. I know for a fact that Lulu wasn't happy. Underneath her formerly flashy outsides hid a shy little farm girl from Oklahoma. I didn't hate the limelight as much as she. I'd had to recite monolithic poems and other stuff in front of an audience in Boston. Didn't like it then either. But I did it then, and I did it now.

Another dog moment featuring Mr. Gallagher, who'd rounded up a greyhound from one of his dog-show friends. His itty-bitty Italian greyhound looked like a runt in comparison.

Another musical moment, this time with Calvin Buck, Lenny Jackson, and Ernie. Ernie tapped while the other two played their instruments. "Sweet Georgia Brown" was the tune. I was in awe of Ernie's skill and poise. He had hidden depths I'd never even dreamed of.

More dogs. Miss Padgett compared and contrasted her two hounds. It seemed that she was more enamored of her canine pals than she was afraid of speaking in front of an audience. Mrs. Swale had offered to show Boris and Bevin, but Miss Padgett declined her offer with thanks. And inflexibility. Miss Padgett had hidden depths too, I guess.

Charles, Marian, and the three little girls tapped next. Marian had choreographed a fun dance piece to the "Charleston" tune. Those little girls were adorable.

Time for Mrs. Swale's gigantic mastiffs.

Then we all took to the stage. The dogs, little girls, Lenny Autley, and Lulu, Sue, and I stayed in the background doing easy steps while Charles and Marian performed the big act. Marian would probably bring the audience to its feet as she danced to "I Wish I Could Shimmy Like My Sister Kate." Marian shimmied amazingly well. I envied her. I also doubted that her sister Kate, if she had one, could have shimmied as well.

Then I remembered Lucille and why we were going through all this effort and almost cried.

At the very end of the show, Ernie came out again and asked

for donations to the Los Angeles S.P.C.A. Collective bow to wild applause (we hoped).

As all of the above was going on, Phil and his crew were supposed to be circulating through the crowd. After doing some policemanly research, the coppers had discovered that a warrant for Mr. Autley's arrest had been issued in Colorado. Mr. Madison also proved to be a wanted man in Colorado.

Personally, I wouldn't want either one of them but bless Colorado's heart.

I'm sorry about that one.

No, I'm not.

At any rate, after the finale, we discussed the show and decided it was engaging and would probably earn at least a few bucks to donate to the S.P.C.A. The kids were giddy. I hoped they'd calm down by noon tomorrow, when we were supposed to do this for real.

Everyone agreed to meet at my house at ten o'clock on the morrow. There and then, we would don our costumes, and Lulu would do all the girls' makeup. The girls included Sue and me. Marian knew how to do her own stage makeup.

A suggestion that makeup might be appropriate for the men too met with a stern rebuff from Ernie. "I had to wear that goop when I was a kid. I might have to dance tomorrow, but I'll be cursed if I dance in face paint.

"Yeah," said Lenny Autley. "I don't wanna wear paint either." His eyes widened, and I do believe he was stricken by a thought. I suspect it was alone in his brain. The kid wasn't teeming with intellectual acumen. "Unless I can be an Indian!" He turned to Ernie, of whom he'd ceased to be afraid after about an hour had passed, and Lenny still lived. "C'n I be an Indian? Please?"

"No," said Ernie.

Lenny said not another word.

TWENTY-SEVEN

The following morning, a whole herd of dogs, their handlers, cops, children, and their parents arrived at my home on Bunker Hill at or about ten a.m. I can't tell you how glad I was that I wasn't the only adult in the place. Mrs. Buck seemed especially good at making kids behave. Then there was Ernie. He'd proved his worth, both as a dancer and a disciplinarian at last night's dress rehearsal.

As mentioned earlier, Ernie'd recruited Junior to be in our show. He couldn't tap or sing, but he was an expert at fulfilling odd jobs. He would take Buttercup in hand. Junior and Buttercup fell in love at first sight.

Mrs. Buck provided fresh doughnuts and muffins. She set them on the sideboard in the breakfast room. She was a marvel. She commandeered one of the cops in uniform to stand guard over the foodstuffs and make sure the kids didn't spill anything. Nothing like a uniform to convey authority. Lenny Autley seemed to be especially wary of the police contingent.

When we were all costumed and made up, various vehicles drove us to Chinatown. There, Charley Wu and his relatives (he had thousands of them, including Lily, the flute-player) had set up a stage on Hill Street between the two sections of Chinatown. The stage's platform was accessible by three wooden steps. They'd also partitioned off a portion of the east plaza for folks to use for costume changes and to sit while others were performing.

For the record, Charlie and Ernie were friends of longstanding. Ernie played on the All-Chinatown Baseball Team when they needed him. Thanks to me, most of the Chinese community adored Ernie for having saved Charley from a murder charge. Then there were the kidnapped girls Ernie had also saved. Mind you, it was I who had forced Ernie to get involved in the Chinatown mess in the first place. But it was Ernie who garnered the applause, not to mention the mazuma.

I tell you, life isn't fair. You've probably already figured that out on your own, haven't you? Anyhow, I tried not to resent my exclusion from the thanks. We women were second-class citizens the world over. Any attempts at rebellion were futile. I resented it anyway.

Our show didn't go precisely as planned. Our opening was swell, and the audience—most of whom stood in the street to watch—seemed to love Ernie. The three little girls and Lenny Autley got lots of applause too. Lenny didn't make any mistakes. I don't know if he feared Ernie or his father more, but he behaved himself.

I heard Marian whisper a fervent, "Thank God," as the children took two bows and then marched off the stage.

Junior and Buttercup were a crowd favorite. The watchers laughed, clapped, and made comments about dogs as the two of them danced. Calvin Buck and his crew played a lively rendition

ALICE DUNCAN

of "Honey," to which they danced. Everyone probably thought
Buttercup's name was Honey, but not even Buttercup cared.

Then Charles and Marian performed a spectacular routine,
featuring tap-dancing, ballet moves, and acrobatics. Charles
picked Marian up and whirled her around, drawing gasps of awe
from the watchers. Then Marian performed a dance number
complete with somersaults and back flips. She was amazing. Both
of them were, by gad.

Mr. Gallagher's Afghan hound and saluki also provoked
murmurs of interest and gasps of surprise. I've often wondered
since then if, after the show was over, the audience considered
themselves educated. I suspect not. But they appeared to enjoy
being lectured at about dogs. If they were anything like me, they
preferred learning about dogs to learning mathematics.

And then it was time for Lulu, Sue, and me! The opening
chords of "Crazy Blues" provoked the audience to clap in
rhythm. That was nice, especially for Lulu and me, who occasionally forgot our choreography or missed a step. Sue never lost
her pace.

"Good luck to us," whispered Lulu.

"Knock 'em dead," said Sue.

"Hope we do all right," I said.

Very well, so my comment wasn't as positive as Sue's or
Lulu's; I meant it with all my heart. Sue immediately tapped to
the front of the stage while Lulu and I tapped in behind her. Was
that a cheer I heard from the crowd?

By Jupiter, it was!

Sue did a truly spectacular job. At the end of our bit, the
three of us joined hands, bowed, and smiled at the audience.
We heard a loud "Encore!" from a number of people. I had no
idea what to do, but Calvin Buck did. He played a riff that
goosed Sue to start dancing again. Lulu and I didn't lag behind
too long, but took our places on the back of the stage (I know

that's not proper stage language) and tapped our tap-dance again.

Once more, the audience went wild. I was tired and hoped to heaven they weren't going to make us do it a third time. Lucky for us, Ernie came out onstage, clapping, smiling, and nodding. He gestured for us to leave the stage, so we did.

After we wiped our brows, we watched from the sidelines as Mr. Gallagher compared his Italian greyhound to a full-sized greyhound. The audience seemed suitably fascinated.

The introduction to "Sweet Georgia Brown" hit the air, and Ernie hit the stage. The man was amazing. He tapped with his cane; he tapped with his hat; and he tapped by himself without using his props. He spun like a top, leaped like a…what leaps? Oh, a kangaroo. It soon became apparent that he hadn't lost any of his ability, agility, or showmanship. Maybe he practiced at home at night? I aimed to ask him as soon as possible.

A laudatory roar rose from the audience when Ernie swept the hat from his head, twirled his cane, and took a final bow.

Boris and Bevan took their places onstage, one on either side of Miss Padgett, who started out soft but gained volume as she extolled the beauties and talents of her two hounds. According to Miss Padgett, both Boris and Bevan could take down a wolf if a wolf should appear in their orbit. I hoped one wouldn't. Impressed clapping sounded from the crowd.

The onlookers adored the number Marian, Charles, and the three little girls tapped to the music of the "Charleston." I could dance the Charleston, but not nearly as well as those little girls. I got confused when you had to switch your hands on your knees; I decided I'd ask Marian to give me a private lesson.

Gasps of awe and wonder rose from the audience when Caesar and Augustus took the stage with Mrs. Swale. I noticed people who had been standing close to the stage stepped backward in alarm. Perfectly understandable. Mrs. Swale lectured on the wonders and history of mastiffs and seemed to enjoy tales of her dogs' ancestors ripping people apart. I shuddered.

After making a speech about the good work done by the S.P.C.A., Ernie gestured to the donation barrel and invited the audience to chip in for the dogs and cats and kids. Intense clapping followed his announcement, so maybe this show would actually help the S.P.C.A. as well as the L.A.P.D. and the Murrays.

Our last number! The dogs and their owners (Buttercup led by Junior), Lenny Autley, the three little girls, and the Three Musketeers (Lulu, Sue, and I) trooped onto the stage. The dogs and we lesser lights stuck to the back of the stage, the dogs sitting placidly while we tapped in place, when Marian and Charles danced to the front of the stage.

Their act was phenomenal. They tapped, somersaulted, flipped, jumped, and danced marvelously. When Marian tapped to the foreground and began dancing to "I Wish I Could Shimmy like My Sister Kate," the crowd went wild. I don't know how many encores she had to make, but it was more than two.

Because I wasn't doing anything but tapping in place, I surveyed the scene. It was gratifying to see so many people enjoying our production. Even more gratifying were the people throwing money into the S.P.C.A. barrel over which Ernie stood and smiled. I expect he stayed there to make sure no one removed money from the barrel.

And then I saw Mr. Horshank! Mr. Horshank, who was supposed to be in jail for obstructing the course of a police investigation. Only for a moment, I entertained the idea that he really *might* have a rude twin. But no. One of him was more than enough. He looked cranky, and he and a big fat man seemed to eye the stage as they murmured to each other. Crumb. I hope Phil and his coppers were paying as much attention to the crowd as I was.

As I scanned the mob of people, I attempted to locate Phil.

Even a uniform would satisfy me. No luck. Where the heck were they?

I heard a sharp, "Mercy!" from Lulu and stopped watching the crowd. I'd tapped out of step. Whoops! So I decided to trust the police, even though I had ample reason not to, and corrected my dance steps.

At long last, the audience agreed to allow Marian to stop shimmying and take several bows. Or curtseys. Whatever tap-dancing ladies did at the ends of their numbers. Lest you wonder, we had posted signs praising the Murray Dance Academy all over the place, and Ernie had mentioned the academy as a swell place to learn any kind of dancing you wanted to learn.

At long, *long* last, we were allowed to leave the stage. Whew! The day wasn't warm, but my body didn't understand that.

"I'm sweating like a pig," said Lulu.

"Me too," said I.

"On ladies, sweat is called dew," said Sue.

I muttered an inelegant, "Poppycock," but said no more because suddenly the three of us were surrounded by a horde of big, burly men. They took our various arms and dragged us away from the privacy enclosure. I opened my mouth to scream, only to have a rag stuffed in it. It was a dirty rag too. I had no idea what was going on, but I sure didn't like it.

It seemed to me that those horrible men frog-marched us for three miles and three hours across bumpy cement. All at once, I heard a door open, and I was shoved into a dark place. I knew Lulu and Sue were there, too, because they both fell on me. I spat out my rag, and Sue and Lulu did likewise with theirs.

"Thank God we're together!" I said.

"Where are we?" asked Lulu.

"I smell something sweet," said Sue.

After sniffing the air, I said, "We're still in Chinatown." Glancing around, I realized the room, while not illuminated by electrical lamps, wasn't completely black because several dirty windows let in a little sunshine. "I think they dumped us into one of the curio shops on the plaza."

"Who are they?" said Lulu.

"No idea," I said, "although I think they have something to do with that stupid gold mine and the murders. I swear I saw Mr. Horshank talking to Mr. Autley."

"I thought Horshank was in jail!" said Lulu.

"So did I," I groused.

"Oh, lord, they aren't going to murder us, are they?" Sue sounded scared. For good reason.

"I have no clue what their plans are," I told her and Lulu, "but I don't aim to be murdered. We can still use our arms and voices. Let's yell."

"Everyone outside is already yelling," said Sue morosely. And reasonably, dang it.

She was correct. The noise outside was…well, noisy. Because of our show. Guess the audience liked it.

"Well, let's see if there's something in this shop we can use as either a weapon or a way to batter ourselves out of here." I hadn't worked for Ernie for so long without learning anything. Ernie would probably dispute that, but he wasn't in that wretched room with us. "We'd better do something quick, because those men might come back and tie us up and muzzle us."

"What can we do?" asked Lulu.

Pushing myself up from the floor, I realized that while my assessment of where we were being held might be accurate, there didn't seem to be any weapons handy. I was hoping to find a big statue of Kwan Yen or something equally helpful. Buddha would do, although he wasn't as pointy as Kwan Yen.

"We can search this place and see what's here," I said.

So, squinting as I walked the perimeter of the small room, I felt around for something that might serve as a weapon or a battering ram. A key would be great, but I doubted our abductors would have left a key lying around.

"I don't see anything but empty shelves." I heard doubt in Lulu's voice.

"If we could find a long-enough rope, you could lasso them," I said, the realization that Lulu was a talented rope-handler having just occurred to me.

"There's not enough room in here to swing a rope like that."

"Well, piffle," I said. "Maybe there's something long enough to make the creatures trip when they come here to tie us up."

"Do you think they'll do that?" said Sue.

"I don't know, but I imagine they will. Why would they want to kidnap us, unless they didn't want to get us out of the way?"

"They might use us as bargaining chips," Lulu mentioned.

"Oh," I said. "I hadn't thought of that."

"But for what?" said Sue. "We don't know anything about anything. We just took tap-dance lessons, and everybody started talking about invisible gold mines and killing other people."

"True," I agreed. "But somebody thinks we know more than we know. I guess. I honestly have no idea why anyone would kidnap us."

"For ransom?" Lulu's voice held well-deserved skepticism.

"Who'd pay ransom for us?" I asked. "I'm the only person I know who has money, and I won't pay ransom for my freedom. Although," I hastily added, thinking of my pals, "I'd pay ransom to get you two out of this mess."

"Let's not worry about that now," said sensible Sue. "Let's look for a way out."

We did. The three of us searched the little space—I think it might have been a closet or an empty storeroom—for what seemed like eternity, muttering as we did so. I found some old rags and a small statue of some Chinese god. A couple of soap cakes. They smelled nice, but I didn't think they'd be helpful. From the surrounding grumbles, Lulu and Sue were having the same luck.

"Botheration," I muttered, frustrated and irate.

"Did you recognize any of the men?" asked Sue.

Lulu and I chorused, "No."

"I wonder why—" My wondering was interrupted by the sound of heavy footsteps coming from somewhere. Couldn't figure out where.

Then a door we hadn't noticed before opened, and the same huge, ugly, menacing man who'd been talking to Mr. Horshank appeared. He had his fists planted on his hips, and he scowled at us. Don't ask me why, but I suddenly knew he was Mr. Autley, Lenny's father. Figures. Bullies beget bullies, I reckon.

Lulu stood up and hollered, "Let us out of here!"

"Not until you tell us where it is," the man rumbled. He had a voice like gravel.

Now I was not merely afraid but confused as well.

"Tell you where what is?" I asked, bewildered.

"Don't kid a kidder, kid," growled the man.

"I don't even know what that means," muttered Sue.

"You can get out of here as soon as you tell us where it is," the man said.

"What are you looking for?" I asked. I thought it was a reasonable question.

The big, burly, bad man evidently didn't share my sentiment. "Don't play dumb with me, girlie."

I decided a trace of firmness would not be amiss in this situation. I didn't see a gun on him, so that was...well, not a good sign, but it was better than seeing a gun. "I have no idea what you're talking about! Are you Lenny Autley's father, by the way?"

"Huh? Yeah. Lenny's my kid," said Mr. Autley.

"Well, Mr. Autley, I don't know what you're talking about. What are you looking for?"

"I ain't lookin' for it! That's 'cause I don't know where it is!" Mr. Autley roared.

Not sure about Lulu or Sue, but I recoiled. Firming my resolve once more, I said, "If you'd tell us what it is, we might be able to help you find it."

"Don't play dumb," he grumbled. He took a step forward and entered the little room in which we three were trapped. I noticed that his bigness was more fat than firm, but he was still bigger and stronger than any of us. Curses.

Suddenly Lulu said, "I know where it is!"

I blinked at her. So did Sue. Mr. Autley grinned.

"I knew you knew," he said smugly. "So spill it."

Lulu took a step toward Mr. Autley, her chin lifted and a determined expression on her face. "Not until you let Mercy and Sue go," she said.

"No way," said Mr. Autley, sneering. He sneered really well.

"Then I won't tell you."

"To hell with you." Taking a giant step into our tiny prison, Mr. Autley loomed over Lulu, Sue, and me for a second. "I know how to make you talk."

"Applesauce," said Lulu.

Not sure about Sue, but I stared at Lulu and feared for her life. This man had already killed or been involved in the killing of three people.

Then a miracle occurred. Out of nowhere, Lulu threw a bunch of—well, I didn't know what they were, but Lulu later declared them to be chips of soap—into Mr. Autley's face. He hollered, I suspect because soap had got into his eyes. Lulu, Sue, and I took his moment of distraction to escape. Using the door Autley had used, we scampered like frightened rabbits out of the closet and into a curio shop. There, on the other side of the room, was a door to the plaza! We raced like…some fast animals. Cheetahs? We raced like three cheetahs through the curio shop behind which we had been trapped.

We made it to the door of the shop, which was locked. Dang. Lulu, having more experience in rescue than either Sue or me, picked up what I think was a Fu dog and smashed a window. We had to jump on a table, but using the Fu dog for help, Lulu knocked the remaining glass from the sill. Sue and I climbed out. Even with Lulu and the Fu dog's help, I managed to get a substantial cut on my left leg, although I didn't know it at the time. As soon as we hit the ground, we started running.

Instantly a high, squeaky male voice squealed, "Stop! Stop!"

The squealer was Mr. Horshank, of course. I didn't have any idea why the police had let him out of jail, but there he was, rat-faced, skinny and, to judge by the color of his face, mad as heck. He attempted to catch me, but I sidestepped his hands and kept running. As Sue ran beside me, she clearly had dodged him too.

TWENTY-EIGHT

Our bottle caps made lots of noise as we raced to the stage. When we arrived, panting and sweating—or "dewing"—Marian, Charles, Phil Bigelow, Rob, and Ernie stared at us surprised.

"Where the devil have you come from?" Ernie asked grumpily.

"We were kidnapped!"

"*What?*"

"Mr. Autley and Mr. Horshank kidnapped us!" I gasped. "Lulu's the one who saved our bacon."

"Where is Lulu?" asked Rob.

Surprised by his question, Sue and I looked around us. No Lulu! Where was Lulu? I glanced over my shoulder, hoping to see Lulu running to catch up with us. But she wasn't running after us. And she wasn't with us.

"What's that blood coming from?" said Ernie, pointing at the pavement under my feet. "Did they stab you?"

"No. We had to get out of a window. Lulu used a Fu dog to break the window, but some of the glass was still there." I yanked my bloody self away from Ernie's grasping hands. "Forget the blood! We've got to find Lulu." I whirled around until I had Phil in my headlamps. "Why the heck did you let Mr. Horshank out of the clink?"

"What?" said Phil. He looked confused

"I won't forget the blood," snapped Ernie. "You need medical attention."

"Not as much as I need Lulu," I snarled, not allowing him to reach for me again. "Get your coppers and come with me, Phil," I commanded. "Sue and I will show you where those animals jailed us."

"I'm not sure I know which shop is the right one," said Sue.

"I'm not either." Glancing at the plaza surface, I noticed a substantial blot of blood. Rather than fuss about it, I hollered, "Follow the bloodstains!" and commenced running.

"Mercy, wait!" Ernie called as I took off.

I didn't wait. I didn't get very far either. After running three or four yards—that's only a guess on my part—my head suddenly got swimmy and I began to wobble. I probably took another two or three steps before the Chinatown plaza spun crazily for a second, and then—well, I don't know what happened.

When I awoke, I didn't recognize my surroundings. Ernie loomed over me, and Mrs. Buck was talking to a stranger across the room. My left leg hurt like holy heck and was wrapped up like a mummy. Buttercup was there, though, so I knew I must be either at home or close to it. Safe. I was safe.

"She's awake!" called Ernie too loudly, hurting my ears.

"Glory!" exclaimed Mrs. Buck. She rushed to the bed.

The bed? What bed? It wasn't my bed.

"God almighty, Mercy, you scared me almost to death! What were you thinking?"

Squinting up at Ernie, I pondered his question for a second. I couldn't answer it because my brain seemed to be empty. Then I remembered.

"Lulu! Where's Lulu?" The voice that came from my mouth didn't sound right. I frowned and squinted some more.

"Lulu is safe and sound and with Rob," said Ernie, his voice a good deal softer.

"Where am I?"

"You're at home, Miss Mercy," said Mrs. Buck. "And I've got some good beef broth for you. You need to drink it up and get better."

"Where at home am I?" I didn't recognize the room, although it looked faintly familiar.

"Mrs. Buck made up a bed for you in a room downstairs," said Ernie. "How the heck many rooms are *in* this joint of yours, anyhow?" He sounded crabby.

"I don't know. Is Lulu all right? Did those horrid men hurt her?"

"The only one who got hurt was you," said Ernie. "As usual."

"That's not fair! We were trying to escape, and I cut my leg on some glass. The stupid fringes in my dress kept hitting the cut. At least, I think they did. Where are Lulu and Rob? Are you sure Lulu's not injured?" I'd spoken too many words. My body rebelled and my head, which I'd lifted, fell back onto the pillow again.

Sue entered my field of vision. It looked to me as if she'd bathed and changed. "Lulu and Rob are in the living room, Mercy. You worried us *so* much! When you collapsed on the plaza and I saw all the blood around you, I thought those men had killed you!"

"So did I," growled Ernie.

The strange man to whom Mrs. Buck had been talking walked over to my bed. He smiled down at me.

"Who are you?" I asked impolitely.

"This is Dr. Chambers," said Ernie. "He patched you up."

"You lost a good deal of blood before I could do so," said Dr. Chambers with an expression he probably thought was reassuring. I wasn't reassured, although I'm glad he doctored me.

I said, "Oh. Thanks."

"You'll be weak for quite a while," Dr. Chambers said, sticking a thermometer in my mouth.

Because I wasn't sick, but injured, I didn't understand the reason for the thermometer. Therefore, I pulled out of my mouth.

"Stop that," roared Ernie.

"Stop yelling," I tried to roar back at him. Couldn't. Crumb. I felt too weak to holler. This was an alarming situation.

"I won't stop it," said Ernie, taking the thermometer from my fingers and stuffing it back into my mouth. "I thought those bastards had killed you!"

"So did I." Sue's eyes had begun to leak tears. "I was so terrified for you."

I grabbed the thermometer again and shoved it under my pillow so Ernie couldn't get it back. "But...I don't know what happened. Will someone please tell me what happened? All I know is that Lulu wasn't with us, and I was headed back to the shop where those awful men had thrown us."

"That's what happened," snarled Ernie. "Like an idiot and bleeding like a...I don't know what bleeds that much...you started running away from us."

"I wasn't running away from you," I corrected him. "I was taking you to Lulu."

"Yeah, well, you didn't make it," he grumbled.

"But you found Lulu?"

"Yes," said Sue, using a hankie to wipe her eyes. "Oh, Mercy, I was *so* frightened!"

"I'm sorry, Sue." Something then occurred to me. "Did you catch Mr. Autley and Mr. Horshank?"

"Yes," said Ernie. "They're in police custody."

"Good," I said. "Do you know what Mr. Autley was talking about when he asked us where it was?"

Ernie, his brow furrowing, said, "Huh?"

"Yes," said Sue. "It was a map. Mr. Madison had it."

"Mr. Madison was there too?" I hadn't seen Mr. Madison.

"Yes, he was there too," grumbled Ernie. "He was there, and so were Horshank and Autley. The coppers corralled them all."

"That's nice," I said, attempting to smile. Boy, was I weak!

"That's enough for now, Mr. Ernie," said Mrs. Buck. She gently tugged Ernie away from my bed and set a steaming cup on the bedside table.

I couldn't recall precisely which room I was in. My house did indeed have too many rooms. A young, single woman didn't need so many rooms, even if she rented some of them out. But my head was too foggy at the moment to come to any conclusions about the house situation.

Pulling up a chair, Mrs. Buck sat on it, lifted the cup from the table, and dipped a spoon into it. "Here's some beef broth. You need to heal and get your blood flowing in your veins again."

"Yeah," grumped Ernie. "You lost most of the blood you used to have on the plaza in Chinatown."

Like an obedient baby, I opened my mouth to receive the soup. It was good, although it didn't have any vegetables or anything floating in it. I guess that's why Mrs. Buck had called it broth. I definitely needed to learn more about cooking.

Dr. Chambers frowned and said, "What did you do with my thermometer?"

"She pushed it under her pillow," said Ernie.

"Young woman," said Dr. Chambers sternly. "You suffered a life-threatening injury—"

ALICE DUNCAN

"I did?" The spoonful of broth Mrs. Buck had put in my mouth went down the wrong way.

"Yes, you did, you idiot," growled Ernie.

I wished I could give him a good slug across the chops, but I was choking to death at the moment, and the coughing was making my left leg pound as if someone were sawing it off my body. Did soldiers in early wars—when there were no pain-relieving drugs—have to go through this? Why were people—nearly always men—so eager to start wars? I choked until my eyes leaked.

"Cripes, I'm sorry!" said Ernie, kneeling at my bedside. "Mercy, I didn't mean to call you an idiot. You just scared the bejesus out of me. Stop coughing, all right?" Turning his head, he called over his shoulder, "Doctor, what's wrong with her? Can you fix her? You have to fix her!"

"I was attempting to do just that when she hid my thermome-ter," said a caustic Dr. Chambers. "She sustained a severe injury, and if it becomes infected, it might still be dangerous. I think she just swallowed the wrong way."

As my coughing fit abated, I wiped leakage away with my right hand. The salty tears made the hand sting. When I stared at it, I realized it was all scraped up. How had that happened?

"How'd my hand get scratched?" I managed to say in broken syllables.

Ernie bowed his head until his forehead was resting on my bed covers. After attempting to sit up and failing, I frowned at him. He still didn't answer.

A tapping came at a door. I squinted around, unsure where the door to this room actually was. Ah, there it was. I could tell because it was opening.

"Lulu!" I shrieked when I saw her tiptoe into the room. "I'm so glad you're not dead!" My eyes began leaking again, but this time with relief.

"We all thought *you* were dead," said Lulu, walking slowly to the bed and me. Her gaze shifted and landed on the doctor, Mrs. Buck, Sue, and then Ernie. "Is she able to talk?"

My earlier shriek had shredded what was left of my voice, and when I tried to say, "Yes," it didn't come out. Blast!

Dr. Chambers said, "She's very weak, and she can't talk for long." He frowned at Lulu, who didn't deserve to be frowned at.

Ernie lifted his head, and I saw his eyes were bloodshot. Had he been crying? Drinking? The only thing I'd ever seen Ernie drink other than coffee, tea, or soda pop was apple cider. Peering at him closely, I couldn't read the expression on his face.

"Come over here, Lulu," he said. "Did I hear the telephone ringing a few minutes ago?"

Lulu walked to my bed and looked down at me, clasping her hands to her bosom, thereby wrinkling the piece of paper she held. "Mercy, I'm so glad you're not dead!"

Interesting. I said, "Likewise," because it was the truth.

"Who was on the telephone?" asked Ernie. "If it was anybody from Boston, Mercy doesn't need to know."

"I know," said Lulu, smiling faintly. She'd met my parents. She'd also met my obnoxious brother George. "It wasn't from Boston. It was a lady named"—she glanced at the crunched piece of paper in her hand—"Thelma Grabgrinder."

"Who?" said Ernie.

"Thelma Grabgrinder," repeated Lulu.

"Why'd she call me?" I asked, never having heard the name before.

"I'm not sure," said Lulu. "She said something about a book and a contract."

Shocked, I once more attempted to rise. Once more, I failed. "Book! She called about my *book*?"

Nodding, Lulu said, "Yes. She asked me to ask you to put

through a trunk call to her when you're able. I told her you were sick."

"Did she say anything else?" I said, almost hyperventilating.

"Calm down, young lady," Dr. Chambers said. "It's not good for you to get agitated."

"Agitated?" I whispered—I wanted to scream. "I'm not agitated. I'm astounded."

Ernie's squint traveled from me to Lulu and back again. "Did you send your book to a publisher?"

I nodded. "Halliday, Smith, and Ransom."

"Wow," said Lulu. "You never told me that."

"I didn't tell anybody."

"Cripes," said Ernie. "I don't think editors with big publishing firms call people whose books they're rejecting. I think she might have called with an offer to buy your book, Mercy." He was astounded too; I could tell.

Wriggling on the bed in an attempt to leave it, I had to give up when I blacked out once more. When I opened my eyes, Ernie, Lulu, Mrs. Buck, Sue, and Dr. Chambers were all looming over me. I felt like a goldfish in a tank of water.

"You can't get up yet, Mercy," said Ernie.

The faces withdrew.

"But—"

He interrupted me. "You can't get up yet, Mercy." It sounded as if he put a period at the end of each word.

"But—"

Turning to Lulu, Ernie said, "Did she give you a number to call?"

"Yes." Lulu handed Ernie the paper.

"I'll set up a trunk call to this woman," he said to me. "I'll tell her I'm representing you."

"But—"

"You damn near died today, Mercy Allcutt! With a deep gash on your leg, you recklessly hared off after a couple of murderers, dammit, and you almost died for your effort."

"But—"

"That's not entirely true, Ernie," said Lulu. Glad someone stuck up for me.

"It isn't," agreed Sue. "She was trying to save Lulu."

His face looking like a thundercloud, Ernie said, "She should have told us about it. We'd have found Lulu. We *did* find Lulu. Mercy almost croaked. And it's not going to happen again. We're going to get married, and your days of running around after criminals are over."

"We are?" I whispered, bewildered. "They are?"

"Yes. As soon as we can, we're getting married. Then we're moving out of Los Angeles. Then you can write books."

"Oh, Mercy!" Sue clasped her hands to her bosom.

"Yes!" cried Lulu. Her hands were already clasped at her bosom.

I continued squinting at Ernie. "Is that a proposal?"

"No," said a grumpy Ernie. "It's a command."

"I don't run around after criminals," I protested feebly. In truth, I felt lousy. My leg hurt dreadfully, and my body had evidently been bruised here and there during our escape—or maybe when I collapsed.

Ernie rose from his knees. He no longer looked like he wanted to cry. He looked kind of like he wanted to murder me. Pointing at me, he said, "Don't move. I'll put a call through to this Grabgrinder person."

"Tell her yes," I whispered.

"Depends on what she says," said Ernie.

Darn him! I really, really, *really* wanted to be a published author of detective fiction!

Too bad, Mercy Allcutt. My heart sank when I saw him leave the room.

After that, I must have blacked out again, because I don't remember anything until later that day. Afternoon. Evening. Night. Whatever it was.

TWENTY-NINE

T hus ended my tap-dancing career. There was good news, however, that more than made up for it.

After resting in bed for two days, Dr. Chambers told Ernie that I could get out of bed, but he advised against doing so. By then, I realized the injury to my leg had been much worse than I'd originally thought. In actual fact, I'd nearly died. Uncomfortable notion.

Ernie, however, had called the operator and had a trunk call placed to Miss Thelma Grabgrinder, editor at Halliday, Smith, and Ransom in New York City. Dr. Chambers had found a wheelchair somewhere, and Ernie wheeled me into my office off the living room. The time was approximately ten a.m. on Friday of that week.

When the telephone rang in my office, Ernie answered it. "Miss Allcutt's residence."

The operator must have put through the trunk call, because Ernie said, "Yes, this is Miss Allcutt's home. Is this Miss Grab-grinder?"

Whoever was on the other end of the wire must have said,

"No," because Ernie rolled his eyes and said, "We're returning her telephone call to Miss Allcutt."

Silence. At least that's all I heard.

Ernie must have heard something else because he said, "Yes. I'll hold the wire." Covering the mouthpiece, he said to me, "Her secretary answered the 'phone. She's getting her."

Pronouns can be so confusing sometimes, but I figured out that sentence even with parts of my brain still not working properly. Golly, I'd always known blood was important, but I'd never had a personal connection with losing so much of it before.

Ernie jerked a little and said, "Yes? Is this Miss Grabgrinder?"

He must have received a positive response because he said, "Yes, she's here. I'll hand her the receiver." And he did.

"Hello?" I said in a small voice. I cleared my throat and told myself to be brave.

"Miss Allcutt?"

"Yes, this is Miss Allcutt."

"Excellent," said Miss Grabgrinder.

It was? I hoped she'd explain.

She did.

"Miss Allcutt, I'm calling today because I've read your manuscript, and I think it would be a good fit for our mystery line."

"You do?"

"You sound surprised." And Miss Grabgrinder sounded amused.

"I am," I said.

"You needn't be," she said. "Your writing is first-rate, and your manuscript was much cleaner than most of the ones we receive."

Told you I was a good secretary. I typed like the wind, and I could take shorthand like nobody's business too.

"I'm glad. Thank you."

"Thank *you*."

Crumb. I hoped we weren't going to go through an endless round of thank-yous. Fortunately, Miss Grabgrinder got to the point.

"We would like to offer you a contract for this book. Do you have any other finished manuscripts ready?"

Good lord, what did the woman think I did all day? I had to go to work, for pity's sake. Very well, so I didn't *need* to go to work. Still, I had a job.

"No, although I've begun writing another book."

"Excellent. Are you using some of the same characters in your next novel?"

"You mean Gloria Packard? The girl in the book who helps the police and has a private detective as a boss?"

"Yes." A laugh trilled over the wire. "Miss Packard is quite the character. She made me laugh out loud several times."

She did? I thought she was a sober-sided prude who didn't know anything about detecting. She had muddled through to victory in my novel, but she'd done it more or less by accident.

"Yes," I said. "Miss Gloria Packard is in the book I'm writing now. And the P.I., Henry Hudson, is in it too." I hurried to add, "If you think it's a good idea."

"It's a marvelous idea," said Miss Grabgrinder. "And please continue to write books featuring those two."

"Very well," I said obediently.

Ernie made motions indicative of him wanting to talk to the editor again. I frowned at him, but he became insistent.

"In that case," said Miss Grabgrinder, "We'd like to offer you a contract for three books. The terms of the contract are—"

Ernie, who evidently had preternaturally good hearing, snatched the receiver from my hand. I tried to scowl at him, but I'd begun to feel awfully weak and couldn't summon the energy.

"Miss Grabgrinder?" he said into the mouthpiece.

I presume she said she was because Ernie then said, "Miss Allcutt suffered a severe accident two days ago. I'm Mr. Ernest Templeton, Miss Allcutt's fiancé."

He was? That was nice.

Silence, according to me.

"Yes. She's getting better, but she's very weak," said Ernie. "It might be better if you told me what you intend to offer Miss Allcutt, and she and I can discuss the matter."

More nothing, according to me. Ernie picked up a pencil and slid a piece of paper toward himself. With his pencil poised, he wrote something on the paper. I couldn't see it. Darn it, this was *my* life! I didn't want Ernie usurping my life and writing career! Future writing career. I hoped.

Finally, Ernie said, "Yes. Thank you. Miss Allcutt, an attorney friend of ours, and I will discuss this and get back to you on Monday. Will that meet with your approval?"

She must have said yes, because Ernie said, "Thank you."

Then he and she hung up their respective receivers. I bopped Ernie on the arm closest to me. "You can't just take over my life, you know, Mr. Ernest Templeton."

With a grin and a chuckle, Ernie said, "I know that, Mercy. Quite well, in fact. However, you're extremely weak at the moment, and I think it would be a good idea for Rob to look at the details of their offer. He's not a literary lawyer, but at least he knows more about legal stuff than I do."

He had a point. I'd have told him so, but I couldn't quite make myself talk.

"I'm rolling you back to bed now," he said. "We'll talk about this later."

I said something that sounded like, "Guh." Then I slept until I don't know when. When I awoke, Ernie was sitting beside my bed reading a book. Squinting, I couldn't make out the title.

"What're you reading?" My voice was soft, but it jerked Ernie to attention.

"You're awake!" he said.

"Obviously," I said back.

"Grump."

"Yes."

"I'm reading *The Murder of Roger Ackroyd*, by Agatha Christie."

Perking up a bit, I said, "Oh, I loved that one."

"Found it on your bookcase in the den."

"What time is it?"

Ernie shook his sleeve down—he wore no suit jacket—and peered at his wristwatch. "Six p.m."

"Ah." Then, because I couldn't help myself, I said, "What did Miss Grabgrinder say?"

"Hold that thought," he said. Then he got up out of his chair and headed to the door!

I'd have screeched at him had I been able. As I wasn't, I lay in the bed and stewed. Fortunately, I didn't have to stew for long. Maybe a minute and a half later, Ernie returned to my sickroom. He was accompanied by Lulu and Rob. The open door allowed succulent aromas to enter the room, and I realized I was hungry. I couldn't remember being hungry for a long time.

Rushing to my bed, Lulu said, "Mercy! We were all so scared for you! You lost so much blood!"

"You didn't go to the stage with Sue and me."

"That weasel Horshank grabbed my arm. Made me fall. But I kicked him in the groin and got to the stage at about the same time you collapsed. I thought...I thought you were dead." She sniffled into a hankie, and Rob put his arm around her shoulder.

"Oh my," I said. "You're so resourceful, Lulu. That's the second villain you've kicked in the groin, isn't it? You'll have to teach me how to do that."

"I will," she promised.

279

"She won't either," said Ernie. "You won't need to escape from villains any longer. You're going to marry me and write books. You may leave the house every now and then, but not to chase crooks." He grinned, so I figured he wasn't completely serious.

"Spoilsport," I said.

"When it comes to your safety, you bet I am." Now he was serious; I could tell.

"I'm so glad you're going to be all right," said Lulu.

"Me too," said Rob.

"Rob and I are going to bring a table in here, and Mrs. Buck is aiming to serve dinner in this room. As we eat, we can talk to Rob about the contract Miss Grabgrinder offered you."

"What about Sue and Caroline?" I asked.

Ernie's gaze paid a short trip to the ceiling. "They'll dine in the dining room. Mrs. Buck cooked enough for an army."

"Bless her heart," I said.

"Yes," said Lulu.

"She's a treasure," said Ernie.

So, during a delectable meal consisting of roast pork, mashed potatoes and gravy, carrots, applesauce, fruit salad, and I can't even remember what all else, Rob, Ernie, and I decided to accept Miss Grabgrinder's proposed contract for three books from me.

"She has a lot of faith in me," I muttered at one point.

"I have faith in you too," said Ernie. "It's your dream come true." He heaved a huge, fake sigh. "Before this, I thought *I* was your dream come true."

Rob and Lulu laughed. After I swallowed, so did I.

For the record, our performance for the S.P.C.A. brought in a ton of money. There was plenty for the stated cause, and much left over to assist the Murray siblings in keeping their dance academy open.

The Los Angeles Police Department hauled in several criminals as well. All things considered, it was a worthwhile enterprise. Except for my leg injury, and that healed eventually.

———

Rob and Lulu, and Ernie and I were married by a Los Angeles County judge as soon as I was able to walk again, about five weeks after my near-death experience. Chloe and Harvey drove to Los Angeles from Beverly Hills to act as witnesses. They brought Heather Rose, who was beginning to look human. I still couldn't determine any particular beauty in her, but it didn't matter. Her parents and everyone else could, and that's all that counted.

We told our parents we were married about a month after the event took place. My mother was outraged, my father disapproved, and I was unsurprised.

I sold my huge house on Bunker Hill after making sure Sue and Caroline were safely settled elsewhere. With the proceeds from the sale, and with money from Ernie's savings, we bought a lovely home on Holliston Avenue in a little town just north of Pasadena called Altadena.

Mr. and Mrs. Buck moved with us.

I, writing as M.L. Temple, became a bestselling author of detective fiction.

Eighteen months after we spoke our wedding vows, Loretta (after Mrs. Buck) Elizabeth (after Ernie's sister) Templeton was born at the Women's Hospital of Pasadena. Ernie and I, along with all our friends, thought she was the most beautiful child ever born.

We were correct in our judgment.

END

ABOUT THE AUTHOR

Award-winning author Alice Duncan lives with a herd of wild dachshunds (enriched from time to time with fosterees from New Mexico Dachshund Rescue) in Roswell, New Mexico. She's not a UFO enthusiast; she's in Roswell because her mother's family settled there fifty years before the aliens crashed (and living in Roswell, NM, is cheaper than living in Pasadena, CA, unfortunately). Alice would love to hear from you at alice@ aliceduncan.net

www.aliceduncan.net